Richard Lovelace, Dudley Posthumus Lovelace, William Carew Hazlitt

Lucasta

The Poems of Richard Lovelace

Richard Lovelace, Dudley Posthumus Lovelace, William Carew Hazlitt

Lucasta
The Poems of Richard Lovelace

ISBN/EAN: 9783337401054

Printed in Europe, USA, Canada, Australia, Japan

Cover: Foto ©Andreas Hilbeck / pixelio.de

More available books at **www.hansebooks.com**

LUCASTA.

THE POEMS OF RICHARD LOVELACE, ESQ.

NOW FIRST EDITED, AND THE TEXT

CAREFULLY REVISED.

WITH SOME ACCOUNT OF THE AUTHOR,

AND A FEW NOTES,

BY W. CAREW HAZLITT,

OF THE INNER TEMPLE, BARRISTER-AT-LAW.

LONDON:

JOHN RUSSELL SMITH,

SOHO SQUARE.

1864.

TO

WILLIAM HAZLITT, ESQ.,

OF THE MIDDLE TEMPLE, A REGISTRAR OF

THE COURT OF BANKRUPTCY

IN LONDON,

This Little Volume

IS INSCRIBED AS A SLIGHT TESTIMONY OF

THE GREATEST RESPECT, BY HIS

AFFECTIONATE SON,

THE EDITOR.

INTRODUCTION.

HERE is scarcely an *un-dramatic* writer of the Seventeenth Century, whose poems exhibit so many and such gross corruptions as those of the author of *Lucasta*. In the present edition, which is the first attempt to present the productions of a celebrated and elegant poet to the admirers of this class of literature in a readable shape, both the text and the pointing have been amended throughout, the original reading being always given in the foot-notes; but some passages still remain, which I have not succeeded in elucidating to my satisfaction, and one or two which have defied all my attempts at emendation, though, as they stand, they are unquestionably nonsense. It is proper to mention that several rather bold corrections have been hazarded in the course of the volume; but where this has been done, the deviation from the original has invariably been pointed out in the notes.

On the title-page of the copy of *Lucasta*, 1649, preserved among the King's Pamphlets in the British Museum, the original possessor has, according to his usual practice, marked the date of purchase, viz., June

21 ; perhaps, and indeed probably, that was also the date of publication. A copy of *Lucasta*, 1649, occasionally appears in catalogues, purporting to have belonged to Anne, Lady Lovelace ; but the autograph which it contains was taken from a copy of Massinger's *Bondman* (edit. 1638, 4to.), which her Ladyship once owned. This copy of Lovelace's *Lucasta* is bound up with the copy of the *Posthume Poems*, once in the possession of Benjamin Rudyerd, Esq., grandson and heir of the distinguished Sir Benjamin Rudyerd, as appears also from his autograph on the title.[1]

In the original edition of the two parts of *Lucasta*, 1649-59, the arrangement of the poems appears, like that of the text, to have been left to chance, and the result has been a total absence of method. I have therefore felt it part of my duty to systematise the contents of the volume, and, so far as it lay in my power, to place the various pieces of which it consisted in their proper order ; all the odes, sonnets, &c. addressed or referring to the lady who is concealed under the names of *Lucasta* and *Amarantha* have now been, for the first time, brought together ; and the copies of commendatory and gratulatory verses, with one exception prefixed by Lovelace to various publications by friends during his life-time, either prior to the appearance of the first part of his own poems in 1649, or between that date and the

---

[1] Mr. B. R. was a somewhat diligent collector of books, both English and foreign. On the fly-leaves of his copy of Rosse's *Mystagogus Poeticus*, 1648, 8vo., he has written the names of a variety of works, of which he was at the time seemingly in recent possession.

issue of his Remains ten years later, have been placed by themselves, as an act of justice to the writer, of whose style and genius they are, as is generally the case with all compositions of the kind, by no means favourable specimens. The translations from Catullus, Ausonius, &c. have been left as they stood ; they are, for the most part, destitute of merit ; but as they were inserted by the Poet's brother, when he edited the posthumous volume, I did not think it right to disturb them, and they have been retained in their full integrity.

Lovelace's *Lucasta* was included by the late S. W. Singer, Esq., in his series of " Early English Poets ;" but that gentleman, besides striking out certain passages, which he, somewhat unaccountably and inconsistently, regarded as indelicate, omitted a good deal of preliminary matter in the form of commendatory verses which, though possibly of small worth, were necessary to render the book complete ; it is possible, that Mr. Singer made use of a copy of *Lucasta* which was deficient at the commencement. It may not be generally known that, independently of its imperfections in other respects, Mr. Singer's reprint abounds with the grossest blunders.

The old orthography has been preserved intact in this edition ; but with respect to the employment of capitals, the entirely arbitrary manner in which they are introduced into the book as originally published, has made it necessary to reduce them, as well as the singularly capricious punctuation, to modern rules. At the same time, in those cases where capitals seemed more characteristic or appropriate, they have been retained.

It is a singular circumstance, that Mr. Singer (in

common with Wood, Bliss, Ellis, Headley, and all other biographers,) overlooked the misprint of *Aramantha* for *Amarantha*, which the old compositor made, with one or two exceptions, wherever the word occurred. In giving a correct representation of the original title-page, I have been obliged to print *Aramantha*.

In the hope of discovering the exact date of Lovelace's birth and baptism, I communicated with the Rev. A. J. Pearman, incumbent of Bethersden, near Ashford, and that gentleman obligingly examined the registers for me, but no traces of Lovelace's name are to be found.

W. C. H.

Kensington, *August* 12, 1863.

BIOGRAPHICAL NOTICE.

WITH the exception of Sir Egerton Brydges, who contributed to the *Gentleman's Magazine* for 1791-2 a series of articles on the life and writings of the subject of the present memoir, all the biographers of RICHARD LOVELACE have contented themselves with following the account left by Anthony Wood of his short and unhappy career. I do not think that I can do better than commence, at least, by giving word for word the narrative of Wood in his own language, to which I purpose to add such additional particulars in the form of notes or otherwise, as I may be able to supply. But the reader must not expect much that is new: for I regret to say that, after the most careful researches, I have not improved, to any large extent, the state of knowledge respecting this elegant poet and unfortunate man.

" Richard Lovelace," writes Wood, " the eldest son of

Sir William Lovelace[1] of Woollidge in Kent, knight, was

---

[1] Pedigree of the family of Richard Lovelace, the poet.

Richard Lovelace, of Queenhithe (temp. Hen. VI.).

Lancelot Lovelace.

| Richard Lovelace, d. s. p. | William Lovelace (ob. 1501). | John, (ancestor of the Lords Lovelace, of Hurley (co. Berks). |

| John | William Lovelace. |

William Lovelace, Serjeant at Law, ob. 1576.

Sir William Lovelace, ob. 1629 = Elizabeth, daughter of Edward
(according to Berry).   Aucher, Esq., of Bishops-
      bourne.

Sir William Lovelace = Anne, daughter and heir of Sir
      William Barnes, of Woolwich.

| RICH-= ? AL- ARD THEA. LOVE- LACE, born 1618 | Fran- cis. | Wil- liam. | Tho- mas. | Dud- ley | = Mary Love- lace, (? his cousin). | Jo- hanna | = Ro- bert Cæsar Esq. |

| Mar-= Henry Coke, Esq. 5th garet son of the Chief Jus- tice, and ancestor of the Earls of Leicester. | A daugh- ter, b. 1678. | Anne. | Juli- ana. | Jo- hanna. |

| Richard. | Ciriac. | . . . . | . . . . |

The above has been partly derived from a communication to the *Gentleman's Magazine* for Dec. 1791, by Sir Egerton Brydges, who chiefly compiled it from Hasted, compared with Berry's *Kent Genealogies*, 474, where there are a few inaccuracies. It is, of course, a mere skeleton-tree, and furnishes no information as to the collateral branches, the connexion between the houses of Stanley and Lovelace, &c. Sir Egerton Brydges' series of articles on Lovelace in the *Gentleman's Magazine*, with the exception of that from which the foregoing table is taken, does not contain

born in that country [in 1618], educated in grammar

---

much, if anything, that is new. On the 3rd of May, 1577, Henry Binneman paid "vi^d. and a copie" to the Stationers' Company for the right to print "the Briefe Course of the Accidents of the Deathe of Mr. Serjeant Lovelace;" and on the 30th of August following, Richard Jones obtained a licence to print "A Short Epitaphe of Serjeant Lovelace." This was the same person who is described in the pedigree as dying in 1576. His death happened, no doubt, like that of Sir Robert Bell and others, at the Oxford Summer assizes for 1576. See Stow's *Annales*, fol. 1154.

In 1563, Barnaby Googe the poet dedicated his *Eglogs, Epitaphes, and Sonnettes, newly written*, to "the Ryght Worshypfull M. Richard Lovelace, Esquier, Reader of Grayes Inne."

The following is a list of the members of the Lovelace family who belonged to the Honourable Society of Gray's Inn from 1541 to 1646:—

Thomas Lovelace, admitted 1541.

William Lovelace,	„ 1548.	Called to the bar in 1551.
Richard Lovelace,	„ 1557.	Reader in 1563. Barnaby Googe's friend.
Lancelot Lovelace,	„ 1571.	
William Lovelace,	„ 1580.	
Lancelot Lovelace,	„ 1581.	Recorder of Canterbury, ob. 1640, æt. 78.
Francis Lovelace,	„ 1609.	Perhaps the same who was Recorder of Canterbury in 1638.
Francis Lovelace (of Canterbury),	„ 1640.	Probably the poet's younger brother.
William Lovelace,	„ 1646.	

For these names and dates I am indebted to the courtesy of the Steward of Gray's Inn.

Sir William Lovelace, the poet's grandfather who, according to Berry, died in 1629, was a correspondent of Sir Dudley Carleton (see *Calendars of State Papers, Domestic Series*, 1611-18, pp. 443, 521, 533; *Ibid.* 1618-23, p. 17). It appears from some Latin lines before the first portion of *Lucasta*, that the poet's father served with distinction in Holland, and probably it was this circumstance which led to Lovelace himself turning his at-

learning in Charterhouse[1] School near London, became
a gent. commoner of Gloucester Hall in the beginning of
the year 1634,[2] and in that of his age sixteen, being
then accounted the most amiable and beautiful person
that ever eye beheld ; a person also of innate modesty,
virtue, and courtly deportment, which made him then,
but especially after, when he retired to the great city,
much admired and adored by the female sex.   In
1636, when the king and queen were for some days
entertained at Oxon, he was, at the request of a great
lady belonging to the queen, made to the Archbishop of
Canterbury [Laud], then Chancellor of the University,
actually created, among other persons of quality, Master of Arts, though but of two years' standing ; at which
time his conversation being made public, and conse-
quently his ingenuity and generous soul discovered, he
became as much admired by the male, as before by the
female, sex.   After he had left the University, he re-

___

tention in a similar direction : for the latter was on service in
the Low Countries, perhaps under his father (of whose death we
do not know the date, though Hasted intimates that he fell at the
Gryll), when his friend Tatham, afterwards the city poet, addressed to him some verses printed in a volume entitled *Ostella*
(printed in 1650).

[1] Mr. A. Keightley, Registrar of the Charterhouse, with his
usual kindness, examined for me the books of the institution, in
the hope of finding the date of Lovelace's admission, &c., but
without success. Mr. Keightley has suggested to me that perhaps
Lovelace was not on the foundation, which is of course highly
probable, and which, as Mr. Keightley seems to think, may account for the omission of his name from the registers.

[2] " He was matriculated at Gloucester Hall, June 27, 1634,
as ' filius Gul. Lovelace de Woolwich in Com. Kant. arm. au.
nat. 16.' "—Dr. BLISS, in a note on this passage in his edition of
the *Athenæ.*

tired in great splendour to the court, and being taken
into the favour of Lord George Goring, afterwards Earl
of Norwich, was by him adopted a soldier, and sent in
the quality of an ensign, in the Scotch expedition, an.
1639. Afterwards, in the second expedition, he was
commissionated a captain in the same regiment, and in
that time wrote a tragedy called *The Soldier*, but never
acted, because the stage was soon after suppressed.
After the pacification of Berwick, he retired to his native
country, and took possession [of his estate] at Lovelace
Place, in the parish of Bethersden,[1] at Canterbury,

---

[1] Bethersden is a parish in the Weald of Kent, eastward of
Smarden, near Surrenden. "The manor of Lovelace," says Hasted (*History of Kent*, iii. 239), "is situated at a very small distance *south-westward* from the church [of Bethersden]. It was
in early times the property of a family named Grunsted, or
Greenstreet, as they were sometimes called ; the last of whom,
Henry de Grunsted, a man of eminent repute, as all the records
of this county testify, in the reigns of both King Edward II.
and III., passed away this manor to *Kinet*, in which name it
did not remain long; for *William Kinet*, in the 41st year of King
Edward III, conveyed it by sale to *John Lovelace*, who erected
that mansion here, which from hence bore his name in addition,
being afterwards styled *Bethersden-Lovelace*, from which sprang
a race of gentlemen, who, in the military line, acquired great reputation and honour, and by their knowledge in the municipal
laws, deserved well of the Commonwealth ; from whom descended
those of this name seated at *Bayford* in *Sittingburne*, and at
Kingsdown in this county, the Lords Lovelace of Hurley, and
others of the county of Berks." The same writer, in his *History
of Canterbury*, has preserved many memorials of the connexion of
the Lovelaces from the earliest times with Canterbury and its
neighbourhood. William Lovelace, in the reign of Philip and
Mary, died possessed of the mansion belonging to the abbey of
St. Lawrence, near Canterbury; after the death of his son

Chart. Halden, &c., worth, at least, £500 per annum. About which time he [being then on the commission of the peace] was made choice of by the whole body of the county of Kent at an assize, to deliver the Kentish petition[1] to the House of Commons, for the restoring

---

William, it passed to other hands. In 1621, Lancelot Lovelace, Esq., was Recorder of Canterbury; in 1638, Richard Lovelace, Esq., held that office; and in the year of the Restoration, Richard Lovelace, the poet's brother, was Recorder. In the Public Library at Plymouth, there is a folio MS. (mentioned in Mr. Halliwell's catalogue, 1853), containing "Original Papers of the Molineux and *Lovelace* Families." I regret that I have not had an opportunity of inspecting it. Mr. Halliwell does not seem to have examined the volume; at all events, that gentleman does not furnish any particulars as to the nature of the contents, or as to the period to which the papers belong. This information, in the case of a MS. deposited in a provincial library in a remote district, would have been peculiarly valuable. It is possible that the documents refer only to the Lovelaces of Hurley, co. Berks.

[1] "The Humble Petition of the Gentry, Ministers, and Commonalty, for the county of Kent, agreed upon at the General Assizes for that county." See *Journals of the House of Lords,* iv. 675-6-7. The "framers and contrivers" of this petition were Sir Edward Dering, Bart., of Surrenden-Dering; Sir Roger Twysden, the well-known scholar; Sir George Strode, and Mr. Richard Spencer. On the 21st May, 1641, Dering had unsuccessfully attempted to bring in a bill for the *abolition* of church-government by bishops, archbishops, &c., whereas one of the articles of the petition of 1642 (usually known as *Dering's Petition*) was a prayer for the restoration of the Liturgy and the maintenance of the episcopal bench in its integrity. A numerously signed petition had also been addressed to both Houses by the county in 1641, in which the strongest reasons were given for the adoption of Dering's proposed act. From 1641 to 1648, indeed, the Houses were overwhelmed by Kentish petitions of various kinds. This portion of Wood's narrative is confirmed by Marvell's lines prefixed to *Lucasta,* 1649:—

the king to his rights, and for settling the government,
&c. For which piece of service he was committed
[April 30, 1642] to the Gatehouse at Westminster,[1]

> " And one the Book prohibits, because Kent
> Their first Petition by the Authour sent."

" Sir William Boteler, of Kent, returning about the beginning
of *April* 1642, from his attendance (being then Gentleman Pen-
tioner) on the king at *Yorke*, then celebrating St. *George's* feast,
was by the earnest solicitation of the Gentry of Kent ingaged to
joyn with them in presenting the most honest and famous Petition
of theirs to the House of Commons, delivered by Captain *Richard
Lovelace,* for which service the Captain was committed Prisoner
to the *Gate House,* and *Sir William Boteler* to the Fleet, from
whence, after some weeks close imprisonment, no impeachment in
all that time brought in against him [Boteler], many Petitions
being delivered and read in the House for his inlargement, he
was at last upon bail of £20,000 [£15,000] remitted to his
house in *London,* to attend *de die in diem* the pleasure of the
House."—*Mercurius Rusticus,* 1646 (edit. 1685, pp. 7, 8). The
fact was that, although on the 7th of April, 1642, the Kentish
petition in favour of the Liturgy, &c. had been ordered by the
House of Commons to be burned by the common hangman (*Parliaments and Councils of England,* 1839, p. 384), Boteler and
Lovelace had the temerity, on the 30th of the same month, to
come up to London, and present it again to the House. It was this
which occasioned their committal. In the *Verney Papers* (Camd.
Soc. 1845, p. 175) there is the following memorandum :—

> " Captaine Lovelace committed to the Gatehouse ⎱ Concerning
> Sir William Butler committed to the Fleete   ⎰ Deering's
> ⎰ petition."

[1] " Gatehouse, a prison in Westminster, near the west end of
the Abbey, which leads into Dean's Yard, Tothill Street, and the
Almonry "—Cunningham's *Handbook of London, Past and Present.* But for a more particular account, see Stow's *Survey,* ed.
1720, ii. lib. 6.

> " The Gatehouse for a Prison was ordain'd,
> When in this land the third king *Edward* reign'd:

where he made that celebrated song called, *Stone Walls do not a Prison make*, &c. After three or four months' [six or seven weeks'] imprisonment, he had his liberty upon bail of £40,000 [£4000?] not to stir out of the lines of communication without a pass from the speaker. During the time of this confinement to London, he lived beyond the income of his estate, either to keep up the credit and reputation of the king's cause by furnishing men with horses and arms, or by relieving ingenious men in want, whether scholars, musicians, soldiers, &c. Also, by furnishing his two brothers, Colonel Franc. Lovelace, and Captain William Lovelace (afterwards slain at Caermarthen)[1] with men and money for the king's cause, and his other brother, called Dudley Posthumus Lovelace, with moneys for his maintenance in Holland, to study tactics and fortification in that school of war. After the rendition of Oxford garrison, in 1646, he formed a regiment for the service of the French king, was colonel of it, and wounded at Dunkirk;[2] and in 1648, returning into England, he,

---

Good lodging roomes, and diet it affords,
But I had rather lye at home on boords."
         TAYLOR's *Praise and Virtue of a Jayle and Jaylers*,
                  (Works, 1630, ii. 130).

[1] By an inadvertence, I have spoken of *Thomas*, instead of *William*, Lovelace having perished at Caermarthen, in a note at p. 125.

[2] It appears from the following copy of verses, printed in Tatham's *Ostella*, 1650, 4to., that Lovelace made a stay in the Netherlands about this time, if indeed he did not serve there with his regiment.

with Dudley Posthumus before mentioned, then a captain under him, were both committed prisoners to

---

UPON MY NOBLE FRIEND RICHARD LOVELACE, ESQ., HIS
BEING IN HOLLAND.   AN INVITATION.

Come, Adonis, come again ;
　　What distaste could drive thee hence,
Where so much delight did reign,
　　Sateing ev'n the soul of sense?
And though thou unkind hast prov'd,
Never youth was more belov'd.
　　　Then, lov'd Adonis, come away,
　　　For Venus brooks not thy delay.

Wert thou sated with the spoil
　　Of so many virgin hearts,
And therefore didst change thy soil,
　　To seek fresh in other parts?
Dangers wait on foreign game;
We have deer more sound and tame.
　　　Then, lov'd Adonis, come away,
　　　For Venus brooks not thy delay.

Phillis, fed with thy delights,
　　In thy absence pines away;
And love, too, hath lost his rites,
　　Not one lass keeps holiday.
They have changed their mirth for cares,
And do onely sigh thy airs.
　　　Then, lov'd Adonis, come away,
　　　For Venus brooks not thy delay.

Elpine, in whose sager looks
　　Thou wert wont to take delight,
Hath forsook his drink and books,
　　'Cause he can't enjoy thy sight:
He hath laid his learning by,
'Cause his wit wants company.
　　　Then, lov'd Adonis, come away,
　　　For friendship brooks not thy delay.

Peter House,[1] in London, where he framed his poems for the press, entitled, *Lucasta : Epodes, Odes, Sonnets,*

All the swains that once did use
    To converse with Love and thee,
In the language of thy Muse,
    Have forgot Love's deity :
They deny to write a line,
And do only talk of thine.
     Then, lov'd Adonis, come away,
     For friendship brooks not thy delay.

By thy sweet Althea's voice,
    We conjure thee to return ;
Or we'll rob thee of that choice,
    In whose flames each heart would burn :
That inspir'd by her and sack,
Such company we will not lack :
     That poets in the age to come,
     Shall write of our Elisium.

[1] Peter, or rather *Petre* House, in Aldersgate Street, belonged at one time to the antient family by whose name it was known. The third Lord Petre, dying in 1638, left it, with other possessions in and about the city of London, to his son William. (Collins's *Peerage*, by Brydges, vii. 10, 11.) When Lovelace was committed to Peter House, and probably long before (*Mercurius Rusticus*, ed. 1685, pp. 76-79), this mansion was used as a house of detention for political prisoners ; but in Ward's *Diary* (ed. Severn, p. 167), there is the following entry (like almost all Ward's entries, unluckily without date) :—" My Lord Peters is an Essex man ; hee hath a house in Aldersgate Street, wherein lives the Marquis of Dorchester : " implying that at that period (perhaps about 1660), the premises still belonged to the Petre family, though temporarily let to Lord Dorchester. Another celebrated house in the same street was London House, which continued for some time to be the town residence of the Bishops of London. When it had ceased to be an episcopal abode, it was adapted to the purposes of an ordinary dwelling, and, among the occupants, at a somewhat later period, was Tom Rawlinson, the great book-collector. See Stow, ed. 1720, ii. lib. iii. p. 121.

Songs, &c., Lond. 1649, Oct. The reason why he gave that title was because, some time before, he had made his amours to a gentlewoman of great beauty and fortune, named Lucy Sacheverell, whom he usually called *Lux casta ;* but she, upon a stray report that Lovelace was dead of his wound received at Dunkirk, soon after married.[1] He also wrote *Aramantha* [Amarantha], a *Pastoral,* printed with *Lucasta.*[2] Afterwards a musical composition of two parts was set to part of it by Henry Lawes,[3] sometimes servant to king Charles I., in his public and private music.

---

[1] How different was the conduct, under similar circumstances, of the lady whom Charles Gerbier commemorates in his *Elogium Heroinum,* 1651, p. 127. "Democion, the Athenian virgin," he tells us, " hearing that Leosthenes, to whom she was contracted, was slain in the wars, she killed herself; but before her death she thus reasoned with herself: ' Although my body is untoucht, yet should I fall into the imbraces of another, I should but deceive the second, since I am still married to the former in my heart.'"

[2] Wood's story about *Lucasta* having been a Lucy Sacheverell, "a lady of great beauty and fortune," may reasonably be doubted. Lucasta, whoever she was, seems to have belonged to Kent; the *Sacheverells* were not a Kentish family. Besides, the corruption of Lucy Sacheverell into Lucasta is not very obvious, and rather violent; and the probability is that the author of the *Athenæ* was misled by his informant on this occasion. The plate etched by Lely and engraved by Faithorne, which is found in the second part of *Lucasta,* 1659, can scarcely be regarded as a portrait; it was, in all likelihood, a mere fancy sketch, and we are not perhaps far from the truth in our surmise that the artist was nearly, if not quite, as much in the dark as to who Lucasta was, as we are ourselves at the present day.

[3] This is a mistake on the part of Wood, which (with many others) ought to be corrected in a new edition of the *Athenæ.* Lawes did not set to music *Amarantha, a Pastoral,* nor any portion of it; but he harmonized two stanzas of a little poem to

" After the murther of king Charles I. Lovelace was set at liberty, and, having by that time consumed all his estate,[1] grew very melancholy (which brought him at length into a consumption), became very poor in body and purse, was the object of charity, went in ragged cloaths (whereas when he was in his glory he wore cloth of gold and silver), and mostly lodged in obscure and dirty places, more befitting the worst of beggars and poorest of servants, &c. After his death his brother Dudley, before mentioned, made a collection of his poetical papers, fitted them for the press, and entitled them *Lucasta: Posthume Poems*, Lond. 1659,[2] Oct., the second part, with his picture before them.[3] These are all the things that he hath extant; those that were never published were his tragedy, called *The Soldier* or *Soldiers*,

---

be found at p. 29 of the present volume, and called " To Amarantha; that she would dishevel her Hair."

[1] Hasted states that soon after the death of Charles I. the manor of Lovelace-Bethersden passed by purchase to Richard Hulse, Esq.

[2] On the title-page of this portion of *Lucasta*, as well as on that which had appeared in 1649, the author is expressly styled, *Richard Lovelace, Esq.*: yet in Berry's *Kent Genealogies*, p. 474, he is, curiously enough, called *Sir Richard Lovelace, Knt.* It is scarcely necessary to observe that the error is on Berry's side.

[3] The most pleasing likeness of Lovelace, the only one, indeed, which conveys any just idea to us of the " handsomest man of his time," is the picture at Dulwich, which has been twice copied, in both instances with very indifferent success. One of these copies was made for Harding's *Biographical Mirror*. Bromley (*Dictionary of Engraved British Portraits*, 1793, p. 101) correctly names F[rancis] Lovelace, the writer's brother, as the designer of the portrait before the *Posthume Poems*.

before mentioned; and his comedy, called *The Scholar*,[1] which he composed at sixteen years of age, when he came first to Gloucester hall, acted with applause afterwards in Salisbury Court. He died in a very mean lodging in Gunpowder Alley,[2] near Shoe Lane,[3] and was

---

[1] Winstanley, perhaps, intended some allusion to these two lost dramas from the pen of Lovelace, when he thus characterizes him in his *Lives of the Poets*, 1687, p. 170:—" I can compare no man," he says, " so like this Colonel *Lovelace* as *Sir Philip Sidney*, of which latter it is said by one in an epitaph made of him :—

  ' Nor is it fit that more I should acquaint,
      Lest men adore in one
  A Scholar, *Souldier*, Lover, and a Saint.' "

As to the comparison, Winstanley must be understood to signify a resemblance between Lovelace and Sidney as men, rather than as writers. Winstanley's extract is from *Wits' Recreations*, but the text, as he gives it, varies from that printed by the editor of the reprint of that work in 1817.

[2] Gunpowder Alley still exists, but it is not the Gunpowder Alley which Lovelace knew, having been rebuilt more than once since 1658. It is now a tolerably wide and airy court, without any conspicuous appearance of squalor. There is no tradition, I am sorry to say, respecting Lovelace; all such recollections have long been swept away. When one of the old inhabitants told me (and there are one or two persons who have lived here all their life) that a great poet once resided thereabout, I naturally became eager to catch the name; but it turned out to be Dr. Johnson, not Lovelace, the latter of whom might have been contemporary with Homer for aught they knew to the contrary in Gunpowder Alley. It appears from Decker and Webster's play of *Westward Hoe*, 1607 (Webster's Works, ed. Hazlitt, i. 67), that there was another Gunpowder Alley, near Crutched Friars.

[3] Hone (*Every-Day Book*, ii. 561, edit. 1827) states, under date of April 28, that " during this month in 1658 the accomplished Colonel Richard Lovelace died *in the Gatehouse at Westminster*, whither he had been committed," &c. No authority,

buried at the west-end of the church of S. Bride, alias
Bridget, in London, near to the body of his kinsman Will.
Lovelace, of Gray's Inn, Esq., in sixteen hundred fifty
and eight,[1] having before been accounted by all those
that well knew him to have been a person well versed in
the Greek[2] and Latin[3] poets, in music, whether practical
or theoretical, instrumental or vocal, and in other things
befitting a gentleman.   Some of the said persons have
also added, in my hearing, that his common discourse
was not only significant and witty, but incomparably

---

however, is given for an assertion so wholly at variance with the
received view on the subject, and I am afraid that Hone has here
fallen into a mistake.

[1] Aubrey, in what are called his *Lives of Eminent Men*, but
which are, in fact, merely rough biographical memoranda, states
under the head of LOVELACE :—" Obiit in a cellar in Long acre, a
little before the restauration of his Ma^lle. Mr. Edm. Wyld, &c.
had made collections for him, and given him money. . . . . Geo.
Petty, haberdasher, in Fleet street, carried xx^s. to him every
Monday morning from S^r . . . . Many and Charles Cotton, Esq.
for . . . . moneths, *but was never repayd.*" Aubrey was certainly a
contemporary of Lovelace, and Wood seems to have been indebted
to him for a good deal of information ; but all who are acquainted
with Aubrey are probably aware that he took, in many instances,
very little trouble to examine for himself, but accepted state-
ments on hearsay.   Wood does not, in the case of Lovelace,
adopt Aubrey's account, and it is to be observed that, *if* the poet
died as poor as he is represented by both writers to have died,
he would have been buried by the parish, and, dying in Long
Acre, the parochial authorities would not have carried him to
Fleet Street for sepulture.

[2] See p. 149, *note* 3.   His acquaintance with Hellenic literature possibly extended very little beyond the pages of the *An-
thologia.*

[3] His favourites appear to have been Ausonius and Catullus.

graceful, which drew respect from all men and women. Many other things I could now say of him, relating either to his most generous mind in his prosperity, or dejected estate in his worst state of poverty, but for brevity's sake I shall now pass them by. At the end of his Posthume Poems are several elegies written on him by eminent poets of that time, wherein you may see his just character."

Such is Wood's account ; it is to be regretted that that writer did not supply the additional information, which he tantalizes us by saying that he possessed, and could have published, had he not been afraid of being tedious. His love of brevity is, in this case, most provoking.

As might be expected, the Journals of Parliament cast additional light on the personal connexion of Lovelace with the Kentish Petition of 1642, which was for the *general* redress of existing grievances, not, as the editor of the *Verney Papers* seems to have considered, merely for the adjustment of certain points relative to the Militia. Parliamentary literature has not a very strong fascination for the editors of old authors, and the biographers of Lovelace have uniformly overlooked the mine of information which lies in the *Lords' and Commons' Journals.* The subject was apparently introduced, for the first time, into Parliament on the 28th March, 1642, when a conference of both Houses took place, respecting " a petition from Kent, which, praying for a Restoration of the Bishops, Liturgy and Common Prayer, and other constitutional measures, was voted seditious and against privilege and the peace of the kingdom ;" on the same occasion, Lord Bristol and Mr. Justice Mallet were committed to the Tower for having in their possession a copy of the document. On the 7th April it was ordered by both Houses, that the Kentish Petition should be burned by the hands of the common hangman.

On the 28th April, the Commons acquainted the Upper House, by Mr. Oliver Cromwell, "that a great meeting was to be held next day on Blackheath, to back the rejected Kentish Petition."[1]

Two days later, a strange scene occurred at Westminster. Let the Commons' Journals tell the story in their own language :—

"30 April, 1642. The House being informed that divers gentlemen of the county of Kent were at the door, that desired to present a Petition to the House;

"They were called in, presented their Petition, and withdrew.

"And their Petition was read, and appeared to be the same that was formerly burnt, by order of both Houses, by the hands of the common hangman. Captain *Leigh* reports that, being at the Quarter Sessions held at *Maidstone,* he observed certain passages which he delivered in writing.

"Captain LOVELACE, who presented the Petition, was called in: and Mr. Speaker was commanded to ask him, from whose hand he had this Petition, and who gave him warrant to present it.

---

[1] On the 5th May, 1642, a counter-petition was presented by some Kentish gentlemen to the House of Commons, disclaiming and condemning the former one.—*Journals of the H. of C.* ii. 558.

" ' Mr. *Geo. Chute* delivered him [he replied] the Petition the next day after the Assizes.'

" ' The gentlemen [he continued], that were assembled at *Blackheath*, commanded him to deliver it.'

" [The Speaker then inquired] whether he knew that the like was burnt by order of this House, and that some were here questioned for the business.

" ' He understood a general rumour, that some gentlemen were questioned.

" ' He had heard a fortnight since, that the like Petition was burnt by the hand of the common hangman.

" ' He knew nothing of the bundle of printed petitions.'

" He likewise said, ' that there was a petition at the Quarter Sessions, disavowed by all the Justices there, which he tore.'

" Sir William Boteler was likewise called in, [and] asked when he was at Yorke.

" [He] answered, ' On Wednesday last was sevennight, he came from Yorke, and came to his house in London.

" ' He heard of a petition that was never delivered.

" ' He never heard of any censure of the Parliament.

" ' He heard that a paper was burnt for being irregularly burnt [? presented].

" ' He had heard that the Petition, that went under the name of the Kentish Petition, was burnt by the hands of the common hangman.

" ' He never heard of any order of either, [or] of both, the Houses concerning [the Petition].

" ' He was at Hull on Thursday or Friday was a sevennight: as he came from Yorke, he took Hull in the way. He had heard, that Sir Roger Twisden was questioned for the like Petition.

" ' He was yesterday at *Black-heath.*'

" Resolved, upon the question, that Captain Love-lace shall be presently committed prisoner to the Gate-house.

" Resolved, upon the question, that Sir William Boteler shall be presently committed prisoner to the Fleet.

" Ordered, that the sergeant shall apprehend them, and carry them in safe custody, and deliver them as prisoners to the several prisons aforesaid."

On the 4th May, 1642, the House of Commons ordered Mr. Whittlock and others to prepare a charge against Mr. Lovelace and Sir William Boteler with all expedition; but nothing further is heard of the matter till the 17th June, when Lovelace[1] and Boteler petitioned the House separately for their release from custody. Hereupon Sir William was discharged on finding personal bail to the extent of £10,000, with a surety for £5000 ; and in the case of his companion in misfortune it was ordered, on the question, that " he be forthwith bailed upon GOOD security." This " good security," surely, did not reach the sum mentioned by Wood, namely, £40,000; but it is likely that the

---

[1] " The humble petition of Richard Lovelace, Esquire, a pri-soner in the Gate-house, by a former order of this House."— *Journals,* ii. 629.

author of the *Athenæ* is *only* wrong by a cypher, and that the amount fixed was £4000, as it has been already suggested. Thus Lovelace's confinement did not exceed seven weeks in duration, and the probability, is that the sole inconvenience, which he subsequently experienced, was the loss of the bail.

The description left by Wood and Aubrey of the end of Lovelace can only be reconciled with the fact, that his daughter and heiress conveyed Kingsdown, Hever,[1] and a moiety of Chipsted, to the Cokes by marriage with Mr. Henry Coke, by presuming that those manors were entailed; while Lovelace Place, as well perhaps as Bayford and Goodneston, not being similarly secured, were sold to defray the owner's incumbrances. At any rate it is not, upon the whole, very probable that he died in a hovel, in a state of absolute poverty;[2] that he received a pound a week (equal to about £4 of our money) from two friends, Cotton and another, Aubrey himself admits; and we may rest satisfied that, however painful the contrast may have been between the opening and close of that career, the deplorable account given in the *Athenæ*, and in the so-called *Lives of Eminent Men*, is much exaggerated and over-drawn.

It has not hitherto been remarked, that among the

---

[1] This property, which was of considerable extent and value, was purchased of the Cheney family, toward the latter part of the reign of Henry VI, by Richard Lovelace, of Queenhithe.

[2] I do not think that there is any proof, that Gunpowder-alley was, at the time when Lovelace resided there, a particularly poor or mean locality.

Kentish gentry who, from time to time, elected to change the nature of their tenure from gavelkind to primogeniture, were the Lovelaces themselves, in the person of Thomas Lovelace,[1] who, by Act of Parliament 2 and 3 Edw. VI. obtained, concurrently with several other families, the power of conversion. This Thomas Lovelace was not improbably the same, who was admitted a student of Gray's Inn in 1541; and that he was of the Kentish Lovelaces there is not much reason to doubt; although, at the same time, I am unable to fix the precise degree of consanguinity between him and Serjeant William Lovelace of Gray's Inn, who died in 1576, and who was great-grandfather to the author of *Lucasta.* The circumstance that the real property of Thomas Lovelace aforesaid, situated in Kent, was released by Act of Parliament, 2 and 3 Edw. VI. from the operations of gavelkind tenure (assuming, as is most likely to have been the case, that he was of the same stock as the poet, though not an immediate ancestor,) seems to explain the following allusion by Dudley Lovelace in the verses prefixed by him to *Lucasta,* 1649 :—

> " Those by the landed have been writ,
> Mine's but a younger-brother wit."

As well as the subjoined lines by Lovelace in the poem entitled, " To Lucasta, from Prison," (see p. 44 of present edition) :—

> " Next would I court my *Liberty,*
> And then my birthright, *Property.*"

---

[1] See Lambarde (*Perambulation of Kent,* 1570, ed. 1826, p. 533).

There is evidence to prove that Lovelace was on intimate terms with some of the wits of his time, and that he had friendly relations with many of them—such as Hall, Rawlins, Lenton, and particularly the Cottons. John Tatham, the City Poet, and author of *The Fancies Theater*, 1640, knew him well, and addressed to him some stanzas, not devoid of merit, during his stay abroad. In 1643, Henry Glapthorne, a celebrated dramatist and poet of the same age, dedicated to Lovelace his poem of *Whitehall*, printed in that year in a quarto pamphlet, with elegies on the Earls of Bedford and Manchester.[1] The pages of *Lucasta* bear testimony to the acquaintance of the author with Anthony Hodges, of New College, Oxford, translator of *Clitophon and*

---

[1] As so little is known of the personal history of Lovelace, the reader may not be displeased to see this Dedication, and it is therefore subjoined :—

"To MY NOBLE FRIEND AND GOSSIP, CAPTAIN RICHARD LOVELACE.

"SIR,

"I HAVE so long beene in your debt that I am almost desperate in my selfe of making you paiment, till this fancy by ravishing from you a new curtesie in its patronage, promised me it would satisfie part of my former engagements to you. Wonder not to see it invade you thus on the sudden; gratitude is aëriall, and, like that element, nimble in its motion and performance; though I would not have this of mine of a French disposition, to charge hotly and retreat unfortunately: there may appeare something in this that may maintaine the field courageously against Envy, nay come off with honour; if you, Sir, please to rest satisfied that it marches under your ensignes, which are the desires of

"Your true honourer,

"HEN. GLAPTHORNE."

Leucippe from the Greek of Achilles Tatius (or rather probably from a Latin version of the original), and with other[1] members of the University.[2]

Although it is stated by Wood that *Lucasta* was prepared for the press by Lovelace himself, on his return from the Continent in 1648, it is impossible to believe that any care was bestowed on the correction of the text, or on the arrangement of the various pieces which compose the volume: nor did his brother Dudley Pos-

---

[1] It has never, so far as I am aware, been suggested that the friend to whom Sir John Suckling addressed his capital ballad:—

"I tell thee, Dick, where I have been,"

may have been Lovelace. It was a very usual practice (then even more so than now) among familiar acquaintances to use the abbreviated Christian name in addressing each other; thus Suckling was *Jack;* Davenant, *Will;* Carew, *Tom,* &c.; in the preceding generation Marlowe had been *Kit;* Jonson, *Ben;* Greene, *Robin,* and so forth; and although there is no positive proof that Lovelace and Suckling were intimate, it is extremely probable that such was the case, more especially as they were not only brother poets, but both country gentlemen belonging to neighbouring counties. Suckling had, besides, some taste and aptitude for military affairs, and could discourse about strategics in a city tavern over a bowl of canary with the author of *Lucasta,* notwithstanding that he was a little troubled by nervousness (according to report), when the enemy was too near.

[2] From Andrew Marvell's lines prefixed to *Lucasta,* 1649, it seems that Lovelace and himself were on tolerably good terms, and that when the former presented the Kentish petition, and was imprisoned for so doing, his friends, who exerted themselves to procure his release, suspected Marvell of a share in his disgrace, which Marvell, according to his own account, earnestly disclaimed. See the lines commencing:—

"But when the beauteous ladies came to know," &c.

thumus, who edited the second part of the book in 1659, perform his task in any degree better. In both instances, the printer seems to have been suffered to do the work in his own way, and very infamously he has done it. To supply all the short-comings of the author and his literary executor at this distance of time, is, unfortunately, out of the power of any editor; but in the present republication I have taken the liberty of rearranging the poems, to a certain extent, in the order in which it may be conjectured that they were written; and where Lovelace contributed commendatory verses to other works, either before or after the appearance of the first portion of *Lucasta*, the two texts have been collated, and improved readings been occasionally obtained.

The few poems, on which the fame of Lovelace may be said to rest, are emanations not only of the stirring period in which he lived, but of the peculiar circumstances into which he was thrown at different epochs of his life. Lovelace had not the melodious and exquisite taste of Herrick, the wit of Suckling, or the power of Randolph (so often second only to his master Jonson). Mr. Singer has praised the exuberant fancy of Lovelace; but, in my thinking, Lovelace was inferior in fancy, as well as in grace, both to Carew and the author of *Hesperides*. Yet Lovelace has left behind him one or two things, which I doubt if any of those writers could have produced, and which our greatest poets would not have been ashamed to own. Winstanley was so far right in instituting a comparison between Lovelace and Sydney, that it is hard to name any one in the entire circle of early English literature except Sydney and Wither, who could have attempted, with any chance of success, the *Song to Althea from Prison;* and how differently Sydney at least would have handled it! We know what Herrick would have made of it; it would have furnished the theme for one more invocation to JULIA. From Suckling we should have had a bantering playfulness, or a fescennine gaiety, equally unsuited to the subject. Waller had once an opportunity of realizing the position, which has been described by his contemporary in immortal stanzas; but Waller, when he was under confinement, was thinking too much of his neck to write verses with much felicity, and preferred waiting, till he got back to Beaconsfield (when his inspiration had evaporated), to pour out his feelings to Lady Dorothy or Lady Sophia. Wither's song, "Shall I wasting in Despair," is certainly superior to the *Song to Althea.* Wither was frequently equal to Lovelace in poetical imagery and sentiment, and he far excelled him in versification. The versification of Lovelace is indeed more rugged and unmusical than that of any other writer of the period, and this blemish is so conspicuous throughout *Lucasta,* and is noticeable in so many cases, where it might have been avoided with very little trouble, that we are naturally led to the inference that Lovelace, in writing, accepted from indolence or haste, the first word which happened to occur to his mind. Daniel, Drayton, and others were, it is well known, indefatigable revisers of their poems; they "added and altered many times," mostly for the better, occasionally for the worse. We can scarcely picture to ourselves Lovelace blotting a line, though it would have been well for his reputation, if he had blotted many.

In the poem of the *Loose Saraband* (p. 34) there is some resemblance to a piece translated from Meleager in Elton's *Specimens of Classic Poets*, i. 411, and entitled by Elton " Playing at Hearts."

> " Love acts the tennis-player's part,
>   And throws to thee my panting heart;
>   Heliodora! ere it fall,
>   Let desire catch swift the ball:
>   Let her in the ball-court move,
>   Follow in the game with love.
>   If thou throw me back again,
>   I shall of foul play complain."

And an address to the Cicada by the same writer, (*Ibid.* i. 415) opens with these lines :—

> " Oh, shrill-voiced insect that, with dew-drops sweet
>   Inebriate, dost in desert woodlands sing."

In the poem called " The Grasshopper" (p. 94), the author speaks of the insect as

> " Drunk ev'ry night with a delicious tear,
>   Dropped thee from heaven."——

The similarity, in each case, I believe to have been entirely accidental : nor am I disposed to think that Lovelace was under any considerable or direct obligations to the classics. I have taken occasion to remark that Lovelace seems to have helped to furnish a model to Cleveland, who carried to an extraordinary length that fondness for words and figures derived from the alchymist's vocabulary; but as regards the author of *Lucasta* himself, it may be asserted that there are few writers whose productions exhibit less of book-lore than his, and even in those places, where he has employed phrases or images similar to some found in Peele, Middleton, Herrick, and others, there is great room to question, whether the circumstance can be treated as amounting to more than a curious coincidence.

The Master of Dulwich College has obligingly informed me, that the picture of *Althea*, as well as that of Lovelace himself, bequeathed by Cartwright the actor to Dulwich College in 1687, bears no clue to date of composition, or to the artist's name, and that it does not assist in the identification of the lady. This is the more vexatious, inasmuch as it seems probable that *Althea*, whoever she was, became the poet's wife, after *Lucasta's* marriage to another. The *Chloes*, &c. mentioned in the following pages were merely more or less intimate acquaintances of Lovelace, like the *Electra*, *Perilla*, *Corinna*, &c. of Herrick. But at the same time an obscurity has hitherto hung over some of the persons mentioned under fictitious names in the poems of Lovelace, which a little research and trouble would have easily removed. For instance, no one who reads "Amarantha, a Pastoral," doubts that *Lucasta* and *Amarantha* are one and the same person. *Alexis* is Lovelace himself. *Ellinda* is a female friend of the poet, who occasionally stayed at her house, and on one occasion (p. 79) had a serious illness there. *Ellinda* marries *Amyntor*, under which disguise, I suspect, lurks the well known Mæcenas of his time, Endymion Porter. If Porter be *Amyntor*, of course *Ellinda* must be the

Lady Olivia Porter, his wife. *Arigo* (see the poem of *Amyntor's Grove*) signifies Porter's friend, Henry Jermyn. It may be as well to add that the *Lettice* mentioned at p. 121, was the Lady Lettice Goring, wife of Lovelace's friend, and third daughter of Richard Boyle, first Earl of Cork. This lady died before her husband, to whom she brought no issue.

The following lines are prefixed to *Fons Lachry-marum, &c.* by John Quarles, 1648, 8vo., and are subscribed, as will be seen, *R. L.*; they may be from the pen of Lovelace; but, if so, it is strange that they were not admitted, with other productions of a similar character, into the volume published by the poet himself in 1649, or into that edited by his brother in 1659.

To my Dear Friend the Author.

The Son begins to rise, the Father's set:
Heav'n took away one light, and pleas'd to let
Another rise. Quarles, thy light's divine,
And it shall teach Darkness it self to shine.
Each word revives thy Father's name, his art
Is well imprinted in thy noble heart.
I've read thy pleasing lines, wherein I find
The rare Endeavors of a modest mind.
Proceed as well as thou hast well begun,
That we may see the Father by the Son.

                                    R. L.

Arms of Lovelace of Bethersden: Gules, on a chief indented argent, three martlets sable.

CONTENTS.

PART I.

---

[1] Since the note at p. 133 was written, the following description by Aubrey (*Lives*, &c., ii. 332), of a picture of the Lady
Venetia Digby has fallen under my notice. " Also, at Mr.

Rose's, a jeweller in Henrietta Street, in Covent Garden, is an excellent piece of hers, drawne after she was newly dead. She had
a most lovely sweet-turned face, delicate darke browne haire.
She had a perfect healthy constitution; strong; good skin; well-
proportioned; inclining to a *Bona-Roba*."

d

III. COMMENDATORY VERSES, PREFIXED TO VARIOUS PUBLICATIONS BETWEEN 1652 AND 1657.

LUCASTA
BY
R L
Esq:

P. Lilly Invt.   W. Faithorne Sculp:

LUCASTA:

EPODES, ODES, SONNETS, SONGS, &c.

TO WHICH IS ADDED

ARAMANTHA,

A

PASTORALL.

BY

RICHARD LOVELACE,

Efq.

LONDON,

Printed by THO. HARPER, and are to be fold
by THO. EVVSTER, at the GUN, in
Ivie Lane. 1649.

ɒ

THE DEDICATION.

TO THE RIGHT HON. MY LADY ANNE LOVELACE.[1]

O the richest Treasury
That e'er fill'd ambitious eye ;
To the faire bright Magazin
Hath impoverisht Love's Queen ;
To th' Exchequer of all honour
(All take pensions but from her) ;
To the taper of the thore
Which the god himselfe but bore ;
To the Sea of Chaste Delight ;
Let me cast the Drop I write.
And as at Loretto's shrine
Cæsar shovels in his mine,

---

[1] This lady was the wife of the unfortunate John, second Lord Lovelace, who suffered so severely for his attachment to the King's cause, and daughter to the equally unfortunate Thomas, Earl of Cleveland, who was equally devoted to his sovereign, and whose estates were ordered by the Parliament to be sold, July 26, 1650. See *Parliaments and Councils of England*, 1839, p. 507.

DEDICATION.

Th' Empres spreads her carkanets,
The lords submit their coronets,
Knights their chased armes hang by,
Maids diamond-ruby fancies tye ;
Whilst from the pilgrim she wears
One poore false pearl, but ten true tears :
   So among the Orient prize,
(Saphyr-onyx eulogies)
Offer'd up unto your fame,
Take my GARNET-DUBLET name,
And vouchsafe 'midst those rich joyes
(With devotion) these TOYES.

                RICHARD LOVELACE.

TO MY BEST BROTHER ON HIS POEMS
CALLED "LUCASTA."

NOW y' have oblieg'd the age, thy wel known
    worth
    Is to our joy auspiciously brought forth.
Good morrow to thy son, thy first borne flame
Which, as thou gav'st it birth, stamps it a name,
That Fate and a discerning age shall set
The chiefest jewell in her coronet.

Why then needs all this paines, those season'd pens,
That standing lifeguard to a booke (kinde friends),
That with officious care thus guard thy gate,
As if thy Child were illigitimate?
Forgive their freedome, since unto their praise
They write to give, not to dispute thy bayes.

As when some glorious queen, whose pregnant wombe
Brings forth a kingdome with her first-borne Sonne,
Marke but the subjects joyfull hearts and eyes:
Some offer gold, and others sacrifice;
This slayes a lambe, that, not so rich as hee,
Brings but a dove, this but a bended knee;

And though their giftes be various, yet their sence
Speaks only this one thought, Long live the prince.

So, my best brother, if unto your name
I offer up a thin blew-burning flame,
Pardon my love, since none can make thee shine,
Vnlesse they kindle first their torch at thine.
Then as inspir'd, they boldly write, nay that,
Which their amazed lights but twinkl'd at,
And their illustrate thoughts doe voice this right,
Lucasta held their torch; thou gav'st it light.

FRANCIS LOVELACE, Col.

AD EUNDEM.

EN puer Idalius tremulis circumvolat alis,
   Quem propè sedentem[1] castior[2] uret amor.
Lampada sic videas circumvolitare Py-
      raustā,[3]
   Cui contingenti est flamma futura rogus.
Ergo procul fugias, Lector, cui nulla placebunt
   Carmina, ni fuerint turpia, spurca, nigra.
Sacrificus Romæ lustralem venditat undam:
   Castior est illâ Castalis unda mihi:
Limpida, et εὐλικρινὴς, nullâ putredine spissa,
   Scilicet ex puro defluit illa jugo.
Ex purâ veniunt tam dia poemata mente,
   Cui scelus est Veneris vel tetigisse fores.

THOMAS HAMERSLEY, Eques Auratus.

---

[1] Old ed. *sidentem.*   [2] Old ed. *cartior.*
[3] See Scheller's *Lex. Tot. Lat.* voce *Pyrausta* and *Pyralis*

ON THE POEMS.

HOW humble is thy muse (Deare) that can
    daign
    Such servants as my pen to entertaine !
    When all the sonnes of wit glory to be
Clad in thy muses gallant livery.
I shall disgrace my master, prove a staine,
And no addition to his honour'd traine ;
Though all that read me will presume to swear
I neer read thee : yet if it may appear,
1 love the writer and admire the writ,
I my owne want betray, not wrong thy wit.
Did thy worke want a prayse, my barren brain
Could not afford it : my attempt were vaine.
It needs no foyle : All that ere writ before,
Are foyles to thy faire Poems, and no more.
Then to be lodg'd in the same sheets with thine,
May prove disgrace to yours, but grace to mine.

Norris Jephson, Col.

TO MY MUCH LOVED FRIEND, RICHARD LOVELACE Esq.

Carmen Eroticum.

DEARE Lovelace, I am now about to prove
    I cannot write a verse, but can write love.
    On such a subject as thy booke I coo'd
Write books much greater, but not half so good.

But as the humble tenant, that does bring
A chicke or egges for's offering,
Is tane into the buttry, and does fox [1]
Equall with him that gave a stalled oxe:
So (since the heart of ev'ry cheerfull giver
Makes pounds no more accepted then a stiver),[2]
Though som thy prayse in rich stiles sing, I may
In stiver-stile write love as well as they.
I write so well that I no criticks feare ;
For who'le read mine, when as thy booke 's so neer,
Vnlesse thy selfe? then you shall secure mine
From those, and Ile engage my selfe for thine.
They'l do't themselves ; thē this allay you'l take,
I love thy book, and yet not for thy sake.

JOHN JEPHSON, Col. [3]

---

[1] *To fox* usually means to intoxicate. To fox oneself is *to get drunk*, and to fox a person is *to make him drunk*. The word in this sense belongs to the cant vocabulary. But in the present case, fox merely signifies *to fare* or *to feast*.

[2] A Dutch penny. It is very likely that this individual had served with the poet in Holland.

[3] Three members of this family, or at least three persons of this name, probably related, figure in the history of the present period, viz., Colonel John Jephson, apparently a military associate of Lovelace; Norris Jephson, who contributed a copy of verses to *Lucasta*, and to the first folio edition of Beaumont and Fletcher's plays, 1647 ; and William Jephson, whose name occurs among the subscribers to the *Solemn League and Covenant*, 1643.

TO MY NOBLE AND MOST INGENIOUS FRIEND,
COLONEL RICHARD LOVELACE,
UPON HIS "LUCASTA."

SO from the pregnant braine of Jove did rise
    Pallas, the queene of wit and beautious
      eyes,
  As faire Lucasta from thy temples flowes,
Temples no lesse ingenious then Joves.
Alike in birth, so shall she be in fame,
And be immortall to preserve thy Name.

ANOTHER, UPON THE POEMS.

NOW, when the wars augment our woes and
    fears,
    And the shrill noise of drums oppresse our
      ears ;
Now peace and safety from our shores are fled
To holes and cavernes to secure their head ;
Now all the graces from the land are sent,
And the nine Muses suffer banishment ;
Whence spring these raptures ? whence this heavenly
    rime,
So calme and even in so harsh a time ?
Well might that charmer his faire Cælia[1] crowne,

---

[1] Many poets have celebrated the charms of a *Cælia;* but I
apprehend that the writer here intends Carew.

And that more polish't Tyterus [1] renowne
His Sacarissa, when in groves and bowres
They could repose their limbs on beds of flowrs :
When wit had prayse, and merit had reward,
And every noble spirit did accord
To love the Muses, and their priests to raise,
And interpale their browes with flourishing bayes ;
But in a time distracted so to sing,
When peace is hurried hence on rages wing,
When the fresh bayes are [2] from the Temple torne,
And every art and science made a scorne ;
Then to raise up, by musicke of thy art,
Our drooping spirits and our grieved hearts ;
Then to delight our souls, and to inspire
Our breast with pleasure from thy charming lyre ;
Then to divert our sorrowes by thy straines,
Making us quite forget our seven yeers paines
In the past wars, unlesse that Orpheus be
A sharer in thy glory : for when he
Descended downe for his Euridice,
He stroke his lute with like admired art,
And made the damned to forget their smart.

JOHN PINCHBACKE, Col.

---

[1] Waller.   [2] Original has *is*.

ΕΞΑΣΤΙΚΟΝ.

Ψεύδεται ὅστις ἔφη· δολιχὸς χρόνος οἶδεν ἀμείβεν
Οὔνομα, καὶ πάντων μνημοσύνην ὀλέσαι.
Ὠδὴν γὰρ ποιεῖν ἀγαθὴν πόνος ἄφθονός ἐστι,
Ὃν μηδεὶς αἰὼν οἶδεν ὀδοῦσι φαγεῖν.
Ὠδὴν σοὶ, φίλε, δῶκε μὲν ἄφθιτον, ὦγαθε, μοῦσα,
Ὡς εἰς αἰῶνας οὔνομα ἦε τέον.

VILLIERS HARINGTON, L.C.

TO HIS MUCH HONOURED FRIEND,
MR. RICHARD LOVELACE,
ON HIS POEMS.

E that doth paint the beauties of your verse,
Must use your pensil, be polite, soft, terse;
Forgive that man whose best of art is love,
If he no equall master to you prove.
My heart is all my eloquence, and that
Speaks sharp affection, when my words fall flat;
I reade you like my mistresse, and discry
In every line the quicknesse of her eye:
Her smoothnesse in each syllable, her grace
To marshall ev'ry word in the right place.
It is the excellence and soule of wit,
When ev'ry thing is free as well as fit;
For metaphors packt up and crowded close
Swath ye minds sweetnes, and display the throws,

And, like those chickens hatcht in furnaces,
Produce or one limbe more, or one limbe lesse
Then nature bids. Survey such when they write,
No clause but's justl'd with an epithite.
So powerfully you draw when you perswade,
Passions in you in us are vertues made;
Such is the magick of that lawfull shell
That where it doth but talke, it doth compell:
  For no Apelles 'till this time e're drew
  A Venus to the waste so well as you.

W. RUDYERD.[1]

HE world shall now no longer mourne nor vex
      For th' obliquity of a cross-grain'd sex;
      Nor beauty swell above her bankes, (and
        made
For ornament) the universe invade
So fiercely, that 'tis question'd in our bookes,
Whether kils most the Amazon's sword or lookes.
Lucasta in loves game discreetly makes
Women and men joyntly to share the stakes,
And lets us know, when women scorne, it is
Mens hot love makes the antiparisthesis;
And a lay lover here such comfort finds
As Holy Writ gives to affected minds.

---

[1] Only son of Sir Benjamin Rudyerd, Kt., known as a poet
and a friend of poets, and as a warm advocate of Episcopacy.
See *Memoirs of Sir B. R.*, edited by Manning, 1841, 8vo., p. 257.

The wilder nymphs, lov's power could not comand,
Are by thy almighty numbers brought to hand,
And flying Daphnes, caught, amazed vow
They never heard Apollo court till now.
'Tis not by force of armes this feat is done,
For that would puzzle even the Knight o' th' Sun ;[1]
But 'tis by pow'r of art, and such a way
As Orpheus us'd, when he made fiends obay.

J. NEEDLER, Hosp. Grayensis.

TO HIS NOBLE FRIEND, MR. RICHARD LOVELACE, UPON HIS POEMS.

SIR,

'VR times are much degenerate from those,
  Which your sweet Muse, which your fair
      fortune chose ;
  And as complexions alter with the climes,
Our wits have drawne th' infection of our times.
That candid age no other way could tell
To be ingenious, but by speaking well.
Who best could prayse, had then the greatest prayse ;

---

[1] A celebrated romance, very frequently referred to by our old writers. Sir Thomas Overbury, in his *Characters*, represents a chambermaid as carried away by the perusal of it into the realms of romance, insomuch that she can barely refrain from forsaking her occupation, and turning lady-errant. The book is better known under the title of *The Mirror of Princely Deedes and Knighthood*, wherein is shewed the worthinesse of the Knight of the Sunne, &c. It consists of nine parts, which appear to have been published at intervals between 1585 and 1601.

'Twas more esteemd to give then wear the bayes.
Modest ambition studi'd only then
To honour not her selfe, but worthy men.
These vertues now are banisht out of towne,
Our Civill Wars have lost the civicke crowne.
He highest builds, who with most art destroys,
And against others fame his owne employs.
I see the envious caterpillar sit
On the faire blossome of each growing wit.

The ayre's already tainted with the swarms
Of insects, which against you rise in arms.
Word-peckers, paper-rats, book-scorpions,
Of wit corrupted the unfashion'd sons.
The barbed censurers begin to looke
Like the grim Consistory on thy booke ;
And on each line cast a reforming eye
Severer then the yong presbytery.
Till, when in vaine they have thee all perus'd,
You shall for being faultlesse be accus'd.
Some reading your *Lucasta* will alledge
You wrong'd in her the Houses priviledge ;
Some that you under sequestration are,
Because you write when going to the Warre ;
And one the book prohibits, because Kent
Their first Petition by the Authour sent.

But when the beauteous ladies came to know,
That their deare Lovelace was endanger'd so :
Lovelace, that thaw'd the most congealed brest,
He who lov'd best, and them defended best,
Whose hand so rudely grasps the steely brand,
Whose hand so gently melts the ladies hand,

They all in mutiny, though yet undrest,
Sally'd, and would in his defence contest.
And one, the loveliest that was yet e're seen,
Thinking that I too of the rout had been,
Mine eyes invaded with a female spight
(She knew what pain 't would be to lose that sight).
O no, mistake not, I reply'd: for I
In your defence, or in his cause, would dy.
But he, secure of glory and of time,
Above their envy or mine aid doth clime.
Him valianst men and fairest nymphs approve,
His booke in them finds judgement, with you, love.

ANDR. MARVELL.

TO COLONEL RICHARD LOVELACE,
ON THE PUBLISHING OF HIS
INGENIOUS POEMS.

 F the desire of glory speak a mind
More nobly operative and more refin'd,
What vast soule moves thee, or what hero's
    spirit
(Kept in'ts traduction pure) dost thou inherit,
That, not contented with one single fame,
Dost to a double glory spread thy name,
And on thy happy temples safely set
Both th' Delphick wreath and civic coronet?
  Was't not enough for us to know how far
Thou couldst in season suffer, act and dare?

But we must also witnesse, with what height
And what Ionick sweetnesse thou canst write,
And melt those eager passions, that are
Stubborn enough t' enrage the god of war
Into a noble love, which may expire [1]
In an illustrious pyramid of fire ;
Which, having gained his due station, may
Fix there, and everlasting flames display.
This is the braver path : time soone can smother
The dear-bought spoils and tropheis of the other.
How many fiery heroes have there been,
Whose triumphs were as soone forgot as seen ?
Because they wanted some diviner one
To rescue thē from night, and make thē known.

    Such art thou to thy selfe.   While others dream
Strong flatt'ries on a fain'd or borrow'd theam,
Thou shalt remaine in thine owne lustre bright,
And adde unto 't *Lvcasta's* chaster light.

    For none so fit to sing great things as he,
That can act o're all lights of poetry.
Thus had Achilles his owne gests design'd,
He had his genius Homer far outshin'd.

Jo. Hall.

---

[1] Original has *aspire.*

[2] The precocious author of *Horæ Vacivæ,* 1646, and of a volume of poems which was printed in the same year.   In the *Lucasta* are some complimentary lines by Lovelace on Hall's translation of the commentary of Hierocles on the Golden Verses of Pythagoras, 1657.

TO THE HONORABLE, VALIANT, AND INGENIOUS
COLONEL RICHARD LOVELACE,
ON HIS EXQUISITE POEMS.

OETS and painters have some near relation,
 Compar'd with fancy and imagination;
 The one paints shadowed persons (in pure
  kind),
The other paints the pictures of the mind
In purer verse. And as rare Zeuxes fame
Shin'd, till Apelles art eclips'd the same
By a more exquisite and curious line
In Zeuxeses (with pensill far more fine),
So have our modern poets late done well,
Till thine appear'd (which scarce have paralel).

 They like to Zeuxes grapes beguile the sense,
But thine do ravish the intelligence,
Like the rare banquet of Apelles, drawn,
And covered over with most curious lawn.

 Thus if thy careles draughts are cal'd the best,
What would thy lines have beene, had'st thou profest
That faculty (infus'd) of poetry,
Which adds such honour unto thy chivalry?
Doubtles thy verse had all as far transcended
As Sydneyes Prose, who Poets once defended.

 For when I read thy much renowned pen,
My fancy there finds out another Ben
In thy brave language, judgement, wit, and art,
Of every piece of thine, in every part:
Where thy seraphique Sydneyan fire is raised high
In valour, vertue, love, and loyalty.

Virgil was styl'd the loftiest of all,
Ovid the smoothest and most naturall;
Martiall concise and witty, quaint and pure,
Iuvenall grave and learned, though obscure.
    But all these rare ones which I heere reherse,
Do live againe in Thee, and in thy Verse:
Although not in the language of their time,
Yet in a speech as copious and sublime.
    The rare Apelles in thy picture wee
Perceive, and in thy soule Apollo see.
Wel may each Grace and Muse then crown thy praise
With Mars his banner and Minerva's bayes.

FRA. LENTON.[1]

TO HIS HONOURED AND INGENIOUS FRIEND,
COLONEL RICHARD LOVELACE,
ON HIS "LUCASTA."

CHAST as Creation meant us, and more
    bright
    Then the first day in's uneclipsed light,
    Is thy *Lucasta*; and thou offerest heere
Lines to her name as undefil'd and cleere;

---

[1] The author of the *Young Gallant's Whirligigg*, 1629, and other poetical works. Singer does not give these lines. In the *Whirligig* there is a curious picture of a young gallant of the time of Charles I., to which Lovelace might have sat, had he been old enough at the time. But Lenton had no want of sitters for his portrait.

Such as the first indeed more happy dayes
(When vertue, wit, and learning wore the bayes
Now vice assumes) would to her memory give:
A Vestall flame that should for ever live,
Plac't in a christal temple, rear'd to be
The Embleme of her thoughts integrity;
And on the porch thy name insculpt, my friend,
Whose love, like to the flame, can know no end.
The marble step that to the alter brings
The hallowed priests with their clean offerings,
Shall hold their names that humbly crave to be
Votaries to th' shrine, and gratefull friends to thee.
So shal we live (although our offrings prove
Meane to the world) for ever by thy love.

THO. RAWLINS.[1]

TO MY DEAR BROTHER, COLONEL
RICHARD LOVELACE.

LE doe my nothing too, and try
To dabble to thy memory.
Not that I offer to thy name
Encomiums of thy lasting fame.
Those by the landed have been writ:
Mine's but a yonger-brother wit;
A wit that's hudled up in scarres,
Borne like my rough selfe in the warres;

---

[1] A well known dramatist and poet. These lines are not in Singer's reprint.

And as a Squire in the fight
Serves only to attend the Knight,
So 'tis my glory in this field,
Where others act, to beare thy shield.

DUDLEY LOVELACE, Capt.[1]

---

[1] The youngest brother of the poet. Besides the present lines, and some to be found in the posthumous volume, of which he was the editor, this gentleman contributed the following commendatory poem to *Ayres and Dialogues* [by Thomas Stanley Esq.] set by John Gamble, 1656. The verses themselves have little merit; and the only object which I had in introducing them, was to add to the completeness of the present edition:—

TO MY MUCH HONORED COZEN, MR. STANLEY,

UPON HIS POEMS SET BY MR. JOHN GAMBLE.

I.

ENOUGH, enongh of orbs and spheres,
  Reach me a trumpet or a drum,
To sound sharp synnets in your ears,
  And beat a deep encomium.

II.

I know not th' Eight Intelligence:
  Those that do understand it, pray
Let them step hither, and from thence
  Speak what they all do sing or say:

III.

Nor what your diapasons are,
  Your sympathies and symphonies;
To me they seem as distant farre
  As whence they take their infant rise.

IV.

But I've a grateful heart can ring
  A peale of ordnance to your praise,
And volleys of small plaudits bring
  To clowd a crown about your baies.

DE DOMINO RICHARDO LOVELACIO,

ARMIGERO ET CHILIARCHA,[1] VIRO INCOMPARABILI.

ECCE tibi, heröi claris natalibus orto ; [2]
 Cujus honoratos Cantia vidit avos.
Cujus adhuc memorat rediviva Batavia
 patrem,
Inter et Herculeos enumerare solet.

V.

Though laurel is thought thunder free,
 That storms and lightning disallows,
Yet Cæsar thorough fire and sea
 Snatches her to twist his conquering brows.

VI.

And now me thinks like him you stand
 I' th' head of all the Poets' hoast,
Whilest with your words you do command,
 They silent do their duty boast.

VII.

Which done, the army ecchoes o're,
 Like Gamble Ios one and all,
And in their various notes implore,
 Long live our noble Generall.

DUDLEY POSTHUMUS LOVELACE.

[1] Strictly speaking, the officer in command of a thousand men, from the Greek χιλιάρχης, or χιλιάρχος, but in the present instance meaning nothing more than Colonel.

[2] I have amended the text of these lines, which in the original is very corrupt. I suppose that the compositor was left to himself, as usual.

Qui tua Grollaferox, laceratus vulnere multo,
  Fulmineis vidit mœnia Pacta globis.
Et cum sæva tuas fudisset Iberia turmas,
  Afflatu pyrii pulveris ictus obit.
Hæc sint magna : tamen major majoribus hic est,
  Nititur et pennis altiùs ire novis.
Sermonem patrium callentem et murmura Celtæ,
  Non piguit linguas edidicisse duas.
Quicquid Roma vetus, vel quicquid Græcia jactat,
  Musarum nutrix alma Calena dedit.
Gnaviter Hesperios compressit Marte cachinnos,
  Devictasque dedit Cantaber ipse manus.
Non evitavit validos Dunkerka lacertos,
  Non intercludens alta Lacuna vias,
Et scribenda gerens vivaci marmore digna,
  Scribere Cæsareo more vel ipse potest.
Cui gladium Bellona dedit, calamumque Minerva,
  Et geminæ Laurûs circuit umbra comam.
Cujus si faciem spectes vultùsque decorem,
  Vix puer Idalius gratior ore fuit.

AD EUNDEM.

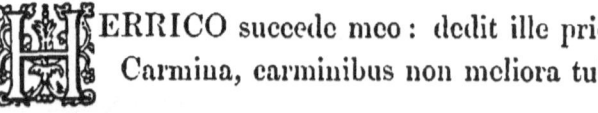ERRICO succede meo : dedit ille priora
  Carmina, carminibus non meliora tuis.[1]

---

[1] Herrick's *Hesperides* had appeared in 1648.

ΠΕΡΙ ΤΟΥ ΑΥΤΟΥ.

Λουλάκιος πολλαπλασίως φίλος ἐστὶν ἐμεῖο.
Τοὔνομά ἐστι φίλος, καὶ τὸ νόημα φίλος.
Καὶ φύλον ἀντιφυλῶ μεγάλοισιν ἀγάκλυτον ἔργοις
Τῆς ἀρετῆς· χειρὸς καὶ φρενὸς ἀγχινόος.
Ὃς νέος ἐν τύτθαις πινυτῶς σελίδεσσιν ἔθηκε
Ποιητῶν ἕκαστον χρῶματ᾽ ἐπαγρόμενος.
Φροῦρον Μουσάων, ποκινῶν ἐσσῆνα Μελισσῶν,
Ἐν Χαρίτεσσι χάριν, καὶ Μελέεσσι μέλι.

Scripsit Jo. Harmarus,
         Oxoniensis, C. W. M.[1]

---

[1] A celebrated scholar and philologist. An account of him will be found in Bliss's edition of Wood's *Athenæ*. He published an Elegy on St. Alban the Protomartyr and an Apology for Archbishop Williams, and edited Scapula. These lines are omitted by Singer.

P. Lilly Inv.

POEMS.

SONG.

SET BY MR. HENRY LAWES.[1]

TO LUCASTA. GOING BEYOND THE SEAS.

I.

F to be absent were to be
  Away from thee;
 Or that when I am gone,
  You or I were alone;
Then my *Lucasta* might I crave
Pity from blustring winde or swallowing wave.

II.

 But I'le not sigh one blast or gale
  To swell my saile,
 Or pay a teare to swage
  The foaming blew-gods rage;
For whether he will let me passe
Or no, I'm still as happy as I was.

---

[1] Of Henry and William Lawes an account may be found in Burney and Hawkins. Although the former (H. Lawes) set many of Lovelace's pieces to music, only two occur in the *Ayres and Dialogues for One, Two, and Three Voyces,* 1653-55-8, folio.

III.

Though seas and land betwixt us both,
　　Our faith and troth,
　　Like separated soules,
　　All time and space controules:
Above the highest sphere wee meet,
Unseene, unknowne, and greet as angels greet,

IV.

So then we doe anticipate
　　Our after-fate,
　　And are alive i'th' skies,
　　If thus our lips and eyes
Can speake like spirits unconfin'd
In Heav'n, their earthy bodies left behind.

SONG.

SET BY MR. JOHN LANIERE.

TO LUCASTA. GOING TO THE WARRES.

I.

ELL me not, (sweet,) I am unkinde,
　　That from the nunnerie
　　Of thy chaste breast and quiet minde
　　To warre and armes I flie.

II.

True: a new Mistresse now I chase,
　　The first foe in the field ;
And with a stronger faith imbrace
　　A sword, a horse, a shield.

III.

Yet this inconstancy is such,
 As you too shall adore;
I could not love thee, dear, so much,
 Lov'd I not Honour more.

A PARADOX.

I.

'IS true the beauteous Starre[1]
 To which I first did bow
Burnt quicker, brighter far,
 Than that which leads me now;
  Which shines with more delight,
  For gazing on that light
  So long, neere lost my sight.

II.

Through foul we follow faire,
 For had the world one face,
And earth been bright as ayre,
 We had knowne neither place.
  Indians smell not their neast;
  A Swisse or Finne tastes best
  The spices of the East.[2]

---

[1] *i. e. Lucasta.*
[2] The East was celebrated by all our early poets as the land of
spices and rich gums:—

III.

So from the glorious Sunne
　Who to his height hath got,
With what delight we runne
　To some black cave or grot!
　　And, heav'nly Sydney you
　　Twice read, had rather view
　　Some odde romance so new.

IV.

The god, that constant keepes
　Unto his deities,
Is poore in joyes, and sleepes
　Imprison'd in the skies.
　　This knew the wisest, who
　　From Juno stole, below
　　To love a bear or cow.

" For now the fragrant East,
　The spicery o' th' world,
　　　Hath hurl'd
A rosie tincture o'er the Phœnix nest."
　Otia Sacra, by Mildmay, Earl of Westmoreland,
　　　1648, p. 37.

SONG.

SET BY MR. HENRY LAWES.

TO AMARANTHA;[1] THAT SHE WOULD DISHEVELL HER HAIRE.

I.

AMARANTHA sweet and faire,
Ah brade[2] no more that shining haire!
As my curious hand or eye,
Hovering round thee, let it flye.

II.

Let it flye as unconfin'd
As it's calme ravisher, the winde,
Who hath left his darling, th' East,
To wanton o're that[3] spicie neast.

III.

Ev'ry tresse must be confest:
But neatly tangled at the best;

---

[1] A portion of this song is printed, with a few orthographical variations, in the *Ayres and Dialogues*, part i. 1653; and it is also found in Cotgrave's *Wits Interpreter*, 1655, where it is called "Amarantha counselled." Cotgrave used the text of Lawes, and only gives that part of the production which he found in *Ayres and Dialogues*.

[2] Forbear to brade—Lawes' *Ayres and Dialogues*, and Cotgrave.

[3] This—Lawes' *Ayres and Dialogues*. Cotgrave reads *his*.

Like a clue of golden thread,
Most excellently ravelled.

IV.

Doe not then winde up that light
In ribands, and o'er-cloud in night,
  Like the sun in's early ray;
But shake your head, and scatter day.

V.

See, 'tis broke! within this grove,
The bower aud the walkes of love,
  Weary lye we downe and rest,
And faune each other's panting breast.

VI.

Heere wee'll strippe and coole our fire,
In creame below, in milke-baths[1] higher:
  And when all wells are drawne dry,
I'll drink a teare out of thine eye.

VII.

Which our very joys shall leave,
That sorrowes thus we can deceive;
  Or our very sorrowes weepe,
That joyes so ripe so little keepe.

---

[1] Milk-baths have been a favourite luxury in all ages. Peele
had probably in his mind the custom of his own time and country when he wrote the following passage:—

"Bright Bethsabe shall wash in David's bower,
In water mix'd with purest almond flower,
And bathe her beauty in the milk of kids."
  King David and Fair Bethsabe, 1599.

SONNET.

SET BY MR. HUDSON.

I.

EPOSE your finger of that ring,
    And crowne mine with't awhile;
Now I restor't. Pray, dos it bring
    Back with it more of soile?
Or shines it not as innocent,
As honest, as before 'twas lent?

II.

So then inrich me with that treasure,
    'Twill but increase your store,
And please me (faire one) with that pleasure
    Must please you still the more.
Not to save others is a curse
The blackest, when y'are ne're the worse.

ODE.

SET BY DR JOHN WILSON.[1]

TO LUCASTA. *THE ROSE.*

I.

WEET serene skye-like flower,
    Haste to adorn her bower;
      From thy long clowdy bed
      Shoot forth thy damaske[2] head.

---

[1] Dr. John Wilson was a native of Feversham in Kent, a gentleman of Charles the First's chapel, and chamber-musician to his majesty. For an account of his works, see Burney's *His-*

II.

New-startled blush of *Flora !*
The griefe of pale *Aurora,*
　　Who will contest no more,
　　Haste, haste, to strowe her floore.

III.

Vermilion ball, that's given
From lip to lip in Heaven ;
　　Loves couches cover-led,
　　Haste, haste, to make her bed.

IV.

Dear offspring of pleas'd *Venus,*
And jollie plumpe *Silenus ;*
　　Haste, haste, to decke the haire,
　　Of th' only sweetly faire.

V.

See ! rosie is her bower,
Her floore is all this flower ;
　　Her bed a rosie nest
　　By a bed of roses prest.

---

tory of *Music,* vol. iii. pp. 399-400, or Hawkins' *History of*
Music, iii. 57, where a portrait of Wilson, taken from the original
painting, will be found. Wood, author of the *Fasti* and *Athenæ,*
says that he was in his time, " the best at the lute in all England." Herrick, in his *Hesperides,* 1648, has these lines in reference to Henry Lawes :—

　　" Then if thy voice commingle with the string,
　　I hear in thee the rare Laniere to sing,
　　Or curious Wilson."

　[2] In a MS. copy of the poem contemporary with the author,
now before me, this word is omitted.

VI.

But early as she dresses,
Why fly you her bright tresses ?
    Ah ! I have found, I feare ;
    Because her cheekes are neere.

LOVE CONQUER'D.

A SONG.

SET BY MR. HENRY LAWES.

I.

THE childish god of love did sweare
        Thus : By my awfull bow and quiver,
Yon' weeping, kissing, smiling pair,
I'le scatter all their vowes i' th' ayr,
        And their knit imbraces shiver.

II.

Up then to th' head with his best art
    Full of spite and envy blowne,
At her constant marble heart,
He drawes his swiftest surest dart,
    Which bounded back, and hit his owne.

III.

Now the prince of fires burnes ;
    Flames in the luster of her eyes ;
Triumphant she, refuses, scornes ;
He submits, adores and mournes,
    And is his votresse sacrifice.

D

IV.

Foolish boy! resolve me now
 What 'tis to sigh and not be heard?
He weeping kneel'd, and made a vow:
The world shall love as you' fast two;
 So on his sing'd wings up he steer'd.

A LOOSE SARABAND.

SET BY MR. HENRY LAWES.

I.

AH me! the little tyrant theefe!
 As once my heart was playing,
He snatcht it up and flew away,
 Laughing at all my praying.

II.

Proud of his purchase,[1] he surveys
 And curiously sounds it,
And though he sees it full of wounds,
 Cruel one, still[2] he wounds it.

---

[1] Prize. It is not uncommonly used by the early dramatists
in this sense; but the verb *to purchase* is more usually found than
the noun.

"Yet having opportunity, he tries,
 Gets her goodwill, and with his purchase flies."

WITHER's *Abuses Stript and Whipt*, 1613.

[2] Here I have hazarded an emendation of the text. In original we read, *cruell still on.* Lovelace's poems were evidently
printed without the slightest care.

III.

And now this heart is all his sport,
    Which as a ball he boundeth
From hand to breast, from breast to lip,
    And all its [1] rest confoundeth.

IV.

Then as a top he sets it up,
    And pitifully whips it;
Sometimes he cloathes it gay and fine,
    Then straight againe he strips it.

V.

He cover'd it with false reliefe, [2]
    Which gloriously show'd it;
And for a morning-cushionet
    On's mother he bestow'd it.

VI.

Each day, with her small brazen stings,
    A thousand times she rac'd it;
But then at night, bright with her gemmes,
    Once neere her breast she plac'd it.

VII.

There warme it gan to throb and bleed;
    She knew that smart, and grieved;
At length this poore condemned heart
    With these rich drugges repreeved.

---

[1] Original reads *it's*.   [2] Original has *belieje*.

VIII.

She washt the wound with a fresh teare,
    Which my *Lucasta* dropped,
And in the sleave[1]-silke of her haire
    'Twas hard bound up and wrapped.

IX.

She proab'd it with her constancie,
    And found no rancor nigh it;
Only the anger of her eye
    Had wrought some proud flesh by it.

X.

Then prest she narde in ev'ry veine,
    Which from her kisses trilled;
And with the balme heald all its paine,
    That from her hand distilled.

XI.

But yet this heart avoyds me still,
    Will not by me be owned;
But 's fled to its physitian's breast;
    There proudly sits inthroned.

---

[1] Soft, like floss.

ORPHEUS TO WOODS.

SONG.

SET BY MR. CURTES.

EARK! Oh heark! you guilty trees,
    In whose gloomy galleries
    Was the cruell'st murder done,
    That e're yet eclipst the sunne.
Be then henceforth in your twigges
Blasted, e're you sprout to sprigges;
Feele no season of the yeere,
But what shaves off all your haire,
Nor carve any from your wombes
Ought but coffins and their tombes.

ORPHEUS[1] TO BEASTS.

SONG.

SET BY MR. CURTES.[2]

1.

ERE, here, oh here! *Euridice*,
    Here was she slaine;
    Her soule 'still'd through a veine:
    The gods knew lesse

---

[1] By Orpheus we may perhaps understand Lovelace himself, and by Euridice, the lady whom he celebrates under the name of Lucasta. Grainger mentions (*Biog. Hist.* ii. 74) a portrait of

That time divinitie,
Then ev'n, ev'n these
Of brutishnesse.

II.

Oh! could you view the melodie
Of ev'ry grace,
And musick of her face,[1]
You'd drop a teare,
Seeing more harmonie
In her bright eye,
Then now you heare.

Lovelace by Gaywood, in which he is represented as Orpheus.
I have not seen it. The old poets were rather fond of likening
themselves to this legendary personage, or of designating themselves his poetical children :—

> "We that are *Orpheus'* sons, and can inherit
> By that great title "—
>
> DAVENANT'S *Works*, 1673, p. 215.

Many other examples might be given. Massinger, in his *City
Madam*, 1658, makes Sir John Frugal introduce a representation
of the story of the Thracian bard at an entertainment given to
Luke Frugal.

[2] A lutenist. Wood says that after the Restoration he became
gentleman or singing-man of Christ Church, Oxford. He was one
of those musicians who, after the abolition of organs, &c. during
the civil war, met at a private house at Oxford for the purpose
of taking his part in musical entertainments.

[1] "Such was Zuleika; such around her shone
The nameless charms unmark'd by her alone;
The light of love, the purity of grace,
The mind, the music breathing from her face."

> BYRON'S *Bride of Abydos*, canto 1.
>
> (*Works*, ed. 1825, ii. 299.)

DIALOGUE.

Lucasta, Alexis.[1]

SET BY MR. JOHN GAMBLE.[2]

I.

Lucasta.

TELL me, *Alexis*, what this parting is,
    That so like dying is, but is not it?

Alexis.

It is a swounding for a while from blisse,
    'Till kind *how doe you* call's us from the fit.

Chorus.

If then the spirits only stray, let mine
Fly to thy bosome, and my soule to thine:
Thus in our native seate we gladly give
Our right for one, where we can better live.

II.

Lu.   But ah, this ling'ring, murdring farewel!
    Death quickly wounds, and wounding cures the ill.
Alex. It is the glory of a valiant lover,
    Still to be dying, still for to recover.

---

[1] *i. e.* the poet himself.

[2] "John Gamble, apprentice to Ambrose Beyland, a noted musician, was afterwards musician at one of the play-houses; from thence removed to be a cornet in the King's Chapel. After that he became one in Charles the Second's band of violins, and composed for the theatres. He published *Ayres and Dialogues to the Theorbo and Bass Viol*, fol. Lond., 1659."—HAWKINS.

Cho.　Soldiers suspected of their courage goe,
　　　　That ensignes and their breasts untorne show :
　　　　Love nee're his standard, when his hoste he sets,
　　　　Creates alone fresh-bleeding bannerets.

III.

Alex.　But part we, when thy figure I retaine
　　　　　Still in my heart, still strongly in mine eye?
Lu.　Shadowes no longer than the sun remaine,
　　　　But whē his beams, that made 'em, fly, they fly.
Cho.　Vaine dreames of love! that only so much blisse
　　　　Allow us, as to know our wretchednesse ;
　　　　And deale a larger measure in our paine
　　　　By showing joy, then hiding it againe.

IV.

Alex.　No, whilst light raigns, *Lucasta* still rules here,
　　　　　And all the night shines wholy in this sphere.
Lu.　I know no morne but my *Alexis* ray,
　　　　To my dark thoughts the breaking of the day.

Chorus.

Alex.　So in each other if the pitying sun
　　　　　Thus keep us fixt, nere may his course be run !
Lu.　And oh! if night us undivided make ;
　　　　Let us sleepe still, and sleeping never wake !

The close.

　　　　Cruel *adieus* may well adjourne awhile
　　　　The sessions of a looke, a kisse, or smile,
　　　　And leave behinde an angry grieving blush ;
　　　　But time nor fate can part us joyned thus.

SONNET.

SET BY MR. WILLIAM LAWES.

I.

WHEN I by thy faire shape did sweare,
    And mingled with each vowe a teare,
      I lov'd, I lov'd thee best,
      I swore as I profest.
For all the while you lasted warme and pure,
    My oathes too did endure.
But once turn'd faithlesse to thy selfe and old,
They then with thee incessantly[1] grew cold.

II.

I swore my selfe thy sacrifice
By th' ebon bowes[2] that guard thine eyes,
    Which now are alter'd white,
    And by the glorious light
Of both those stars, which of[3] their spheres bereft,
    Only the gellie's left.
Then changed thus, no more I'm bound to you,
Then swearing to a saint that proves untrue.

---

[1] *i. e.* at once, immediately.   [2] Her eyebrows.
[3] Original reads *of which.*

LUCASTA WEEPING.

SONG.

SET BY MR. JOHN LANEERE.

I.

 UCASTA wept, and still the bright
  Inamour'd god of day,
With his soft handkercher of light,
  Kist the wet pearles away.

II.

But when her teares his heate or'ccame,
  In cloudes he quensht his beames,
And griev'd, wept out his eye of flame,
  So drowned her sad streames.

III. [1]

At this she smiled, when straight the sun
  Cleer'd by her kinde desires;
And by her eyes reflexion
  Fast kindl'd there his fires.

---

[1] This stanza is not found in the printed copy of *Lucasta*, 1649, but it occurs in a MS. of this poem written, with many compositions by Lovelace and other poets, in a copy of Crashaw's *Poems*, 1648, 12mo, a portion of which having been formed of the printer's proof-sheets, some of the pages are printed only on one side, the reverse being covered with MSS. poems, among the rest with epigrams by *Mr. Thomas Fuller* (about fifty in number). There can be little doubt, from the character of the majority of these little poems, that by " Mr. Thomas Fuller " we may understand the church-historian.

TO LUCASTA. FROM PRISON.

AN EPODE.[1]

I.

ONG in thy shackels, liberty
I ask not from these walls, but thee ;
Left for awhile anothers bride,
To fancy all the world beside.

II.

Yet e're I doe begin to love,
See, how I all my objects prove ;
Then my free soule to that confine,
'Twere possible I might call mine.

III.

First I would be in love with *Peace*,
And her rich swelling breasts increase ;
But how, alas ! how may that be,
Despising earth, she will love me ?

IV.

Faine would I be in love with *War*,
As my deare just avenging star ;

---

[1] This was written, perhaps, during the poet's confinement in Peterhouse, to which he was committed a prisoner on his return from abroad in 1648. At the date of its composition, there can be little doubt, from expressions in stanzas vi. and xii. that the fortunes of Charles I. were at their lowest ebb, and it may be assigned without much risk of error to the end of 1648.

But War is lov'd so ev'rywhere,
Ev'n he disdaines a lodging here.

v.

Thee and thy wounds I would bemoane,
Faire thorough-shot *Religion;*
But he lives only that kills thee,
And who so bindes thy hands, is free.

vi.

I would love a *Parliament*
As a maine prop from Heav'n sent;
But ah! who's he, that would be wedded
To th' fairest body that's beheaded?

vii.

Next would I court my *Liberty,*
And then my birth-right, *Property;*
But can that be, when it is knowne,
There's nothing you can call your owne?

viii.

A *Reformation* I would have,
As for our griefes a *Sov'raigne* salve;
That is, a cleansing of each wheele
Of state, that yet some rust doth feele.

ix.

But not a reformation so,
As to reforme were to ore'throw,
Like watches by unskilfull men
Disjoynted, and set ill againe.

X.

The *Publick Faith*[1] I would adore,
But she is banke-rupt of her store:
Nor how to trust her can I see,
For she that couzens all, must me.

XI.

Since then none of these can be
Fit objects for my love and me;
What then remaines, but th' only spring
Of all our loves and joyes, the King?

XII.

He who, being the whole ball
Of day on earth, lends it to all;
When seeking to eeclipse his right,
Blinded we stand in our owne light.

XIII.

And now an universall mist
Of error is spread or'e each breast,
With such a fury edg'd as is
Not found in th' inwards of th' abysse.

---

[1] " The publick faith? why 'tis a word of kin,
  A nephew that dares *cozen* any sin;
  A term of art, great *Behomoth's* younger brother,
  Old *Machaviel* and half a thousand other;
  Which, when subscrib'd, writes *Legion*, names on truss,
  Abaddon, *Belzebub*, and *Incubus*."
       CLEAVELAND'S *Poems*, ed. 1669, p. 91.

XIV.

Oh, from thy glorious starry waine
Dispense on me one sacred beame,
To light me where I soone may see
How to serve you, and you trust me !

LUCASTA'S FANNE, WITH A LOOKING-GLASSE IN IT.[1]

I.

ASTRICH![2] thou featherd foole, and easie
prey,
  That larger sailes to thy broad vessell
  needst ;
Snakes through thy guttur-neck hisse all the day,
  Then on thy iron messe at supper feedst.[3]

II.

O what a glorious transmigration
  From this to so divine an edifice
Hast thou straight made ! heere[4] from a winged stone
  Transform'd into a bird of paradice !

---

[1] This adaptation of the fan to the purposes of a mirror, now so common, was, as we here are told, familiar to the ladies of Lovelace's time. Mr. Fairholt, in his *Costume in England*, 1846, p. 496, describes many various forms which were given at different periods to this article of use and ornament ; but the present passage in *Lucasta* appears to have escaped his notice.

[2] Ostrich. Lyly, in his *Euphues*, 1579, sig. c 4, has *Estridge*. The fan here described was composed of ostrich-feathers set with precious stones.

[3] In allusion to the digestive powers of this bird.

[4] Original reads *neere*.

III.

Now doe thy plumes for hiew and luster vie
  With th' arch of heav'n that triumphs or'e past wet,
And in a rich enamel'd pinion lye
  With saphyres, amethists and opalls set.

IV.

Sometime they wing her side,[1] the strive to drown
  The day's eyes piercing beames, whose am'rous heat
Sollicites still, 'till with this shield of downe
  From her brave face his glowing fires are beat.

V.

But whilst a plumy curtaine she doth draw,
  A chrystall mirror sparkles in thy breast,
In which her fresh aspect when as she saw,
  And then her foe[2] retired to the west.

VI.

Deare engine, that oth' sun got'st me the day,
  'Spite of his hot assaults mad'st him retreat!
No wind (said she) dare with thee henceforth play
  But mine own breath to coole the tyrants heat.

VII.

My lively shade thou ever shalt retaine
  In thy inclosed feather-framed glasse,
And but unto our selves to all remaine
  Invisible, thou feature of this face!

---

[1] The poet means that Lucasta, when she did not require her fan for immediate use, wore it suspended at her side or from her girdle.
[2] The sun.

VIII.

So said, her sad swaine over-heard and cried :
　　Yee Gods ! for faith unstaind this a reward !
Feathers and glasse t'outweigh my vertue tryed !
　　Ah ! show their empty strength ! the gods accord.

IX.

Now fall'n the brittle favourite lyes and burst !
　　Amas'd *Lucasta* weepes, repents and flies
To her *Alexis,* vowes her selfe acurst,
　　If hence she dresse her selfe but in his eyes.

LUCASTA, TAKING THE WATERS AT

TUNBRIDGE.[1]

I.

YEE happy floods ! that now must passe
　　The sacred conduicts of her wombe,
Smooth and transparent as your face,
　　When you are deafe, and windes are
　　　dumbe.

II.

Be proud ! and if your waters be
　　Foul'd with a counterfeyted teare,
Or some false sigh hath stained yee,
　　Haste, and be purified there.

---

[1] From this it might be conjectured, though the ground for doing so would be very slight, that *Lucasta* was a native of Kent or of one of the adjoining shires ; but against this supposition we have to set the circumstance that elsewhere this lady is called a "northern star."

III.

And when her rosie gates y'have trac'd,
  Continue yet some Orient wet,
'Till, turn'd into a gemme, y'are plac'd
  Like diamonds with rubies set.

IV.

Yee drops, that dew th' Arabian bowers,
  Tell me, did you e're smell or view
On any leafe of all your flowers
  Soe sweet a sent, so rich a hiew?

V.

But as through th' Organs of her breath
  You trickle wantonly, beware:
Ambitious Seas in their just death
  As well as Lovers, must have share.

VI.

And see! you boyle as well as I;
  You, that to coole her did aspire,
Now troubled and neglected lye,
  Nor can your selves quench your owne fire.

VII.

Yet still be happy in the thought,
  That in so small a time as this,
Through all the Heavens you were brought
  Of Vertue, Honour, Love and Blisse.

E

TO LUCASTA.

ODE LYRICK.

I.

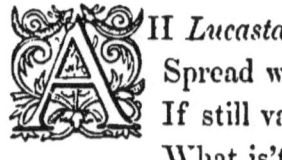

AH *Lucasta*, why so bright ?
Spread with early streaked light !
If still vailed from our sight,
What is't but eternall night ?

II.

Ah *Lucasta*, why so chaste ?
With that vigour, ripenes grac't,
Not to be by Man imbrac't
Makes that Royall coyne imbace't,
And this golden Orchard waste !

III.

Ah *Lucasta*, why so great,
That thy crammed coffers sweat ?
Yet not owner of a seat
May shelter you from Natures heat,
And your earthly joyes compleat.

IV.

Ah *Lucasta*, why so good ?
Blest with an unstained flood
Flowing both through soule and blood ;
If it be not understood,
'Tis a Diamond in mud.

v.

Lucasta! stay! why dost thou flye?
Thou art not bright but to the eye,
Nor chaste but in the mariage-tye,
Nor great but in this treasurie,
Nor good but in that sanctitie.

vi.

Harder then the Orient stone,
Like an apparition,
Or as a pale shadow gone,
Dumbe and deafe she hence is flowne.

vii.

Then receive this equall dombe:
Virgins, strow no teare or bloome,
No one dig the Parian wombe;
Raise her marble heart i'th' roome,
And 'tis both her coarse and tombe.

LUCASTA PAYING HER OBSEQUIES TO THE CHAST MEMORY OF MY DEAREST COSIN MRS. BOWES BARNE[S].[1]

I.

SEE! what an undisturbed teare
She weepes for her last sleepe:
But, viewing her, straight wak'd a Star.
She weepes that she did weepe.

---

[1] This lady was probably the wife of a descendant of Sir William Barnes, of Woolwich, whose only daughter and heir, Anne, married the poet's father, and brought him the seat in Kent. See *Gents. Magazine* for 1791, part ii. 1095.

II.

Griefe ne're before did tyranize
  On th' honour of that brow,
And at the wheeles of her brave eyes
  Was captive led til now.

III.

Thus, for a saints apostacy
  The unimagin'd woes
And sorrowes of the Hierarchy
  None but an angel knowes.

IV.

Thus, for lost soules recovery
  The clapping of all wings
And triumphs of this victory
  None but an angel sings.

V.

So none but she knows to bemone
  This equal virgins fate,
None but *Lucasta* can her crowne
  Of glory celebrate.

VI.

Then dart on me (*Chast Light*[1]) one ray,
  By which I may discry
Thy joy cleare through this cloudy day
  To dresse my sorrow by.

---

[1] A translation of *Lucasta*, or *Lux Casta*, for the sake of the metre.

UPON THE CURTAINE OF LUCASTA'S PICTURE, IT WAS THUS WROUGHT.[1]

II, stay that covetous hand; first turn all eye,
All depth and minde; then mystically spye
IIer soul's faire picture, her faire soul's, in all
So truely copied from th' originall,
That you will sweare her body by this law
Is but its shadow, as this, its;—now draw.

LUCASTA'S WORLD.

EPODE.

I.

OLD as the breath of winds that blow
To silver shot descending snow,
    Lucasta sigh't;[2] when she did close
    The world in frosty chaines!
And then a frowne to rubies frose
    The blood boyl'd in our veines:
Yet cooled not the heat her sphere
Of beauties first had kindled there.

---

[1] Pictures used formerly to have curtains before them. It is still done in some old houses. In *Westward Hoe*, 1607, act ii. scene 3, there is an allusion to this practice:—

"*Sir Gosling.* So draw those curtains, and let's see the pictures under 'em."—WEBSTER's *Works*, ed. Hazlitt, i. 133.

[2] Original reads *sight*.

II.

Then mov'd, and with a suddaine flame
Impatient to melt all againe,
  Straight from her eyes she lightning hurl'd,
    And earth in ashes mournes ;
  The sun his blaze denies the world,
    And in her luster burnes :
Yet warmed not the hearts, her nice
Disdaine had first congeal'd to ice.

III.

And now her teares nor griev'd desire
Can quench this raging, pleasing fire ;
  Fate but one way allowes ; behold
    Her smiles' divinity !
  They fann'd this heat, and thaw'd that cold,
    So fram'd up a new sky.
Thus earth, from flames and ice repreev'd,
E're since hath in her sun-shine liv'd.

THE APOSTACY OF ONE, AND BUT
ONE LADY.

I.

THAT frantick errour I adore,
  And am confirm'd the earth turns round ;
  Now satisfied o're and o're,
    As rowling waves, so flowes the ground,
And as her neighbour reels the shore :
  Finde such a woman says she loves ;
  She's that fixt heav'n, which never moves.

II.

In marble, steele, or porphyrie,
    Who carves or stampes his armes or face,
Lookes it by rust or storme must dye :
    This womans love no time can raze,
Hardned like ice in the sun's eye,
    Or your reflection in a glasse,
    Which keepes possession, though you passe.

III.

We not behold a watches hand
    To stir, nor plants or flowers to grow ;
Must we infer that this doth stand,
    And therefore, that those do not blow ?
This she acts calmer, like Heav'ns brand,
    The stedfast lightning, slow loves dart,
    She kils, but ere we feele the smart.

IV.

Oh, she is constant as the winde,
    That revels in an ev'nings aire !
Certaine as wayes unto the blinde,
    More reall then her flatt'ries are ;
Gentle as chaines that honour binde,
    More faithfull then an Hebrew Jew,
    But as the divel not halfe so true.

AMYNTOR[1] FROM BEYOND THE SEA TO ALEXIS.[2]

A DIALOGUE.

Amyntor.

ALEXIS! ah Alexis! can it be,
 Though so much wet and drie
  Doth drowne our eye,
Thou keep'st thy winged voice from me?

Alexis.

Amyntor, a profounder sea, I feare,
 Hath swallow'd me, where now
  My armes do row,
I floate i'th' ocean of a teare.

Lucasta weepes, lest I look back and tread
 Your Watry land againe.
Amyn. I'd through the raine;
Such showrs are quickly over-spread.

Conceive how joy, after this short divorce,
 Will circle her with beames,
  When, like your streames,
You shall rowle back with kinder force,

---

[1] Endymion Porter? [2] Lovelace himself.

And call the helping winds to vent your thought.

Alex.   Amyntor! Chloris! where
Or in what sphere
Say, may that glorious fair be sought?

Amyn. She's now the center of these armes e're blest,
Whence may she never move,
Till Time and Love.
Haste to their everlasting rest.

Alex.   Ah subtile swaine! doth not my flame rise high
As yours, and burne as hot?
Am not I shot
With the selfe same artillery?

And can I breath without her air?—*Amyn.*
Why, then,
From thy tempestuous earth,
Where blood and dearth
Raigne 'stead of kings, agen

Wafte thy selfe over, and lest storms from far
Arise, bring in our sight
The seas delight,
Lucasta, that bright northerne star.

Alex.   But as we cut the rugged deepe, I feare
The green god stops his fell
Chariot of shell,
And smooths the maine to ravish her.

Amyn. Oh no, the prince of waters' fires are done ;
　　　　He as his empire's old,
　　　　　　And rivers, cold ;
　　　　His queen now runs abed to th' sun ;

　　　　But all his treasure he shall ope' that day :
　　　　Tritons shall sound : his fleete
　　　　　　In silver meete,
　　　　And to her their rich offrings pay.

Alex.　We flye, Amyntor, not amaz'd how sent
　　　　By water, earth, or aire :
　　　　　　Or if with her
　　　　　　By fire : ev'n there
　　　　I move in mine owne element.

CALLING LUCASTA FROM HER
RETIREMENT.

ODE.

I.

FROM the dire monument of thy black roome,
　　Wher now that vestal flame thou dost in-
　　　　tombe,
　　As in the inmost cell of all earths wombe.

II.

Sacred Lucasta, like the pow'rfull ray
Of heavenly truth, passe this Cimmerian way,
Whilst all the standards of your beames display.

III.

Arise and climbe our whitest, highest hill;
There your sad thoughts with joy and wonder fill,
And see seas calme[1] as earth, earth as your will.

IV.

Behold ! how lightning like a taper flyes,
And guilds your chari't, but ashamed dyes,
Seeing it selfe out-gloried by your eyes.

V.

Threatning and boystrous tempests gently bow,
And to your steps part in soft paths, when now
There no where hangs a cloud, but on your brow.

VI.

No showrs but 'twixt your lids, nor gelid snow,
But what your whiter, chaster brest doth ow,[2]
Whilst winds in chains colder for[3] sorrow blow.

VII.

Shrill trumpets doe only sound to eate,
Artillery hath loaden ev'ry dish with meate,
And drums at ev'ry health alarmes beate.

VIII.

All things Lucasta, but Lucasta, call,
Trees borrow tongues, waters in accents fall,
The aire doth sing, and fire is[4] musicall.

---

[1] Original has *colme.*   [2] *i. e.* own.   [3] Original reads *your.*
[4] Original has *fire's,* but *fire is* is required by the metre, and
it is probably what the poet wrote.

IX.

Awake from the dead vault in which you dwell,
All's loyall here, except your thoughts rebell
Which, so let loose, often their gen'rall quell.

X.

See! she obeys! By all obeyed thus,
No storms, heats, colds, no soules contentious,
Nor civill war is found; I meane, to us.

XI.

Lovers and angels, though in heav'n they show,
And see the woes and discords here below,
What they not feele, must not be said to know.

AMARANTHA.

A PASTORALL.[1]

UP with the jolly bird of light
 Who sounds his third retreat to night;
 Faire Amarantha from her bed
 Ashamed starts, and rises red
As the carnation-mantled morne,
Who now the blushing robe doth spurne,
And puts on angry gray, whilst she,
The envy of a deity,
Arayes her limbes, too rich indeed
To be inshrin'd in such a weed;

---

[1] The punctuation of this piece is in the original edition singularly corrupt. I have found it necessary to amend it throughout.

Yet lovely 'twas and strait, but fit ;
Not made for her, but she to it :
By nature it sate close and free,
As the just bark unto the tree :
Unlike Love's martyrs of the towne,
All day imprison'd in a gown,
Who, rackt in silke 'stead of a dresse,
Are cloathed in a frame or presse,
And with that liberty and room,
The dead expatiate in a tombe.

No cabinets with curious washes,
Bladders and perfumed plashes ;
No venome-temper'd water's here,
Mercury is banished this sphere :
Her payle's all this, in which wet glasse
She both doth cleanse and view her face.

Far hence, all Iberian smells,
Hot amulets, Pomander spells,
Fragrant gales, cool ay'r, the fresh
And naturall odour of her flesh,
Proclaim her sweet from th' wombe as morne.
Those colour'd things were made, not borne,
Which, fixt within their narrow straits,
Do looke like their own counterfeyts.
So like the Provance rose she walkt,
Flowerd with blush, with verdure stalkt ;
Th' officious wind her loose hayre curles,
The dewe her happy linnen purles,
But wets a tresse, which instantly
Sol with a crisping beame doth dry.

Into the garden is she come,

Love and delight's Elisium ;
If ever earth show'd all her store,
View her discolourd budding floore ;
Here her glad eye she largely feedes,
And stands 'mongst them, as they 'mong weeds :
The flowers in their best aray
As to their queen their tribute pay,
And freely to her lap proscribe
A daughter out of ev'ry tribe.
Thus as she moves, they all bequeath
At once the incense of their breath.
  The noble Heliotropian
Now turnes to her, and knowes no sun.
  And as her glorious face doth vary,
So opens loyall golden Mary[1]
Who, if but glanced from her sight,
Straight shuts again, as it were night.
  The violet (else lost ith' heap)
Doth spread fresh purple for each step.
With whose humility possest,
Sh' inthrones the Poore Girle[2] in her breast :
The July-flow'r[3] that hereto thriv'd,
Knowing her self no longer-liv'd,
But for one look of her upheaves,
Then 'stead of teares straight sheds her leaves.
  Now the rich robed Tulip who,
Clad all in tissue close, doth woe
Her (sweet to th' eye but smelling sower).

---

[1] The marigold.   [2] A flower so called.
[3] More commonly know as *the gilliflower.*

She gathers to adorn her bower.

But the proud Hony-suckle spreads
Like a pavilion her heads,
Contemnes the wanting commonalty,
That but to two ends usefull be,
And to her lips thus aptly plac't,
With smell and hue presents her tast.

So all their due obedience pay,
Each thronging to be in her way :
Faire Amarantha with her eye
Thanks those that live, which else would dye :
The rest, in silken fetters bound,
By crowning her are crown and crown'd.[1]

And now the sun doth higher rise,
Our Flora to the meadow hies :
The poore distressed heifers low,
And as sh' approacheth gently bow,
Begging her charitable leasure
To strip them of their milkie treasure.

Out of the yeomanry oth' heard.
With grave aspect, and feet prepar'd,
A rev'rend lady-cow drawes neare,
Bids Amarantha welcome here ;
And from her privy purse lets fall
A pearle or two, which seeme[s] to call
This adorn'd adored fayry
To the banquet of her dayry.

Soft Amarantha weeps to see
'Mongst men such inhumanitie.

---

[1] *i. e.* the lady gathers the flowers, and binds them in her hair
th a silken fillet, making of them a kind of chaplet or crown.

That those, who do receive in hay,
And pay in silver[1] twice a day,
Should by their cruell barb'rous theft
Be both of that and life bereft.

But 'tis decreed, when ere this dies,
That she shall fall a sacrifice
Unto the gods, since those, that trace
Her stemme, show 'tis a god-like race,
Descending in an even line
From heifers and from steeres divine,
Making the honour'd extract full
In Iö and Europa's bull.
She was the largest goodliest beast,
That ever mead or altar blest;
Round [w]as her udder, and more white
Then is the Milkie Way in night;
Her full broad eye did sparkle fire;
Her breath was sweet as kind desire,
And in her beauteous crescent shone,
Bright as the argent-horned moone.

But see! this whitenesse is obscure,
Cynthia spotted, she impure;
Her body writheld,[2] and her eyes

---

[1] *i. e.* silvery or white milk.

[2] An uncommon word, signifying *wrinkled.* Bishop Hall seem
to be, with the exception of Lovelace, almost the only write
who used it.   Compare, however, the following passage:—

"Like to a *writhel'd* Carion I have seen
(Instead of fifty, write her down fifteen)
Wearing her bought complexion in a box,
And ev'ry morn her closet-face unlocks."

Plantagenet's Tragicall Story, by T. W. 1649, p. 105

Departing lights at obsequies:
Her lowing hot to the fresh gale,
Her breath perfumes the field withall;
To those two suns that ever shine,
To those plump parts she doth inshrine,
To th' hovering snow of either hand,
That love and cruelty command.

    After the breakfast on her teat,
She takes her leave oth' mournfull neat
Who, by her toucht, now prizeth her [1] life,
Worthy alone the hollowed knife.

    Into the neighbring wood she's gone,
Whose roofe defies the tell-tale Sunne,
And locks out ev'ry prying beame;
Close by the lips of a cleare streame,
She sits and entertaines her eye
With the moist chrystall and the frye [2]
With burnisht-silver mal'd, whose oares [3]
Amazed still make to the shoares;
What need she other bait or charm,
What hook [4] or angle, but her arm?
The happy captive, gladly ta'n,
Sues ever to be slave in vaine,
Who instantly (confirm'd in's feares)
Hasts to his element of teares.

    From hence her various windings roave
To a well-orderd stately grove;
This is the pallace of the wood

---

[1] Original has *prize their.*
[2] The fish with their silvery scales.
[3] Fins.
[4] Original reads *but look.*

F

And court oth' Royall Oake, where stood
The whole nobility: the Pine,
Strait Ash, tall Firre, and wanton Vine;
The proper Cedar, and the rest.
Here she her deeper senses blest;
Admires great Nature in this pile,
Floor'd with greene-velvet Camomile,
Garnisht with gems of unset fruit,
Supply'd still with a self recruit;
Her bosom wrought with pretty eyes
Of never-planted Strawberries;
Where th' winged musick of the ayre
Do richly feast, and for their fare,
Each evening in a silent shade,
Bestow a gratefull serenade.
   Thus ev'n tyerd with delight,
Sated in soul and appetite;
Full of the purple Plumme and Peare,
The golden Apple, with the faire
Grape that mirth fain would have taught her,
And nuts, which squirrells cracking brought her;
She softly layes her weary limbs,
Whilst gentle slumber now beginnes
To draw the curtaines of her eye;
When straight awakend with a crie
And bitter groan, again reposes,
Again a deep sigh interposes.
And now she heares a trembling voyce:
Ah! can there ought on earth rejoyce!
Why weares she this gay livery,
Not black as her dark entrails be?

Can trees be green, and to the ay'r
Thus prostitute their flowing hayr?
Why do they sprout, not witherd dy?
Must each thing live, save wretched I?
Can dayes triumph in blew and red,
When both their light and life is fled?
Fly Joy on wings of Popinjayes
To courts of fools, where [1] as your playes
Dye laught at and forgot; whilst all
That's good mourns at this funerall.
Weep, all ye Graces, and you sweet
Quire, that at the hill inspir'd meet:
Love, put thy tapers out, that we
And th' world may seem as blind as thee;
And be, since she is lost (ah wound!)
Not Heav'n it self by any found.

  Now as a prisoner new cast, [2]
Who sleepes in chaines that night, his last,
Next morn is wak't with a repreeve,
And from his trance, not dream bid live,
Wonders (his sence not having scope)
Who speaks, his friend or his false hope.

  So Amarantha heard, but feare
Dares not yet trust her tempting care;
And as againe her arms oth' ground
Spread pillows for her head, a sound
More dismall makes a swift divorce,
And starts her thus :——Rage, rapine, force!
Ye blew-flam'd daughters oth' abysse,

---

[1] Original has *there*.　　[2] *i. e.* condemned.

Bring all your snakes, here let them hisse;
Let not a leaf its freshnesse keep;
Blast all their roots, and as you creepe,
And leave behind your deadly slime,
Poyson the budding branch in's prime:
Wast the proud bowers of this grove,
That fiends may dwell in it, and move
As in their proper hell, whilst she
Above laments this tragedy:
Yet pities not our fate; oh faire
Vow-breaker, now betroth'd to th' ay'r!
Why by those lawes did we not die,
As live but one, Lucasta! why——
As he Lucasta nam'd, a groan
Strangles the fainting passing tone;
But as she heard, Lucasta smiles,
Posses [1] her round; she's slipt mean whiles
Behind the blind of a thick bush,
When, each word temp'ring with a blush,
She gently thus bespake: Sad swaine,
If mates in woe do ease our pain,
Here's one full of that antick grief,
Which stifled would for ever live,
But told, expires; pray then, reveale
(To show our wound is half to heale),
What mortall nymph or deity
Bewail you thus? Who ere you be,

---

[1] This word does not appear to have any very exact meaning
See Halliwell's *Dictionary of Archaic Words*, art. *Posse*, and
Worcester's Dict. *ibid*, &c. The context here requires *to tur*
sharply or quickly.

The shepheard sigh't,[1] my woes I crave
Smotherd in me, me[2] in my grave;
Yet be in show or truth a saint,
Or fiend, breath anthemes, heare my plaint,
For her and thy breath's symphony,
Which now makes full the harmony
Above, and to whose voice the spheres
Listen, and call her musick theirs;
This was I blest on earth with, so
As Druids amorous did grow,
Jealous of both: for as one day
This star, as yet but set in clay,
By an imbracing river lay,
They steept her in the hollowed brooke,
Which from her humane nature tooke,
And straight to heaven with winged feare,[3]
Thus, ravisht with her, ravish her.

The nymph reply'd: This holy rape
Became the gods, whose obscure shape
They cloth'd with light, whilst ill you grieve
Your better life should ever live,
And weep that she, to whom you wish
What heav'n could give, has all its blisse.
Calling her angell here, yet be
Sad at this true divinity:
She's for the altar, not the skies,

[1] Original has *sight*.
[2] Original reads *I*. The meaning seems to be, "I crave that my woes may be smothered in me, and I may be smothered in my grave."
[3] Reverence.

Whom first you crowne, then sacrifice.
　　Fond man thus to a precipice
Aspires, till at the top his eyes
Have lost the safety of the plain,
Then begs of Fate the vales againe.
　　The now confounded shepheard cries:
Ye all-confounding destinies!
How did you make that voice so sweet
Without that glorious form to it?
Thou sacred spirit of my deare,
Where e're thou hoverst o're us, hear!
Imbark thee in the lawrell tree,
And a new Phebus follows thee,
Who, 'stead of all his burning rayes,
Will strive to catch thee with his layes;
Or, if within the Orient Vine,
Thou art both deity and wine;
But if thou takest the mirtle grove,
That Paphos is, thou, Queene of Love,
And I, thy swain who (else) must die,
By no beasts, but thy cruelty:
But you are rougher than the winde.
Are souls on earth then heav'n [1] more kind?
Imprisoned in mortality
Lucasta would have answered me.
Lucasta, Amarantha said,
Is she that virgin-star? a maid,
Except her prouder livery,
In beauty poore, and cheap as I;

---

[1] *i. e.* in heaven.

Whose glory like a meteor shone,
Or aëry apparition,
Admir'd a while, but slighted known.

    Fierce, as the chafed lyon hies,
He rowses him, and to her flies,
Thinking to answer with his speare——

    Now, as in warre intestine where,
Ith' mist of a black battell, each
Layes at his next, then makes a breach
Through th' entrayles of another, whom
He sees nor knows whence he did come,
Guided alone by rage and th' drumme,
But stripping and impatient wild,
He finds too soon his onely child.

    So our expiring desp'rate lover
Far'd when, amaz'd, he did discover
Lucasta in this nymph; his sinne
Darts the accursed javelin
'Gainst his own breast, which she puts by
With a soft lip and gentle eye,
Then closes with him on the ground
And now her smiles have heal'd his wound.
Alexis too again is found;
But not untill those heavy crimes
She hath kis'd off a thousand times,
Who not contented with this pain,
Doth threaten to offend again.

    And now they gaze, and sigh, and weep,
Whilst each cheek doth the other's steep,
Whilst tongues, as exorcis'd, are calm;
Onely the rhet'rick of the palm

Prevailing pleads, untill at last
They[re] chain'd in one another fast.
Lucasta to him doth relate
Her various chance and diffring fate:
How chac'd by Hydraphil, and tract
The num'rous foe to Philanact,
Who whilst they for the same things fight,
As Bards decrees and Druids rite,
For safeguard of their proper joyes
And shepheards freedome, each destroyes
The glory of this Sicilie;
Since seeking thus the remedie,
They fancy (building on false ground)
The means must them and it confound,
Yet are resolved to stand or fall,
And win a little, or lose all.

From this sad storm of fire and blood
She fled to this yet living wood;
Where she 'mongst savage beasts doth find
Her self more safe then humane [1] kind.

Then she relates, how Cælia—[2]
The lady—here strippes her array,
And girdles her in home-spunne bayes,
Then makes her conversant in layes
Of birds, and swaines more innocent,
That kenne not guile [n]or courtship ment.

Now walks she to her bow'r to dine

---

[1] *i. e.* than among human kind.
[2] It may be presumed that *Lucasta* had adopted the name of *Cælia* during her sylvan retreat.

Under a shade of Eglantine,
Upon a dish of Natures cheere
Which both grew, drest and serv'd up there:
That done, she feasts her smell with po'ses
Pluckt from the damask cloath of Roses.
Which there continually doth stay,
And onely frost can take away;
Then wagers which hath most content
Her eye, eare, hand, her gust or sent.

Intranc't Alexis sees and heares,
As walking above all the spheres:
Knows and adores this, and is wilde,[1]
Untill with her he live thus milde.[2]
So that, which to his thoughts he meant
For losse of her a punishment,
His armes hung up and his sword broke,
His ensignes folded, he betook
Himself unto the humble crook.
And for a full reward of all,
She now doth him her shepheard call,
And in a see of flow'rs install:
Then gives her faith immediately,
Which he returns religiously;
Both vowing in her peacefull cave
To make their bridall-bed and grave.

But the true joy this pair conceiv'd,
Each from the other first bereav'd,
And then found, after such alarmes,
Fast-pinion'd in each other's armes,

---

[1] Impatient.   [2] Tranquil or secluded.

Ye panting virgins, that do meet
Your loves within their winding sheet.
Breathing and constant still ev'n there ;
Or souls their bodies in yon' sphere,
Or angels, men return'd from hell
And separated mindes—can tell.

TO ELLINDA,

THAT LATELY I HAVE NOT WRITTEN.

I.

IF in me anger, or disdaine
In you, or both, made me refraine
From th' noble intercourse of verse,
That only vertuous thoughts rehearse ;
  Then, chaste Ellinda, might you feare
  The sacred vowes that I did sweare.

II.

But if alone some pious thought
Me to an inward sadnesse brought,
Thinking to breath your soule too welle,
My tongue was charmed with that spell ;
  And left it (since there was no roome
  To voyce your worth enough) strooke dumbe.

III.

So then this silence doth reveal
No thought of negligence, but zeal :
For, as in adoration,
This is love's true devotion ;
  Children and fools the words repeat,
  But anch'rites pray in tears and sweat.

ELLINDA'S GLOVE.

SONNET.

I.

THOU snowy farme with thy five tenements![1]
 Tell thy white mistris here was one,
 That call'd to pay his dayly rents;
But she a-gathering flowr's and hearts is
  gone,
And thou left voyd to rude possession.

II.

But grieve not, pretty Ermin cabinet,
 Thy alabaster lady will come home;
 If not, what tenant can there fit
The slender turnings of thy narrow roome,
But must ejected be by his owne dombe?[2]

III.

Then give me leave to leave my rent with thee:
 Five kisses, one unto a place:
 For though the lute's too high for me,
Yet servants, knowing minikin[3] nor base,
Are still allow'd to fiddle with the case.

---

[1] *i. e.* the white glove of the lady with its five fingers.

[2] Doom.

[3] A description of musical pin attached to a lute. It was only brought into play by accomplished musicians. In the address of "The Country Suiter to his Love," printed in Cotgrave's *Wits Interpreter*, 1662, p. 119, the man says:—

 "Fair Wench! I cannot court thy sprightly eyes
 With a base-viol plac'd betwixt my thighs,

BEING TREATED.

TO ELLINDA.

OR cherries plenty, and for corans
    Enough for fifty, were there more on's ;
    For elles of beere,[1] flutes[2] of canary,
    That well did wash downe pasties-Mary ;[3]

    I cannot lisp, nor to a fiddle sing,
      Nor run upon a high-strecht minikin."
In Middleton's *Familie of Love,* 1608 (Works by Dyce, ii. 127)
there is the following passage :—
  " *Gudgeon.*   Ay, and to all that forswear marriage, and can be
content with other men's wives.
  Gerardine. Of which consort you two are grounds ; one touches
the bass, and the other tickles the minikin."
  [1] This expression has reference to the old practice of drinking
beer and wine out of very high glasses, with divisions marked on
them.   A yard of ale is even now a well understood term : nor is
the custom itself out of date, since in some parts of the country
one is asked to take, not a glass, but *a yard.*   The ell was of
course, strictly speaking, a larger measure than a yard ; but it was
often employed as a mere synonyme or equivalent.   Thus, in
Maroccus Extaticus, 1595, Bankes says :—" Measure, Marocco,
nay, nay, they that take up commodities make no difference for
measure between a Flemish elle and an English yard."
  [2] In the new edition of Nares (1859), this very passage is
quoted to. illustrate the meaning of the word, which is defined
rather vaguely to be *a cask.*   Obviously the word signifies something of the kind, but the explanation does not at all satisfy me.
I suspect that a flute *of canary* was so called from the cask having several vent-holes, in the same way that the French call a
lamprey *fleute d'Aleman* from the fish having little holes in the
upper part of its body.
  [3] Forsyth, in his *Antiquary's Portfolio,* 1825, mentions certain

For peason, chickens, sawces high,
Pig, and the widdow-venson-pye ; [1]
With certaine promise (to your brother)
Of the virginity of another,
Where it is thought I too may peepe in
With knuckles far as any deepe in ; [2]

" glutton-feasts," which used formerly to be celebrated period-
ically in honour of the Virgin ; perhaps the pasties used on these
occasions were thence christened *pasties-Mary.*

[1] Venison pies or pasties were the most favourite dish in this
country in former times ; innumerable illustrations might be furnished of the high esteem in which this description of viand was
held by our ancestors, who regarded it as a thoroughly English
luxury. The anonymous author of *Horæ Subsecivæ*, 1620, p. 38
(this volume is supposed to have been written by Giles Brydges,
Lord Chandos), describes an affected Englishman who has been
travelling on the Continent, as "sweating at the sight of a pasty
of venison," and as " swearing that the only delicacies be mush-
rooms, or *caviare*, or snayles."

   " The full-cram'd dishes made the table crack,
      Gammons of bacon, brawn, and what was chief,
      King in all feasts, a tall Sir Loyne of *Bref,*
      Fat venison pasties smoaking, 'tis no fable,
      Swans in their broath came swimming to the table."—
        Poems of BEN JOHNSON Junior, by W. S. 1672, p. 3.

[2] An allusion to the scantiness of forks. " And when your
justice of peace is knuckle-deep in goose, you may without dis-
paragement to your blood, though you have a lady to your mother, fall very manfully to your woodcocks."—DECKER's *Guls
Horn Book,* 1609, ed. Nott, p. 121.

  " *Hodge.* Forks! what be they?
  Mar. The laudable use of forks,
      Brought into custom here, as they are in Italy,
      To the sparing of napkins——"
       JONSON's *The Devil is an Ass,* act v. scene 4.

For glasses, heads, hands, bellies full
Of wine, and loyne right-worshipfull ; [1]
Whether all of, or more behind—a
Thankes freest, freshest, faire Ellinda.
Thankes for my visit not disdaining,
Or at the least thankes for your feigning ;
For if your mercy doore were lockt-well,
I should be justly soundly knockt-well ;
Cause that in dogrell I did mutter
Not one rhime to you from dam-Rotter. [2]

Next beg I to present my duty
To pregnant sister in prime beauty,
Whom well I deeme (e're few months elder)
Will take out Hans from pretty Kelder,
And to the sweetly fayre Mabella,
A match that vies with Arabella ;
In each respect but the misfortune,
Fortune, Fate, I thee importune.

Nor must I passe the lovely Alice,
Whose health I'd quaffe in golden chalice ;
But since that Fate hath made me neuter,
I only can in beaker pewter :

"*Lovell.* Your hand, good sir.
Greedy. This is a lord, and some think this a favour;
But I had rather have my hand in my dumpling."
MASSINGER'S *New Way to Pay Old Debts,* 1633.
[1] The sirloin of beef.
[2] Rotterdam.

But who'd forget, or yet left un-sung
The doughty acts of George the yong-son?
Who yesterday to save his sister
Had slaine the snake, had he not mist her:
But I shall leave him, 'till a nag on
He gets to prosecute the dragon;
And then with helpe of sun and taper,
Fill with his deeds twelve reames of paper,
That Amadis,[1] Sir Guy, and Topaz
With his fleet neigher shall keep no-pace.

 But now to close all I must switch-hard,
 [Your] servant ever;

LOVELACE RICHARD.

TO ELLINDA.

VPON HIS LATE RECOVERY.

A PARADOX.

I.

OW I grieve that I am well!
 All my health was in my sicknes,
Go then, Destiny, and tell,
 Very death is in this quicknes.

---

[1] *Amadis de Gaule.* The translation of this romance by Anthony Munday and two or three others, whose assistance he obtained, made it popular in England, although, perhaps with the exception of the portion executed by Munday himself, the performance is beneath criticism.

II.

Such a fate rules over me,
　　That I glory when I languish,
And do blesse the remedy,
　　That doth feed, not quench my anguish.

III.

'Twas a gentle warmth that ceas'd
　　In the vizard of a feavor;
But I feare now I am cas'd
　　All the flames, since I must leave her.

IV.

Joyes, though witherd, circled me,
　　When unto her voice inured
Like those who, by harmony,
　　Only can be throughly cured.

V.

Sweet, sure, was that malady,
　　Whilst the pleasant angel hover'd,
Which ceasing they are all, as I,
　　Angry that they are recover'd.

VI.

And as men in hospitals,
　　That are maim'd, are lodg'd and dined;
But when once their danger fals,
　　Ah th' are healed to be pined!

VII.

Fainting so, I might before
Sometime have the leave to hand her,
But lusty, am beat out of dore,
And for Love compell'd to wander.

TO CHLOE,

COURTING HER FOR HIS FRIEND.

I.

CHLOE, behold! againe I bowe :
Againe possest, againe I woo ;
From my heat hath taken fire
Damas, noble youth, and fries,[1]
Gazing with one of mine eyes,
Damas, halfe of me expires :
Chloe, behold! Our fate's the same.
Or make me cinders too, or quench his flame.

---

[1] This is not unfrequently used in old writers in the sense of *burn*:—

"But Lucilla, who now began to frie in the flames of love, all the company being departed," &c.—LYLY's *Euphues*, 1579, sig. c v. verso.

"My lady-mistresse cast an amourous eye
Upon my forme, which her affections drew,
Shee was Love's martyr, and in flames did frye."
Egypt's Favorite. The Historie of Joseph. By
Sir F. Hubert, 1631, sig. C.

G

II.

I'd not be King, unlesse there sate
Lesse lords that shar'd with me in state
  Who, by their cheaper coronets, know,
  What glories from my diadem flow:
  Its use and rate[1] values the gem:
  Pearles in their shells have no esteem;
And, I being sun within thy sphere,
'Tis my chiefe beauty thinner lights shine there.

III.

The Us'rer heaps unto his store
By seeing others praise it more;
  Who not for gaine or want doth covet,
  But, 'cause another loves, doth love it:
  Thus gluttons cloy'd afresh invite
  Their gusts from some new appetite;
And after cloth remov'd, and meate,
Fall too againe by seeing others eate.

GRATIANA DAUNCING AND SINGING.

I.

SEE! with what constant motion
  Even and glorious, as the sunne,
    Gratiana steeres that noble frame,
  Soft as her breast, sweet as her voyce,
  That gave each winding law and poyze,
    And swifter then the wings of Fame.

---

[1] The estimation in which it is held, its marketable worth.

II.

She beat the happy pavement
By such a starre-made firmament,
   Which now no more the roofe envies ;
But swells up high with Atlas ev'n,
Bearing the brighter, nobler Heav'n,
   And in her, all the Dieties.

III.

Each step trod out a lovers thought
And the ambitious hopes he brought,
   Chain'd to her brave feet with such arts,
Such sweet command and gentle awe,
As when she ceas'd, we sighing saw
   The floore lay pav'd with broken hearts.

IV.

 So did she move: so did she sing:
Like the harmonious spheres that bring
   Unto their rounds their musick's ayd ;
Which she performed such a way,
As all th' inamour'd world will say:
   The Graces daunced, and Apollo play'd.

AMYNTOR'S GROVE,[1]

HIS CHLORIS, ARIGO,[2] AND GRATIANA.

AN ELOGIE.

T was[3] Amyntor's Grove, that Chloris
For ever ecchoes, and her glories ;
Chloris, the gentlest sheapherdesse,
That ever lawnes and lambes did blesse ;
Her breath, like to the whispering winde,
Was calme as thought, sweet as her minde ;
Her lips like coral gates kept in
The perfume and [4] the pearle within ;

---

[1] In the MS. copy this poem exhibits considerable variations, and is entitled " Gratiana's Eulogy."

[2] *Arigo* or *Arrigo* is the Venetian form of *Henrico.* I have no means of identifying *Chloris* or *Gratiana;* but *Amyntor* was probably, as I have already suggested, Endymion Porter, and *Arigo* was unquestionably no other than Henry Jermyn, or Jarmin, who, though no poet, was, like his friend Porter, a liberal and discerning patron of men of letters.

> " Yet when thy noble choice appear'd, that by
> Their combat first prepar'd thy victory :
> *Endymion* and *Arigo,* who delight
> In numbers—"

DAVENANT'S *Madagascar,* 1638 (Works, 1673, p. 212).

See also p. 247 of Davenant's Works.

Jermyn's name is associated with that of Porter in the noblest dedication in our language, that to *Davenant's Poems,* 1638, 12mo. " If these poems live," &c.

[3] This and the five next lines are not in MS. which opens with " Her lips," &c.

[4] So original ; MS. reads *of.*

Her eyes a double-flaming torch
That alwayes shine, and never scorch ;
Her[1] selfe the Heav'n in which did meet
The all of bright, of faire and sweet.

Here was I brought with that delight
That seperated soules take flight ;
And when my reason call'd my sence
Back somewhat from this excellence,
That I could see, I did begin
T' observe the curious ordering
Of every roome, where 'ts hard to know,
Which most excels in sent or show.
Arabian gummes do breathe here forth,
And th' East's come over to the North ;
The windes have brought their hyre[2] of sweet
To see Amyntor Chloris greet ;
Balme and nard, and each perfume,
To blesse this payre,[3] chafe and consume ;
And th' Phœnix, see ! already fries !
Her neast a fire in Chloris[4] eyes !

---

[1] This and the next thirteen lines are not in MS.
[2] *i. e.* tribute.
[3] *faire*—MS.
[4] *her faire*—MS. The story of the phœnix was very popular,
and the allusions to it in the early writers are almost innumerable.

> " My labour did to greater things aspire,
> To find a *Phœnix* melted in the fire,
> Out of whose ashes should spring up to birth
> A friend "—
> > *Poems of* BEN JOHNSON jun., by W. S., 1672, p. 18.

Next[1] the great and powerful hand
Beckens my thoughts unto a stand
Of Titian, Raphael, Georgone
Whose art even Nature hath out-done;
For if weake Nature only can
Intend, not perfect, what is man,
These certainely we must prefer,
Who mended what she wrought, and her;
And sure the shadowes of those rare
And kind incomparable fayre
Are livelier, nobler company,
Then if they could or speake, or see:
For these[2] I aske without a tush,
Can kisse or touch without a blush,
And we are taught that substance is,
If uninjoy'd, but th'[3] shade of blisse.

Now every saint cleerly divine,
Is clos'd so in her severall shrine;
The gems so rarely, richly set,
For them wee love the cabinet;
So intricately plac't withall,
As if th' imbrordered the wall,
So that the pictures seem'd to be
But one continued tapistrie.[4]

After this travell of mine eyes
We sate, and pitied Dietics;

---

[1] This and the next eleven lines are not in MS.
[2] The MS. reads *she.*
[3] The MS. reads for *but th'* " the."
[4] In the houses of such as could afford the expense, the walls
of rooms were formerly lined with tapestry instead of paper.

Wee bound our loose hayre with the vine,
The poppy, and the eglantine;
One swell'd an oriental bowle
Full, as a grateful, loyal soule
To Chloris! Chloris! Heare, oh, heare!
'Tis pledg'd above in ev'ry sphere.

    Now streight the Indians richest prize
Is kindled in[1] glad sacrifice;
Cloudes are sent up on wings of thyme,
Amber, pomgranates, jessemine,
And through our earthen conduicts sore
Higher then altars fum'd before.

    So drencht we our oppressing cares,
And choakt the wide jawes of our feares.
Whilst ravisht thus we did devise,
If this were not a Paradice
In all, except these harmlesse sins:
Behold! flew in two cherubins,
Cleare as the skye from whence they came,
And brighter than the sacred flame;
The boy adorn'd with modesty,
Yet armed so with majesty,
That if the Thunderer againe
His eagle sends, she stoops in vaine.[2]
Besides his innocence he tooke
A sword and casket, and did looke
Like Love in armes; he wrote but five,
Yet spake eighteene: each grace did strive,

---

[1] So MS.; original has *a*.
[2] An allusion to the fable of Jupiter and Ganymede.

And twenty Cupids thronged forth,
Who first should shew his prettier worth.
But oh, the Nymph! Did you ere know
Carnation mingled with snow?[1]
Or have you seene the lightning shrowd,
And straight breake through th' opposing cloud?
So ran her blood; such was its hue;
So through her vayle her bright haire flew,
And yet its glory did appeare
But thinne, because her eyes were neere.

　　Blooming boy, and blossoming mayd,
May your faire sprigges be neere betrayd
To[2] eating worme or fouler storme;
No serpent lurke to do them harme;
No sharpe frost cut, no North-winde teare,
The verdure of that fragrant hayre;
But[3] may the sun and gentle weather,
When you are both growne ripe together,
Load you with fruit, such as your Father
From you with all the joyes doth gather:
And may you, when one branch is dead,
Graft such another in its stead,
Lasting thus ever in your prime,
'Till th' sithe is snatcht away from Time.[4]

---

[1] *Mix'd with droppinge snow*—MS.

[2] This and the succeeding line are not in MS.

[3] This and the six following lines are not in MS.

[4] Here we have a figure, which reminds us of Jonson's famous lines on the Countess of Pembroke; but certainly in this instance the palm of superiority is due to Lovelace, whose conception of Time having his scythe snatched from him is bolder and finer than that of the earlier and greater poet.

THE SCRUTINIE.

SONG.

SET BY MR. THOMAS CHARLES.[1]

I.

WHY shouldst thou[2] sweare I am forsworn,
 Since thine I vow'd to be ?
Lady, it is already Morn,
 And 'twas last night I swore to thee
 That fond impossibility.

II.

Have I not lov'd thee much and long,
 A tedious twelve moneths[3] space ?
I should[4] all other beauties wrong,
 And rob thee of a new imbrace ;
 Should[5] I still dote upon thy face.

III.

Not but all joy in thy browne haire
 In[6] others may be found ;
But I must search the black and faire,
 Like skilfulle minerallists that sound
 For treasure in un-plow'd-up[7] ground.

---

[1] This poem appears in *Wits Interpreter*, by John Cotgrave, ed. 1662, p. 214, under the title of " On his Mistresse, who unjustly taxed him of leaving her off."

[2] So Cotgrave. *Lucasta* reads *should you*.

[3] So Cotgrave. This is preferable to *hours*, the reading in *Lucasta*.

[4] So Cotgrave. *Lucasta* reads *must*.

[5] So Cotgrave. *Lucasta* has *could*.

[6] So Cotgrave. *Lucasta* reads *By*.

[7] *Unbidden*—Cotgrave.

IV.

Then if, when I have lov'd my[1] round,
　　Thou prov'st the pleasant she;
With spoyles[2] of meaner beauties crown'd,
　　I laden will returne to thee,
　　Ev'n sated with varietie.

PRINCESSE LOYSA[3] DRAWING.

SAW a little Diety,
　Minerva in epitomy,
　Whom *Venus*, at first blush, surpris'd,
Tooke for her winged wagge disguis'd.
But viewing then, whereas she made
Not a distrest, but lively shade
Of *Eccho* whom he had betrayd,
Now wanton, and ith' coole oth' Sunne
With her delight a hunting gone,
And thousands more, whom he had slaine;
To live and love, belov'd againe:
Ah! this is true divinity!
I will un-God that toye! cri'd she;
Then markt she *Syrinx* running fast
To Pan's imbraces, with the haste
Shee fled him once, whose reede-pipe rent
He finds now a new Instrument.

---

[1] *thee*—Cotgrave.
[2] *In spoil*—Cotgrave.
[3] Probably the second daughter of Frederic and Elizabeth of Bohemia, b. 1622. See TOWNEND's *Descendants of the Stuarts,* 1858, p. 7.

Theseus return'd invokes the Ayre
And windes, then wafts his faire ;
Whilst *Ariadne* ravish't stood
Half in his armes, halfe in the flood.

  Proud *Anáxerete* doth fall
At *Iphis* feete, who smiles at[1] all :
And he (whilst she his curles doth deck)
Hangs no where now, but on her neck.
Here *Phœbus* with a beame untombes
Long-hid *Leucothoë*, and doomes
Her father there ; *Daphne* the faire
Knowes now no bayes but round her haire ;
And to *Apollo* and his Sons,
Who pay him their due Orisons,
Bequeaths her lawrell-robe, that flame
Contemnes, Thunder and evill Fame.

  There kneel'd *Adonis* fresh as spring,
Gay as his youth, now offering
Herself those joyes with voice and hand,
Which first he could not understand.

  Transfixed *Venus* stood amas'd,
Full of the Boy and Love, she gaz'd,
And in imbraces seemed more
Seneeless and colde then he before.
Uselesse Childe ! In vaine (said she)
You beare that fond artillerie ;
See heere a pow'r above the slow
Weake execution of thy bow.

  So said, she riv'd the wood in two,
Unedged all his arrowes too,

---

¹ Original has *of*.

And with the string their feathers bound
To that part, whence we have our wound.
  See, see! the darts by which we burn'd
Are bright Loysa's pencills turn'd,
With which she now enliveth more
Beauties, than they destroy'd before.

A

FORSAKEN LADY TO HER FALSE SERVANT

THAT IS DISDAINED BY HIS NEW

MISTRISS.[1]

WERE it that you so shun me, 'cause you wish
(Cruels't) a fellow in your wretchednesse,
Or that you take some small ease in your
  owne
Torments, to heare another sadly groane,
I were most happy in my paines, to be
So truely blest, to be so curst by thee:
But oh! my cries to that doe rather adde,
Of which too much already thou hast had,
And thou art gladly sad to heare my moane;
Yet sadly hearst me with derisiön.

  Thou most unjust, that really dost know,
And feelst thyselfe the flames I burne in. Oh!
How can you beg to be set loose from that
Consuming stake you binde another at?

---

[1] Carew (*Poems*, ed. 1651, p. 53) has some lines, entitled, "In the person of a Lady to her Inconstant Servant," which are of nearly similar purport to Lovelace's poem, but are both shorter and better.

Uncharitablest both wayes, to denie
That pity me, for which yourself must dye,
To love not her loves you, yet know the paiu
What 'tis to love, and not be lov'd againe.

Flye on, flye on, swift Racer, untill she
Whom thou of all ador'st shall learne of thee
The pace t'outfly thee, and shall teach thee groan,
What terrour 'tis t'outgo and be outgon.

Nor yet looke back, nor yet must we
Run then like spoakes in wheeles eternally,
And never overtake? Be dragg'd on still
By the weake cordage of your untwin'd will
Round without hope of rest? No, I will turne,
And with my goodnes boldly meete your scorne ;
My goodnesse which Heav'n pardon, and that fate
Made you hate love, and fall in love with hate.

But I am chang'd ! Bright reason, that did give
My soule a noble quicknes, made me live
One breath yet longer, and to will, and see
Hath reacht me pow'r to scorne as well as thee:
That thou, which proudly tramplest on my grave,
Thyselfe mightst fall, conquer'd my double slave :
That thou mightst, sinking in thy triumphs, moan,
And I triumph in my destructiön.

Hayle, holy cold ! chaste temper, hayle ! the fire
Rav'd[1] o're my purer thoughts I feel t' expire,

---

[1] *Rav'd* seems here to be equivalent to *reav'd*, or *bereav'd*.
Perhaps the correct reading may be " reav'd." See Worcester's
Dictionary, art. RAVE, where Menage's supposition of affinity
between *rave* and *bereave* is perhaps a little too slightingly treated.

And I am candied ice.　Yee pow'rs! if e're
I shall be fore't unto my sepulcher,
Or violently hurl'd into my urue,
Oh make me choose rather to freeze than burne.

THE GRASSEHOPPER.

TO MY NOBLE FRIEND, MR. CHARLES COTTON.[1]

ODE.

I.

H thou, that swing'st upon the waving eare[2]
　Of some well-filled oaten beard,[3]
Drunk ev'ry night with a delicious teare[4]
　Dropt thee from Heav'n, where now
　　th'art reard.

---

[1] Charles Cotton the elder, father of the poet·　He died in
1658.　This poem is extracted in *Censura Literaria*, ix. 352, as
a favourable specimen of Lovelace's poetical genius.　The text
is manifestly corrupt, but I have endeavoured to amend it.
In Elton's *Specimens of Classic Poets*, 1814, i. 148, is a trans·
lation of Anacreon's Address to the Cicada, or Tree-Locust
(Lovelace's grasshopper?), which is superior to the modern
poem, being less prolix, and more natural in its manner.　In all
Lovelace's longer pieces there are too many obscure and feeble
conceits, and too many evidences of a leaning to the metaphysical
and antithetical school of poetry.

[2] Original has *haire*.

[3] *i. e.* a beard of oats.

[4] Meleager's invocation to the tree-locust commences thus in
Elton's translation:—
　　"Oh shrill-voiced insect! that with dew-drops sweet
　　　Inebriate——"
See also Cowley's *Anacreontiques*, No. X.　*The Grasshopper.*

II.

The joyes of earth and ayre are thine intire,
  That with thy feet and wings dost hop and flye ;
And when thy poppy workes, thou dost retire
  To thy carv'd acorn-bed to lye.

III.

Up with the day, the Sun thou welcomst then,
  Sportst in the guilt plats[1] of his beames,
And all these merry dayes mak'st merry men,[2]
  Thy selfe, and melancholy streames.

IV.

But ah, the sickle ! golden cares are cropt ;
  Ceres and *Bacchus* bid good night ;
Sharpe frosty fingers all your flowrs have topt,
  And what sithes spar'd, winds shave off quite.

V.

Poore verdant foole ! and now green ice, thy joys
  Large and as lasting as thy peirch[3] of grasse,

---

[1] *i.e.* horizontal lines tinged with gold. See Halliwell's *Glossary of Archaic Words*, 1860, art. PLAT (seventh and eighth meaning). The late editors of Nares cite this passage from *Lucasta* as an illustration of *guilt-plats,* which they define to be "plots of gold." This definition, unsupported by any other evidence, is not very satisfactory, and certainly it has no obvious application here.

[2] Randolph says :—

   "—— toiling ants perchance delight to hear
   The summer musique of the gras-hopper."
                              Poems, 1640, p. 90.

It is a question, perhaps, whether Lovelace intended by the *grasshopper* the *cicada* or the *locusta.* See Sir Thomas Browne's *Inquiries into Vulgar Errors* (Works, by Wilkins, 1836, iii. 93).

[3] Perch.

Bid us lay in 'gainst winter raine, and poize
    Their flouds with an o'erflowing glasse.

VI.

Thou best of men and friends? we will create
    A genuine summer in each others breast;
And spite of this cold Time and frosen Fate,
    Thaw us a warme seate to our rest.

VII.

Our sacred harthes shall burne eternally
    As vestal flames; the North-wind, he
Shall strike his frost-stretch'd winges, dissolve
       and flye
    This Ætna in epitome.

VIII.

Dropping December shall come weeping in,
    Bewayle th' usurping of his raigne;
But when in show'rs of old Greeke[1] we beginne,
    Shall crie, he hath his crowne againe!

IX.

Night as cleare Hesper shall our tapers whip
    From the light casements, where we play,
And the darke hagge from her black mantle strip,
    And sticke there everlasting day.

X.

Thus richer then untempted kings are we,
    That asking nothing, nothing need:
Though lord of all what seas imbrace, yet he
    That wants himselfe, is poore indeed.

---

[1] *i.e.* old Greek wine.

AN ELEGIE.

ON THE DEATH OF MRS. CASSANDRA COTTON,

ONLY SISTER TO MR. C. COTTON.[1]

HITHER with hallowed steps as is the ground,
　　That must enshrine this saint with lookes
　　　　profound,
　　And sad aspects as the dark vails you weare,
Virgins opprest, draw gently, gently neare ;
Enter the dismall chancell of this roome,
Where each pale guest stands fixt a living tombe ;
With trembling hands helpe to remove this earth
To its last death and first victorious birth :
Let gums and incense fume, who are at strife
To enter th' hearse and breath in it new life ;
Mingle your steppes with flowers as you goe,
Which, as they haste to fade, will speake your woe.

And when y' have plac't your tapers on her urn,
How poor a tribute 'tis to weep and mourn !
That flood the channell of your eye-lids fils,
When you lose trifles, or what's lesse, your wills.
If you'l be worthy of these obsequies,
Be blind unto the world, and drop your eyes ;

---

[1] Cassandra Cotton, only daughter of Sir George Cotton, of
Warblenton, co. Sussex, and of Bedhampton, co. Hants, died
some time before 1649, unmarried. She was the sister of Charles
Cotton the elder, and aunt to the poet. See *Walton's Angler*,
ed. Nicolas, Introduction, clxvi.

Waste and consume, burn downward as this fire
That's fed no more: so willingly expire;
Passe through the cold and obscure narrow way,
Then light your torches at the spring of day,
There with her triumph in your victory.
Such joy alone and such solemnity
Becomes this funerall of virginity.

    Or, if you faiut to be so blest, oh heare!
If not to dye, dare but to live like her:
Dare to live virgins, till the honour'd age
Of thrice fifteen cals matrons on the stage,
Whilst not a blemish or least staine is scene
On your white roabe 'twixt fifty and fifteene;
But as it in your swathing-bands was given,
Bring't in your winding sheet unsoyl'd to Heav'n.
Dære to do purely, without compact good,
Or herald, by no one understood
But him, who now in thanks bows either knee
For th' early benefit and secresie.

Dare to affect a serious holy sorrow,
To which delights of pallaces are narrow,
And, lasting as their smiles, dig you a roome,
Where practise the probation of your tombe
With ever-bended knees and piercing pray'r,
Smooth the rough passe through craggy earth to ay'r;
Flame there as lights that shipwrackt mariners
May put in safely, and secure their feares,
Who, adding to your joyes, now owe you theirs.

    Virgins, if thus you dare but courage take
To follow her in life, else through this lake

Of Nature wade, and breake her earthly bars,
Y' are fixt with her upon a throne of stars,
Arched with a pure Heav'n chrystaline,
Where round you love and joy for ever shine.

But you are dumbe, as what you do lament
More senscles then her very monument,
Which at your weaknes weeps. Spare that vaine teare,
Enough to burst the rev'rend sepulcher.
Rise and walk home ; there groaning prostrate fall,
And celebrate your owne sad funerall :
For howsoe're you move, may heare, or see,
You are more dead and buried then shee.

THE VINTAGE TO THE DUNGEON.

A SONG.[1]

SET BY MR. WILLIAM LAWES.

I.

ING out, pent soules, sing cheerefully !
  Care shackles you in liberty :
  Mirth frees you in captivity.
   Would you double fetters adde ?
   Else why so sadde ?

    Chorus.
 Besides your pinion'd armes youl finde
 Griefe too can manakell the minde.

---

[1] Probably composed during the poet's confinement in Peter-house.

II.

Live then, pris'ners, uncontrol'd;
Drink oth' strong, the rich, the old,
Till wine too hath your wits in hold;
    Then if still your jollitie
    And throats are free—

Chorus.

Tryumph in your bonds and paines,
And daunce to the music of your chaines.

ON THE DEATH OF MRS. ELIZABETH FILMER.[1]

AN ELEGIACALL EPITAPH.

YOU that shall live awhile, before
    Old time tyrs, and is no more:
    When that this ambitious stone
    Stoopes low as what it tramples on:
Know that in that age, when sinne
Gave the world law, and governd Queene,
A virgin liv'd, that still put on
White thoughts, though out of fashion:

---

[1] This lady was perhaps the daughter of Edward Filmer, Esq., of East Sutton, co. Kent, by his wife Eliza, daughter of Richard Argall, Esq., of the same place (See Harl. MS. 1432, p. 300). Possibly, the Edward Filmer mentioned here was the same as the author of " Frenche Court Ayres, with their Ditties eng- lished," 1629, in praise of which Jonson has some lines in his *Underwoods.*

That trac't the stars, 'spite of report,
And durst be good, though chidden for't:
Of such a soule that infant Heav'n
Repented what it thus had giv'n:
For finding equall happy man,
Th' impatient pow'rs snatch it agen.
Thus, chaste as th' ayre whither shee's fled,
She, making her celestiall bed
In her warme alablaster, lay
As cold as in this house of clay:
Nor were the rooms unfit to feast
Or circumscribe this angel-guest;
The radiant gemme was brightly set
In as divine a carkanet;
Of[1] which the clearer was not knowne,
Her minde or her complexion.
Such an everlasting grace,
Such a beatifick face,
Incloysters here this narrow floore,
That possest all hearts before.

Blest and bewayl'd in death and birth!
The smiles and teares of heav'n and earth!
Virgins at each step are afeard,
Filmer is shot by which they steer'd,
Their star extinct, their beauty dead,
That the yong world to honour led;
But see! the rapid spheres stand still,
And tune themselves unto her will.

---

[1] Original reads *for.*

Thus, although this marble must,
As all things, crumble into dust,
And though you finde this faire-built tombe
Ashes, as what lyes in its wombe :
Yet her saint-like name shall shine
A living glory to this shrine,
And her eternall fame be read,
When all but *very vertue's dead.*[1]

TO MY WORTHY FRIEND MR. PETER LILLY :[2]

ON THAT EXCELLENT PICTURE OF HIS MAJESTY AND THE DUKE OF YORKE, DRAWNE BY HIM AT HAMPTON-COURT.

SEE ! what a clouded majesty, and eyes
Whose glory through their mist doth
brighter rise !
See ! what an humble bravery doth shine,
And griefe triumphant breaking through each line,

---

[1] " Which ensuing times shall warble,
When 'tis lost, that 's writ in marble."
WITHER'S *Fair Virtue, the Mistress of Philarete,* 1622.
Headley (*Select Beauties,* ed. 1810, ii. p. 42) has remarked the similarity between these lines and some in Collins' *Dirge in Cymbeline :*—
" Belov'd till life can charm no more ;
And *mourn'd till pity's self be dead.*"
[2] Mr., afterwards Sir Peter, Lely. He was frequently called Lilly, or Lilley, by his contemporaries, and Lilley is Pepys'

How it commands the face! so sweet a scorne
Never did *happy misery* adorne!
So sacred a contempt, that others show
To this, (oth' height of all the wheele) below,
That mightiest monarchs by this shaded booke
May coppy out their proudest, richest looke.

Whilst the true eaglet this quick luster spies,
And by his *sun's* enlightens his owne eyes;
He cures[1] his cares, his burthen feeles, then streight
Joyes that so lightly he can beare such weight;
Whilst either eithers passion doth borrow,
And both doe grieve the same victorious sorrow.

These, my best *Lilly*, with so bold a spirit
And soft a grace, as if thou didst inherit
For that time all their greatnesse, and didst draw
With those brave eyes your royal sitters saw.

Not as of old, when a rough hand did speake
A strong aspect, and a faire face, a weake;

---

spelling. "At Lord Northumberland's, at Sion, is a remarkable picture of King Charles I, holding a letter directed 'au roi monseigneur,' and the Duke of York, æt. 14, presenting a penknife to him to cut the strings. It was drawn at Hampton-Court, when the King was last there, by Mr. Lely, who was earnestly recommended to him. I should have taken it for the hand of Fuller or Dobson. It is certainly very unlike Sir Peter's latter manner, and is stronger than his former. The King has none of the melancholy grace which Vandyck alone, of all his painters, always gave him. It has a sterner countenance, and expressive of the tempests he had experienced."— WALPOLE's *Anecdotes of Painting in England*, ed. 1862, p. 443-4.

[1] Original reads *cares*.

When only a black beard cried villaine, and
By hieroglyphicks we could understand ;
When chrystall typified in a white spot,
And the bright ruby was but one red blot ;
Thou dost the things Orientally the same
Not only paintst its colour, but its flame :
Thou sorrow canst designe without a teare,
And with the man his very hope or feare ;
So that th' amazed world shall henceforth finde
None but my *Lilly* ever drew a *minde.*

THE LADY A. L.[1]

MY ASYLUM IN A GREAT EXTREMITY.

WITH that delight the Royal captiv's[2] brought
　　Before the throne, to breath his farewell
　　　　thought,
　　To tel his last tale, and so end with it,
Which gladly he esteemes a benefit ;
When the brave victor, at his great soule dumbe,
Findes something there fate cannot overcome,
Cals the chain'd prince, and by his glory led,
First reaches him his crowne, and then his head ;
Who ne're 'til now thinks himself slave and poor ;
For though nought else, he had himselfe before.

---

[1] *i. e.* Anne, Lady Lovelace, the poet's kinswoman, who seems
to have assisted him in some emergency, unknown to us except
through the present lines.

[2] Caractacus (?).

He weepes at this faire chance, nor wil allow,
But that the diadem doth brand his brow,
And under-rates himselfe below mankinde,
Who first had lost his body, now his minde,

With such a joy came I to heare my dombe,
And haste the preparation of my tombe,
When, like good angels who have heav'nly charge
To steere and guide mans sudden giddy barge,
She snatcht me from the rock I was upon,
And landed me at life's pavillion :
Where I, thus wound out of th' immense abysse,
Was straight set on a pinacle of blisse.

Let me leape in againe ! and by that fall
Bring me to my first woe, so cancel all :
Ah ! 's this a quitting of the debt you owe,
To crush her and her goodnesse at one blowe?
Defend me from so foule impiety,
Would make friends grieve, and furies weep to see.

Now, ye sage spirits. which infuse in men
That are oblidg'd twice to oblige agen,
Informe my tongue in labour what to say,
And in what coyne or language to repay.
But you are silent as the ev'nings ayre,
When windes unto their hollow grots repaire.[1]

---

[1] The mythology of Greece assigned to each wind a separate cave, in which it was supposed to await the commands of its sovereign Æolus, or Æolos. It is to this myth that Lovelace alludes.

Oh, then accept the all that left me is,
Devout oblations of a sacred wish !

When she walks forth, ye perfum'd wings oth' East,
Fan her, 'til with the Sun she hastes to th' West,
And when her heav'nly course calles up the day,
And breakes as bright, descend, some glistering ray,
To circle her, and her as glistering haire,
That all may say a living saint shines there.
Slow Time, with woollen feet make thy soft pace,
And leave no tracks ith' snow of her pure face ;
But when this vertue must needs fall, to rise
The brightest constellation in the skies ;
When we in characters of fire shall reade,
How cleere she was alive, how spotless, dead.
All you that are a kinne to piety :
For onely you can her close mourners be,
Draw neer, and make of hallowed teares a dearth :
Goodnes and justice both are fled the earth.

If this be to be thankful, I'v a heart
Broaken with vowes, eaten with grateful smart,
And beside this, the vild[1] world nothing hath
Worth anything but her provoked wrath ;
So then, who thinkes to satisfie in time,
Must give a satisfaction for that crime :
Since she alone knowes the gifts value, she
Can onely to her selfe requitall be,
And worthyly to th' life payut her owne story
In its true colours and full native glory ;

---

[1] A very common form of *vile* among early writers.

Which when perhaps she shal be heard to tell,
Buffoones and theeves, ceasing to do ill,
Shal blush into a virgin-innocence,
And then woo others from the same offence ;
The robber and the murderer, in 'spite
Of his red spots, shal startle into white :
All good (rewards layd by) shal stil increase
For love of her, and villany decease ;[1]
Naught[2] be ignote, not so much out of feare
Of being punisht, as offending her.

So that, when as my future daring bayes
Shall bow it selfe[3] in lawrels to her praise,
To crown her conqu'ring goodnes, and proclaime
The due renowne and glories of her name :
My wit shal be so wretched and so poore
That, 'stead of praysing, I shal scandal her,
And leave, when with my purest art I'v done,
Scarce the designe of what she is begunne :
Yet men shal send me home, admir'd, exact ;
Proud, that I could from her so wel detract.

---

[1] This reads like a parody on the fourth Eclogue of Virgil.
The early English poets were rather partial to the introduction
of miniature-pictures of the Golden Age on similar occasions to
the present. Thus Carew, in his poem *To Saxham*, says :—

> "The Pheasant, Partridge, and the Lark
> Flew to thy house, as to the Ark.
> The willing Oxe of himself came
> Home to the slaughter with the Lamb.
> And every beast did thither bring
> Himself, to be an offering."
>
> CAREW'S *Poems*, 1651, p. 34.

[2] Vice.　　　[3] We should read *themselves*.

Where, then, thou bold instinct, shal I begin
My endlesse taske? To thanke her were a sin
Great as not speake, and not to speake, a blame
Beyond what's worst, such as doth want a name;
So thou my all, poore gratitude, ev'n thou
In this wilt an unthankful office do:
Or wilt I fling all at her feet I have:
My life, my love, my very soule, a slave?
Tye my free spirit onely unto her,
And yeeld up my affection prisoner?
Fond thought, in this thou teachest me to give
What first was hers, since by her breath I live;
And hast but show'd me, how I may resigne
Possession of those things are none of mine.

A LADY WITH A FALCON ON HER FIST.

TO THE HONOURABLE MY COUSIN
A[NNE] L[OVELACE.]

I.

THIS Queen of Prey (now prey to you),
 Fast to that pirch of ivory
In silver chaines and silken clue,
 Hath now made full thy victory:

II.

The swelling admirall of the dread
 Cold deepe, burnt in thy flames, oh faire!
Wast not enough, but thou must lead
 Bound, too, the Princesse of the aire?

III.

Unarm'd of wings and scaly oare,
  Unhappy crawler on the land,
To what heav'n fly'st? div'st to what shoare,
  That her brave eyes do not commaud?

IV.

Ascend the chariot of the Sun
  From her bright pow'r to shelter thee:
Her captive (foole) outgases him;
  Ah, what lost wretches then are we!

V.

Now, proud usurpers on the right
  Of sacred beauty, heare your dombe;
Recant your sex, your mastry, might;
  Lower you cannot be or'ccome:

VI.

Repent, ye er'e nam'd he or head,
  For y' are in falcon's monarchy,
And in that just dominion bred,
  In which the nobler is the shee.

A PROLOGUE TO THE SCHOLARS.

A COMEDY PRESENTED AT THE WHITE FRYERS.[1]

 GENTLEMAN, to give us somewhat new,
 Hath brought up *Oxford* with him to show
  you ;
 Pray be not frighted—Tho the scœne and
  gown's
The Universities, the wit 's the town's ;
The lines each honest Englishman may speake :
Yet not mistake his mother-tongue for Greeke,
For stil 'twas part of his vow'd liturgie :—
From learned comedies deliver me !
Wishing all those that lov'd 'em here asleepe,
Promising *scholars*, but no *scholarship*.

 You'd smile to see, how he do's vex and shake,
Speakes naught ; but, if the *prologue* do's but take,
Or the first act were past the pikes once, then—
Then hopes and joys, then frowns and fears agen,
Then blushes like a virgin, now to be
Rob'd of his comicall virginity

---

[1] This was the theatre in Salisbury Court. See Collier, II. E. D. P. iii. 289, and Halliwell's *Dictionary of Old Plays,* art. SCHOLAR. From the terms of the epilogue it seems to have been a piece occupying two hours in the performance. Judging, I presume, from the opening lines, Mr. Halliwell supposes it to have been originally acted at Gloucester Hall. Probably Mr. Halliwell is right.

In presence of you all.   In short, you'd say
More hopes of mirth are in his looks then play.

These feares are for the noble and the wise ;
But if 'mongst you there are such fowle dead eyes,
As can damne unaraign'd, cal law their pow'rs,
Judging it sin enough that it is ours,
And with the house shift their decreed desires,
Faire still to th'*Blacke,Blacke* still to the *White-Fryers ;*[1]
He do's protest he wil sit down and weep
Castles and pyramids   .   .   .
.   .   .   .   .   . No, he wil on,
Proud to be rais'd by such destruction,
So far from quarr'lling with himselfe and wit,
That he wil thank them for the benefit,
Since finding nothing worthy of their hate,
They reach him that themselves must envy at :

THE EPILOGUE.

HE stubborne author of the trifle[2] crime,
That just now cheated you of two hours'
    time,
Presumptuous it lik't him,[3] began to grow
Carelesse, whether it pleased you or no.

---

[1] A quibble on the two adjacent theatres in Whitefriars and Blackfriars.

[2] Perhaps *trifling* was the word written by Lovelace. A *venial offence* is meant.

[3] It would be difficult to point out a writer so unpardonably

But we who ground th' excellence of a play
On what the women at the dores wil say,
Who judge it by the benches, and afford
To take your money, ere his oath or word
His *schollars* school'd, sayd if he had been wise
He should have wove in one two *comedies;*
The first for th' gallery, in which the throne
To their amazement should descend alone,
The rosin-lightning flash, and monster spire
Squibs, and words hotter then his fire.

Th' other for the gentlemen oth' pit,
Like to themselves, all spirit, fancy, wit,
In which plots should be subtile as a flame,
Disguises would make *Proteus* stil the same:
Humours so rarely humour'd and exprest,
That ev'n they should thinke 'em so, not drest;
Vices acted and applauded too, times
Tickled, and th' actors acted, not their crimes,
So he might equally applause have gain'd
Of th' hardned, sooty, and the snowy hand.[1]

Where now one *so so*[2] spatters, t'other: no!
Tis his first play; twere solecisme 'tshould goe;

---

slovenly in his style or phraseology as Lovelace. By " Presumptuous it lik't him," we must of course understand " Presumptuous
that he liked it himself," or presumptuously self-satisfied.

[1] *i.e.* the rough and dirty occupants of the gallery and the
fair spectators in the boxes.

[2] An exclamation of approval, when an actor made a hit.
The phrase seems to be somewhat akin to the Italian " *si, si,*" a
corruption of " *sia, sia.*"

The next 't shew'd pritily, but scarcht within
It appeares bare and bald, as is his chin ;
The towne-wit sentences : *A Scholars Play !*
Pish ! I know not why, but th'ave not the way.[1]

We, whose gaine is all our pleasure, ev'n these
Are bound by justice and religion to please ;
Which he, whose pleasure's all his gaine, goes by
As slightly, as they doe his comædy.

Culls out the few, the worthy, at whose feet
He sacrifices both himselfe and it,
His fancies first fruits : profit he knowes none,
Unles that of your approbation,
Which if your thoughts at going out will pay,
Hee'l not looke farther for a second day.[2]

AGAINST THE LOVE OF GREAT ONES.

NHAPPY youth, betrayd by Fate
To such a love[3] hath sainted hate,
And damned those celestiall bands [4]
Are onely knit with equal hands ;

---

[1] *i.e.* they do not know how to act a play.

[2] This prologue and epilogue were clearly not attached to the play when it was first performed by the fellow-collegians of the poet at Gloucester Hall, as an amateur attempt in the dramatic line, but were first added when "The Scholars" was reproduced in London, and the parts sustained by ordinary actors.

[3] *i.e. that* hath sainted, &c.

[4] So the Editor's MS. copy already described ; the printed copy has *bonds.*

I

The love of great ones is a love,[1]
Gods are incapable to prove :
For where there is a joy uneven,
There never, never can be Heav'n :
'Tis such a love as is not sent
To fiends as yet for punishment;
Ixion willingly doth feele
The gyre of his eternal wheele,
Nor would he now exchange his paine
For cloudes and goddesses againe.

Wouldst thou with tempests lye ? Then bow
To th' rougher furrows of her brow,
Or make a thunder-bolt thy choyce ?
Then catch at her more fatal voyce ;
Or 'gender with the lightning ? trye
The subtler[2] flashes of her eye :
Poore *Semele*[3] wel knew the same,
Who[4] both imbrac't her God and flame ;
And not alone in soule did burne,
But in this love did ashes turne.

How il doth majesty injoy
The bow and gaity oth' boy,
As if the purple-roabe should sit,
And sentence give ith' chayr of wit.

---

[1] So Editor's MS.   Printed copy has—
      " The Love of Great Ones ? 'Tis a Love."
[2] Subtle—*Editor's MS.*
[3] Semele she—*Editor's MS.*
[4] She—*Ibid.*

Say, ever-dying wretch, to whom
Each answer is a certaine doom,[1]
What is it that you would possesse,
The Countes, or the naked Besse ?[2]
Would you her gowne or title do?
Her box or gem, the[3] thing or show?
If you meane *her*, the very *her*,
Abstracted from her caracter,
Unhappy boy! you may as soone
With fawning wanton with the Moone,
Or with an amorous complaint
Get prostitute your very saint;
Not that we are not mortal, or
Fly *Venus* altars, and[4] abhor
The selfesame knack, for which you pine;
But we (defend us!) are divine,
[Not] female, but madam born,[5] and come
From a right-honourable wombe.

---

[1] Dombe—*Lucasta.*

[2] *Bess* is used in the following passage as a phrase for a sort of female *Tom-o-Bedlam*—

"We treat mad-Bedlams, *Toms* and *Besses*,
With ceremonies and caresses!"

DIXON's *Canidia*, 1683, part i. canto 2.

And the word seems also to have been employed to signify the loose women who, in early times, made Covent Garden and its neighbourhood their special haunt. See Cotgrave's *Wits Interpreter*, 1662, p. 236. But here "naked Besse," means only a woman who, in contradistinction to a lady of rank, has no adventitious qualities to recommend her.

[3] Original reads *her.*

[4] Altars, or—*Lucasta.*

[5] Borne—*Lucasta.*

Shal we then mingle with the base,
And bring a silver-tinsell race?
Whilst th' issue noble wil not passe
The gold alloyd[1] (almost halfe brasse),
And th' blood in each veine doth appeare,
Part thick Booreinn, part Lady Cleare;
Like to the sordid insects sprung
From Father Sun and Mother Dung:
Yet lose we not the hold we have,
But faster graspe the trembling slave;
Play at baloon with's heart, and winde
The strings like scaines, steale into his minde
Ten thousand false[2] and feigned joyes
Far worse then they; whilst, like whipt boys,
After this scourge hee's hush with toys.

This[3] heard, Sir, play stil in her eyes,
And be a dying, live[4] like flyes
Caught by their angle-legs, and whom
The torch laughs peece-meale to consume.

---

[1] Allay'd—*Lucasta.*
[2] So Editor's MS. *Lucasta* has *hells.*
[3] From this word down to *lives* is omitted in the MS. copy.
[4] Original has *lives.*

TO ALTHEA.

FROM PRISON.

SONG.

SET BY DR. JOHN WILSON.[1]

I.

WHEN love with unconfined wings
Hovers within my gates;
And my divine *Althea* brings
To whisper at the grates;
When I lye tangled in her haire,[2]
And fetterd to her eye,[3]

---

[1] The first stanza of this famous song is harmonized in *Cheerfull Ayres or Ballads: First composed for one single voice, and since set for three voices.* By John Wilson, Dr. in Music, Professor of the same in the University of Oxford. Oxford, 1660 (Sept. 20, 1659), 4to. p. 10. I have sometimes thought that, when Lovelace composed this production, he had in his recollection some of the sentiments in Wither's *Shepherds Hunting,* 1615. See, more particularly, the sonnet (at p. 248 of Mr. Gutch's Bristol edition) commencing:—

"I that er'st while the world's sweet air did draw."

[2] Peele, in *King David and Fair Bethsabe,* 1599, has a similar figure, where David says:—

"Now comes my lover tripping like the roe,
And brings my longings tangled in her hair."
The "lover" is of course Bethsabe.

[3] Thus Middleton, in his *More Dissemblers besides Women,* printed in 1657, but written before 1626, says:—

"But for modesty,
I should fall foul in words upon fond man,
That can forget his excellence and honour,
His serious meditations, being the end
Of his creation, to learn well to die;
And live a *prisoner to a woman's eye.*"

The birds,[1] that wanton in the aire,
    Know no such liberty.

II.

When flowing cups run swiftly round
    With no allaying *Thames,*
Our carelesse heads with roses bound,
    Our hearts with loyal flames ;
When thirsty griefe in wine we steepe,
    When healths and draughts go free,
Fishes, that tipple in the deepe,
    Know no such libertie.

III.

When (like committed linnets[2]) I
    With shriller throat shall sing

---

[1] Original reads *gods;* the present word is substituted in accordance with a MS. copy of the song printed by the late Dr. Bliss, in his edition of Woods *Athenæ.* If Dr. Bliss had been aware of the extraordinary corruptions under which the text of LUCASTA laboured, he would have had less hesitation in adopting *birds* as the true reading. The "Song to Althea," is a favourable specimen of the class of composition to which it belongs; but I fear that it has been over-estimated.

[2] Percy very unnecessarily altered *like committed linnets* to *linnet-like confined* (Percy's *Reliques,* ii. 247; Moxon's ed.) Ellis (*Specimens of Early English Poets,* ed. 1801, iii. 252) says that this latter reading is "more intelligible." It is not, however, either what Lovelace wrote, or what (it may be presumed) he intended to write, and nothing, it would seem, can be clearer than the passage as it stands, *committed* signifying, in fact, nothing more than *confined.* It is fortunate for the lovers of early English literature that Bp. Percy had comparatively little to do with it. Emendation of a text is well enough; but the wholesale and arbitrary slaughter of it is quite another matter.

The sweetnes, mercy, majesty,
　And glories of my King.
When I shall voyce aloud, how good
　He is, how great should be,
Inlarged winds, that curle the flood,
　Know no such liberty.

IV.

Stone walls doe not a prison make,
　Nor iron bars a cage;
Mindes innocent and quiet take
　That for an hermitage;
If I have freedome in my love,
　And in my soule am free,
Angels alone that sore above
　Enjoy such liberty.

SONNET.

TO GENERALL GORING,[1] AFTER THE PACIFICATION

AT BERWICKE.

A LA CHABOT.[2]

I.

OW the peace is made at the foes rate,[3]
Whilst men of armes to kettles their old
helmes translate,
And drinke in caskes of honourable plate,

---

[1] Particulars of this celebrated man, afterward created Earl of Norwich, may be found in Eachard's *History*, Rushworth's *Collections*, Whitelocke's *Memoirs*, Collins' *Peerage* by Brydges, Pepys' *Diary* (i. 150, ed. 1858), and Peck's *Desiderata Curiosa*, (ed. 1779, ii. 479). Whitelocke speaks very highly of his military character. In a poem called *The Gallants of the Times*, printed in "Wit Restored," 1658, there is the following passage:—

"A great burgandine for *Will Murray's* sake
George Symonds, he vows the first course to take:
When *Stradling* a Græciau dog let fly,
Who took the bear by the nose immediately;
To see them so forward Hugh Pollard did smile,
Who had an old curr of Canary oyl,
And held up his head that *George Goring* might see,
Who then cryed aloud, *To mee, boys, to mee!*"

See, also, *The Answer:*—

"*George*, Generall of Guenefrieds,
He is a joviall lad,
Though his heart and fortunes disagree
Oft times to make him sad."

Consult Davenant's Works, 1673, p. 247, and *Fragmenta Au-*

In ev'ry hand [let] a cup be found,
That from all hearts a health may sound
To *Goring!* to *Goring!* see 't goe round.

II.

He whose glories shine so brave and high,
That captive they in triumph leade each eare and eye,
Claiming uncombated the victorie,
And from the earth to heav'n rebound,
Fixt there eternall as this round :
To *Goring!* to *Goring!* see him crown'd.

III.

To his lovely bride, in love with scars,
Whose eyes wound deepe in peace, as doth his sword
in wars ;
They shortly must depose the Queen of Stars :
Her cheekes the morning blushes give,
And the benighted world repreeve ;
To *Lettice!* to *Lettice!* let her live.

---

lica, 1662, pp. 47, 54. Lord Goring died Jan. 6, 1663 (Smyth's
Obituary, p. 57 ; Camden Soc.).

² *A la Chabot* was a French dance tune, christened after the
admiral of that name, in the same manuer as *a la Bourbon,* mentioned elsewhere in Lucasta, derived its title from another
celebrated person. Those who have any acquaintance with the
history of early English music need not to be informed that it
was formerly the practice of our own composers to seek the
patronage of the gentlemen and ladies about the Court for their
works, and to identify their names with them. Thus we have
" My Lady Carey's Dumpe," &c. &c.

³ Expense.

IV.

Give me scorching heat, thy heat, dry Sun,
That to this payre I may drinke off an ocean :
Yet leave my grateful thirst unquensht, undone ;
Or a full bowle of heav'nly wine,
In which dissolved stars should shine,
To the couple ! to the couple ! th' are divine.

SIR THOMAS WORTLEY'S SONNET

ANSWERED.

[THE SONNET.

I.

NO more
Thou little winged archer, now no more
As heretofore,
Thou maist pretend within my breast to bide,
No more,
Since cruell Death of dearest *Lyndamore*
Hath me depriv'd,
I bid adieu to love, and all the world beside.

II.

Go, go ;
Lay by thy quiver and unbend thy bow
Poore sillie foe,
Thou spend'st thy shafts but at my breast in vain,
Since Death

My heart hath with a fatall icie deart
    Already slain,
Thou canst not ever hope to warme her wound,
     Or wound it o're againe.]

THE ANSWER.

I.

GAINE,
  Thou witty cruell wanton, now againe,
    Through ev'ry veine,
  Hurle all your lightning, and strike ev'ry
   dart,
    Againe,
Before I feele this pleasing, pleasing paine.
    I have no heart,
Nor can I live but sweetly murder'd with
    So deare, so deare a smart.

II.

    Then flye,
And kindle all your torches at her eye,
    To make me dye
Her martyr, and put on my roabe of flame:
    So I,
Advanced on my blazing wings on high,
    In death became
Inthroan'd a starre, and ornament unto
    Her glorious, glorious name.

A GUILTLESSE LADY IMPRISONED:
AFTER PENANCED.

SONG.

SET BY MR. WILLIAM LAWES.

I.

HEARK, faire one, how what e're here is
    Doth laugh and sing at thy distresse;
Not out of hate to thy reliefe,
    But joy t' enjoy thee, though in griefe.

II.

See! that which chaynes you, you chaine here;
    The prison is thy prisoner;
How much thy jaylor's keeper art!
    He bindes your hands, but you his heart.

III.

The gyves to rase so smooth a skin,
    Are so unto themselves within;
But, blest to kisse so fayre an arme,
    Haste to be happy with that harme;

IV.

And play about thy wanton wrist,
    As if in them thou so wert drest;
But if too rough, too hard they presse,
    Oh, they but closely, closely kisse.

V.

And as thy bare feet blesse the way,
    The people doe not mock, but pray,

And call thee, as amas'd they run
  Instead of prostitute, a nun.

VI.

The merry torch burnes with desire
  To kindle the eternall fire,
And lightly daunces in thine eyes
  To tunes of epithalamics.

VII.

The sheet's ty'd ever to thy wast,
  How thankfull to be so imbrac't!
And see! thy very very bonds
  Are bound to thee, to binde such hands.

TO HIS DEARE BROTHER COLONEL F. L.

IMMODERATELY MOURNING MY BROTHERS [1]

UNTIMELY DEATH AT CARMARTHEN.

I.

IF teares could wash the ill away,
  A pearle for each wet bead I'd pay;
But as dew'd corne the fuller growes,
  So water'd eyes but swell our woes.

II.

One drop another cals, which still
(Griefe adding fuell) doth distill;
Too fruitfull of her selfe is anguish,
We need no cherishing to languish.

---

[1] Thomas Lovelace. See *Memoir.*

III.

Coward fate degen'rate man
Like little children uses, when
He whips us first, untill we weepe,
Then, 'cause we still a weeping keepe.

IV.

Then from thy firme selfe never swerve;
Teares fat the griefe that they should sterve;
Iron decrees of destinie
Are ner'e wipe't out with a wet eye.

V.

But this way you may gaine the field,
Oppose but sorrow, and 'twill yield;
One gallant thorough-made resolve
Doth starry influence dissolve.

TO A LADY

THAT DESIRED ME I WOULD BEARE MY
PART WITH HER IN A SONG.

MADAM A. L.[1]

HIS is the prittiest motion:
Madam, th' alarums of a drumme
That cals your lord, set to your cries,
To mine are sacred symphonies.

---

[1] "Madam A. L." is not in MS. copy. "The Lady A. L."
and "Madam A. L." may very probably be two different persons: for Carew in his Poems (edit. 1651, 8vo. p. 2) has a piece
"To A. L.; Persuasions to Love," and it is possible that the

What, though 'tis said I have a voice ;
I know 'tis but that hollow noise
Which (as it through my pipe doth speed)
Bitterns do carol through a reed ;

A. L. of Carew, and the A. L. mentioned above, are identical.
The following poem is printed in Durfey's *Pills to Purge Melancholy*, **v.** 120, but whether it was written by Lovelace, and
addressed to the same lady, whom he represents above as re-
questing him to join her in a song, or whether it was the production of another pen, I cannot at all decide. It is not particularly unlike the style of the author of *Lucasta*. At all events,
I am not aware that it has been appropriated by anybody else,
and as I am reluctant to omit any piece which Lovelace is at all
likely to have composed, I give these lines just as I find them in
Durfey, where they are set to music :—

" *To his fairest* VALENTINE *Mrs*. A. L.

" Come, pretty birds, present your lays,
 And learn to chaunt a goddess praise ;
Ye wood-nymphs, let your voices be
Employ'd to serve her deity :
And warble forth, ye virgins nine,
Some music to my Valentine.

" Her bosom is love's paradise,
 There is no heav'n but in her eyes ;
She's chaster than the turtle-dove,
And fairer than the queen of love :
Yet all perfections do combine
To beautifie my Valentine.

" She's Nature's choicest cabinet,
 Where honour, beauty, worth and wit
Are all united in her breast.
The graces claim an interest :
All virtues that are most divine
Shine clearest in my Valentine."

In the same key with monkeys jiggs,
Or dirges of proscribed piggs,
Or the soft Serenades above
In calme of night,[1] when[2] cats make[3] love.

    Was ever such a consort seen !
Fourscore and fourteen with forteen ?
Yet[4] sooner' they'l agree, one paire,
Then we in our spring-winter aire ;
They may imbrace, sigh, kiss, the rest :
Our breath knows nought but east and west.
Thus have I heard to childrens cries
The faire nurse still such lullabies,
That, well all sayd (for what there lay),
The pleasure did the sorrow pay.

    Sure ther's another way to save
Your phansie,[5] madam ; that's to have
('Tis but a petitioning kinde fate)
The organs sent to Bilingsgate,
Where they to that soft murm'ring quire
Shall teach[6] you all you can admire !

---

[1] Nights—*Editor's MS.*   [2] Where—*Ibid.*   [3] Do—*Ibid.*
[4] There is here either an interpolation in the printed copy, or
an *hiatus* in the MS. The latter reads :—
    " Yet may I 'mbrace, sigh, kisse, the rest," &c.,
thus leaving out a line and a half or upward of the poem, as it
is printed in *Lucasta.*
[5] MS. reads :—" Youre phansie, madam,"
        omitting " that's to have."
[6] Original and MS. have *reach.*

Or do but heare, how love-bang Kate
In pantry darke for freage of mate,
With edge of steele the square wood shapes,
And *Dido*[1] to it chaunts or scrapes.
The merry Phaeton oth' carre
You'l vow makes a melodious jarre;
Sweeter and sweeter whisleth He
To un-anointed[2] axel-tree;
Such swift notes he and 's wheels do run;
For me, I yeeld him Phœbus son.

Say, faire Comandres, can it be
You should ordaine a mutinie?

---

[1] This must refer, I suppose, to the ballad of QUEEN DIDO, which the woman sings as she works. The signification of *love-bang* is not easily determined. *Bang*, in Suffolk, is a term applied to a particular kind of cheese; but I suspect that "love-bang Kate" merely signifies "noisy Kate" here. As to the old ballad of Dido, see Stafford Smith's *Musica Antiqua*, i. 10, ii. 158; and Collier's *Extracts from the Registers of the Stationers' Company*, i. 98. I subjoin the first stanza of "Dido" as printed in the *Musica Antiqua* :—

> "Dido was the Carthage Queene,
>   And lov'd the Troian knight,
> That wandring many coasts had scene,
>   And many a dreadfull fight.
> As they a-hunting road, a show'r
> Drove them in a loving bower,
>   Down to a darksome cave:
> Where Æneas with his charmes
> Lock't Queene Dido in his armes
>   And had what he would have."

A somewhat different version is given in Durfey's *Pills to Purge Melancholy*, vi. 192-3.

[2] *An unanoynted*—MS.

K

For where I howle, all accents fall,
As kings harangues, to one and all.[1]

Ulisses art is now withstood :[2]
You ravish both with sweet and good ;
Saint Syren, sing, for I dare heare,
But when I ope', oh, stop your care.

Far lesse be't æmulation
To passe me, or in trill or[3] tone,
Like the thin throat of Philomel,
And the[4] smart lute who should excell,
As if her soft chords should begin,
And strive for sweetnes with the pin.[5]

Yet can I musick too ; but such
As is beyond all voice or[6] touch ;
My minde can in faire order chime,
Whilst my true heart still beats the time ;
My soule['s] so full of harmonie,
That it with all parts can agree ;
If you winde up to the highest fret,[7]
It shall descend an eight from it,
And when you shall vouchsafe to fall,
Sixteene above you it shall call,

---

[1] This and the three preceding lines are not in MS.

[2] Alluding of course to the very familiar legend of Ulysses. and the Syrens.

[3] A quaver (a well-known musical expression).

[4] *A*—MS.   [5] A musical peg.

[6] *And*—MS.

[7] A piece of wire attached to the finger-board of a guitar.

And yet, so dis-assenting one,
They both shall meet in[1] unison.

Come then, bright cherubin, begin!
My loudest musick is within.
Take all notes with your skillfull eyes;
Hearke, if mine do not sympathise!
Sound all my thoughts, and see exprest
The tablature[2] of my large brest;
Then you'l admit, that I too can
Musick above dead sounds of man;
Such as alone doth blesse the spheres,
Not to be reacht with humane cares.

VALIANT LOVE.

I.

NOW fie upon that everlasting life! I dye!
　　She hates! Ah me! It makes me mad;
　As if love fir'd his torch at a moist eye,
　　Or with his joyes e're crown'd the sad.
Oh, let me live and shout, when I fall on;
　Let me ev'n triumph in the first attempt!
　Loves duellist from conquest 's not exempt,
When his fair murdresse shall not gain one groan,
And he expire ev'n in ovation.

---

[1] Original and MS. read *an.*

[2] The tablature of Lovelace's time was the application of letters, of the alphabet or otherwise, to the purpose of expressing the sounds or notes of a composition.

II.

Let me make my approach, when I lye downe
    With counter-wrought and travers eyes ;[1]
With peals of confidence batter the towne ;
    Had ever beggar yet the keyes ?
No, I will vary stormes with sun and winde ;
    Be rough, and offer calme condition ;
    March in and pread,[2] or starve the garrison.
Let her make sallies hourely : yet I'le find
('Though all beat of) shee's to be undermin'd.

III.

Then may it please your little excellence
    Of hearts t' ordaine, by sound of lips,
That henceforth none in tears dare love comence
    (Her thoughts ith' full, his, in th' eclipse) ;
On paine of having 's launce broke on her bed,
    That he be branded all free beauties' slave,
    And his own hollow eyes be domb'd his grave :
Since in your hoast that coward nere was fed,
Who to his prostrate ere was prostrated.

---

[1] This seems to be a phrase borrowed by the poet from his military vocabulary. He wishes to express that he had fortified his eyes to resist the glances of his fair opponent.

[2] Original reads most unintelligibly and absurdly *March in (and pray'd) or*, &c. *To pread* is *to pillage.*

LA BELLA BONA ROBA.[1]

TO MY LADY H.

ODE.

I.

 ELL me, ye subtill judges in loves treasury,
Inform me, which hath most inricht mine eye,
This diamonds greatnes, or its clarity?

II.

Ye cloudy spark lights, whose vast multitude
Of fires are harder to be found then view'd,
Waite on this star in her first magnitude.

III.

Calmely or roughly! Ah, she shines too much;
That now I lye (her influence is such),
Chrusht with too strong a hand, or soft a touch.

IV.

Lovers, beware! a certaine, double harme
Waits your proud hopes, her looks al-killing charm
Guarded by her as true victorious arme.

V.

Thus with her eyes brave Tamyris spake dread,
Which when the kings dull breast not entered,
Finding she could not looke, she strook him dead.

---

[1] This word, though generally used in a bad sense by early writers, does not seem to bear in the present case any offensive meaning. The late editors of Nares quote a passage from one of Cowley's *Essays*, in which that writer seems to imply by the term merely a fine woman.

I.

CANNOT tell, who loves the skeleton
Of a poor marmoset; nought but boan, boan;
Give me a nakednesse, with her cloath's on.

II.

Such, whose white-sattin upper coat of skin,
Cut upon velvet rich incarnadin,[1]
Has yet a body (and of flesh) within.

III.

Sure, it is meant good husbandry[2] in men,
Who do incorporate with aëry leane,
T' repair their sides, and get their ribb agen.

IV.

Hard hap unto that huntsman, that decrees
Fat joys for all his swet, when as he sees,
After his 'say,[3] nought but his keepers fees.

V.

Then, Love, I beg, when next thou tak'st thy bow,
Thy angry shafts, and dost heart-chasing go,
Passe *rascall deare*, strike me the largest doe.[4]

---

[1] *i. e.* Carnation hue, a species of red. As an adjective, the word is peculiarly rare.

[2] Management or economy.   [3] *i. e.* Essay.

[4] A *rascal deer* was formerly a well-known term among sportsmen, signifying a lean beast, not worth pursuit. Thus in *A C. Mery Talys* (1525), No. 29, we find:—" [they] apoynted thys Welchman to stand still, and forbade him in any wyse to shote

A LA BOURBON.

DONE MOY PLUS DE PITIE OU[1] PLUS DE CREAULTE, CAR
SANS CI IE NE PUIS PAS VIURE, NE MORIR.

I.

IVINE Destroyer, pitty me no more,
    Or else more pitty me ;[2]
Give me more love, ah, quickly give me more,
    Or else more cruelty !
      For left thus as I am,
      My heart is ice and flame ;
    And languishing thus, I
    Can neither live nor dye !

II.

Your glories are eclipst, and hidden in the grave
    Of this indifferency ;

---

at no rascal dere, but to make sure of the greate male, and spare
not." In the new edition of Nares, other and more recent
examples of the employment of the term are given. But in the
Book of Saint Albans, 1486, *Rascal* is used in the signification
merely of a beast other than one of " enchace."

    " And where that ye come in playne or in place,
    I shall you tell whyche ben bestys of enchace.
    One of them is the bucke : a nother is the doo :
    The foxe and the marteron : and the wylde roo.
    And ye shall, my dere chylde, other bestys all,
    Where so ye theym finde, Rascall ye shall them call."

[1] Original reads *au.*

[2] In his poem entitled " Mediocrity in Love rejected," Carew
has a similar sentiment :—

And, Cælia, you can neither altars have.
Nor I, a Diety :
They are aspects divine,
That still or smile, or shine,
Or, like th' offended sky,
Frowne death immediately.

THE FAIRE BEGGER.

I.

COMANDING asker, if it be
Pity that you faine would have,
Then I turne begger unto thee,
And aske the thing that thou dost crave.
I will suffice thy hungry need,
So thou wilt but my fancy feed.

II.

In all ill yeares, was[1] ever knowne
On so much beauty such a dearth ?

" Give me more Love, or more Disdain,
The Torrid, or the Frozen Zone,
Bring equall ease unto my paine ;
The Temperate affords me none :
Either extreme, of Love, or Hate,
Is sweeter than a calme estate."

CAREW's Poems, ed. 1651, p. 14.

And so also Stanley (*Ayres and Dialogues*, set by J. Gamble, 1656, p. 20) :—

" So much of absence and delay,
That thus afflicts my memorie.
Why dost thou kill me every day,
Yet will not give me leave to die ? "

[1] Original reads *wa'st.*

Which, in that thrice-bequeathed gowne,
  Lookes like the Sun eclipst with Earth,
Like gold in canvas, or with dirt
Unsoyled Ermins close begirt.

III.

Yet happy he, that can but tast
  This whiter skin, who thirsty is!
Fooles dote on sattin[1] motions lac'd:
  The gods go naked in their blisse.
At[2] th' barrell's head there shines the vine,
There only relishes the wine.

IV.

There quench my heat, and thou shalt sup
  Worthy the lips that it must touch,
Nectar from out the starry cup:
  I beg thy breath not halfe so much.
So both our wants supplied shall be,
You'l give for love, I, charity.

V.

Cheape then are pearle-imbroderies,
  That not adorne, but cloud[3] thy wast;
Thou shalt be cloath'd above all prise,
  If thou wilt promise me imbrac't.[4]

---

[1] Satin seems to have been much in vogue about this time as a material for female dress.
  " Their glory springs from sattin,
    Their vanity from feather."
A description of woman in *Wits Interpreter*, 1662, p. 115.

[2] Original has *and*.   [3] Original reads *clouds*.

[4] *i.e. to be* embraced.

Wee'l ransack neither chest or shelfe :
Ill cover thee with mine owne selfe.

VI.

But, cruel, if thou dost deny
　　This necessary almes to me,
What soft-soul'd man but with his eye
　　And hand will hence be shut to thee ?
Since all must judge you more unkinde :
I starve your body, you, my minde.

[A DIALOGUE BETWIXT CORDANUS AND AMORET, ON A LOST HEART.

Cordanus.

ISTRESSED pilgrim, whose dark clouded
　　　　eyes
　　Speak thee a martyr to love's cruelties,
　　Whither away ?
Amor.　　　　　　　　What pitying voice I hear,
Calls back my flying steps ?
Cord.　　　　　　　　Pr'ythee, draw near.
Amor. I shall but say, kind swain, what doth become
Of a lost heart, ere to Elysium
It wounded walks ?
Cord.　　　　　　　First, it does freely flye
Into the pleasures of a lover's eye ;
But, once condemn'd to scorn, it fetter'd lies,
An ever-bowing slave to tyrannies.

Amor. I pity its sad fate, since its offence
    Was but for love. Can [1] tears recall it thence?

Cord. O no, such tears, as do for pity call,
    She proudly scorns, and glories at their fall.

Amor. Since neither sighs nor tears, kind shepherd, tell,
    Will not a kiss prevail?

Cord.   Thou may'st as well
    Court Eccho with a kiss.

Amor.   Can no art move
    A sacred violence to make her love?

Cord. O no! 'tis only Destiny or [2] Fate
    Fashions our wills either to love or hate.

Amor. Then, captive heart, since that no humane spell
    Hath power to graspe thee his, farewell.

Cord.[3] Farewell.

Cho. Lost hearts, like lambs drove from their folds
      by fears,
    May back return by chance, but not [4] by tears.][5]

---

[1] So Cotgrave. Lawes, and after him Singer, read *can't*.

[2] So Cotgrave. Lawes and Singer read *and*.

[3] Omitted by Lawes and Singer; I follow Cotgrave.

[4] So Cotgrave. Lawes printed *ne'er*.

[5] This is taken from *Ayres and Dialogues for One, Two, and Three Voyces*, By Henry Lawes, 1653-5-8, where it is set to music for two trebles by H. L. It was not included in the posthumous collection of Lovelace's poems. This dialogue is also found in *Wits Interpreter*, by J. Cotgrave, 1662, 8vo, page 203 (first printed in 1655), and a few improved readings have been adopted from that text.

COMMENDATORY AND OTHER VERSES,
PREFIXED TO VARIOUS PUBLICATIONS
BETWEEN 1638 AND 1647.

AN ELEGIE.
PRINCESSE KATHERINE [1] BORNE, CHRISTENED,
BURIED, IN ONE DAY.

YOU, that can haply[2] mixe your joyes with cries,
　And weave white Iös with black Elegies,
　Can caroll out a dirge, and in one breath
　Sing to the tune either of life, or death;
You, that can weepe the gladnesse of the spheres,
And pen a hymne, in stead of inke, with teares;
Here, here your unproportion'd wit let fall,
To celebrate this new-borne funerall,
And greete that little greatnesse, which from th' wombe
Dropt both a load to th' cradle and the tombe.

---

[1] All historical and genealogical works are deficient in minute information relative to the family of Charles I. Even in Anderson's *Royal Genealogies*, 1732, and in the folio editions of Rapin and Tindal, these details are overlooked. At page 36 of his *Descendants of the Stuarts*, 1858, Mr. Townend observes that two of the children of Charles I. died in infancy, and of these the Princesse Katherine, commemorated by Lovelace, was perhaps one. The present verses were originally printed in *Musarum Oxoniensium Charisteria*, Oxon. 1638, 4to, from which a few better readings have been obtained. With the exceptions mentioned in the notes, the variations of the earlier text from that found here are merely literal.

[2] This reading from *Charisteria*, 1638, seems preferable to *aptly*, as it stands in the *Lucasta*.

Bright soule! teach us, to warble with what feet
Thy swathing linnen and thy winding sheet,
Weepe,[1] or shout forth that fonts solemnitie,
Which at once christn'd and buried[2] thee,
And change our shriller passions with that sound,
First told thee into th' ayre, then to[3] the ground.

Ah, wert thou borne for this? only to call
The King and Queen guests to your buriall!
To bid good night, your day not yet begun,
And shew[4] a setting, ere a rising sun!

Or wouldst thou have thy life a martyrdom?
Dye in the act of thy religion,
Fit, excellently, innocently good,
First sealing it with water, then thy blood?
As when on blazing wings a blest man sores,
And having past to God through fiery dores,
Straight 's roab'd with flames, when the same element,
Which was his shame, proves now his ornament;
Oh, how he hast'ned death, burn't to be fryed,[5]
Kill'd twice with each delay, till deified.

---

[1] So the *Charisteria.* The reading in *Lucasta* is *mourne.*

[2] In *Lucasta* the reading is *buried, and christ'ned.*

[3] This word is omitted in the *Lucasta;* it is here supplied from the *Charisteria.*

[4] *Lucasta* reads *showe's. Shew,* as printed in *Charisteria,* is clearly the true word.

[5] *i. e.* freed. *Free* and *freed* were sometimes formerly pronounced like *fry* and *fryed:* for Lord North, in his *Forest of Varieties,* 1645, has these lines—

"Birds that long have lived free,
Caught and cag'd, but pine and die."

Here evidently *free* is intended to rhyme with *die.*

So swift hath been thy race, so full of flight,
Like him condemn'd, ev'n aged with a night,
Cutting all lets with clouds, as if th' hadst been
Like angels plum'd, and borne a Cherubin.

Or, in your journey towards heav'n, say,
Tooke you the world a little in your way?
Saw'st and dislik'st its vaine pompe, then didst flye
Up for eternall glories to the skye?
Like a religious ambitious one,
Aspiredst for the everlasting crowne?

Ah! holy traytour to your brother prince,
Rob'd of his birth-right and preheminence!
Could you ascend yon' chaire of state e're him,
And snatch from th' heire the starry diadem?
Making your honours now as much uneven,
As gods on earth are lesse then saints in heav'n.

Triumph! sing triumphs, then! Oh, put on all
Your richest lookes, drest for this festivall!
Thoughts full of ravisht reverence, with eyes
So fixt, as when a saint we canonize;
Clap wings with Seraphins before the throne
At this eternall coronation,
And teach your soules new mirth, such as may be
Worthy this birth-day to divinity.

But ah! these blast your feasts, the jubilies
We send you up are sad, as were our cries,
And of true joy we can expresse no more
Thus crown'd, then when we buried thee before.

Princesse in heav'n, forgivenes! whilst we
Resigne our office to the *Hierarchy*.

CLITOPHON AND LUCIPPE TRANSLATED.[1]

TO THE LADIES.

RAY, ladies, breath, awhile lay by
Cælestial Sydney's *Arcady ;*[2]
Heere's a story that doth claime
A little respite from his flame :

---

[1] Achillis Tatii Alexandrini *De Lucippes et Clitophontis Amoribus Libri Octo.* The translation of this celebrated work, to which Lovelace contributed the commendatory verses here republished, was executed by his friend Anthony Hodges, A.M., of New College, Oxford, and was printed at Oxford in 1638, 8vo. There had been already a translation by W. Burton, purporting to be done from the Greek, in 1597, 4to. The text of 1649 and that of 1638 exhibit so many variations, that the reader may be glad to have the opportunity of comparison :—

" *To the Ladies.*
"Fair ones, breathe: a while lay by
Blessed Sidney's *Arcady :*
Here's a story that will make
You not repent *him* to forsake;
And with your dissolving looke
Vntie the contents of this booke;
To which nought (except your sight)
Can give a worthie epithite.
'Tis an abstract of all volumes,
A pillaster of all columnes
Fancie e're rear'd to wit, to be
Little *Love's* epitome,
And compactedly expresse
All lovers happy wretchednesse.

" Brave *Pamela's* majestie
And her sweet sister's modestie
Are fixt in each of you, you are
Alone, what these together were:

Then with a quick dissolving looke
Unfold the smoothnes of this book,

Divinest, that are really
What Cariclea's feigu'd to be ;
That are every one, the Nine ;
And on earth Astræas shine ;
Be our *Leucippe*, and remaine
In *her*, all these o're againe.

"Wonder ! Noble *Clitophon*
Me thinkes lookes somewhat colder on
His beauteous mistresse, and she too
Smiles not as she us'd to doe.
See ! the individuall payre
Are at oddes and parted are ;
Quarrel, emulate, and stand
At strife, who first shall kisse your hand.

"A new warre e're while arose
'Twixt the *Greekes* and *Latines,* whose
Temples should be bound with glory
In best languaging this story :
You, that with one lovely smile
A ten-yeares warre can reconcile ;
Peacefull Hellens awfull see
The jarring languages agree,
And here all armes laid by, they doe
Meet in English to court you."

Rich. Lovelace, Ma: Ar: A: Glou: Eq: Aur:
Fil: Nat: Max.

See Halliwell's *Dictionary of Old Plays*, 1860, art. *Clytophon.*

² There can be no doubt that Sidney's *Arcadia* was formerly
as popular in its way among the readers of both sexes as Sir
Richard Baker's *Chronicle* appears to have been. The former
was especially recommended to those who sought occasional
relaxation from severer studies. See Higford's *Institutions*, 1658,
8vo, p. 46-7. In his poem of *The Surprize*, Cotton describes his
nymph as reading the *Arcadia* on the bank of a river—

To which no art (except your sight)
Can reach a worthy epithite ;
'Tis an abstract of all volumes,
A pillaster of all columnes
Fancy c're rear'd to wit, to be
The smallest gods epitome,
And so compactedly expresse
All lovers pleasing wretchednes.

Gallant Pamela's[1] majesty
And her sweet sisters modesty
Are fixt in each of you ; you are,
Distinct, what these together were ;
Divinest, that are really
What Cariclea's[2] feign'd to be ;
That are ev'ry one the Nine,
And brighter here Astreas shine ;
View our Lucippe, and remaine
In her, these beauties o're againe.

Amazement ! Noble Clitophon
Ev'n now lookt somewhat colder on

" The happy *object* of her eye
   Was *Sidney's* living *Arcady ;*
   Whose amorous tale had so betrai'd
   Desire in this all-lovely maid ;
   That, whilst her cheek a blush did warm,
   I read *Loves* story in her form."
      Poems on Several Occasions. By Charles
         Cotton, Esq. Lond. 1689, 8vo, p. 392.

[1] The Pamela of Sydney's *Arcadia.*

[2] The allusion is to the celebrated story of *Theagenes and Chariclea,* which was popular in this country at an early period. A drama on the subject was performed before the Court in 1574.

L

His cooler mistresse, and she too
Smil'd not as she us'd to do.
See! the individuall payre
Are at sad oddes, and parted are;
They quarrell, æmulate, and stand
At strife, who first shal kisse your hand.

A new dispute there lately rose
Betwixt the Greekes and Latines, whose
Temples should be bound with glory,
In best languaging this story;[1]

Yee heyres of love, that with one *smile*
A ten-yeeres war can reconcile;
Peacefull Hellens! Vertuous! See:
The jarring languages agree!
And here, all armes layd by, they doe
In English meet to wayt on you.

TO MY TRUELY VALIANT, LEARNED FRIEND; WHO IN HIS BOOKE[2] RESOLV'D THE ART GLADIATORY INTO THE MATHEMATICKS.

I.

EARKE, reader! wilt be learn'd ith' warres?
    A gen'rall in a gowne?
Strike a league with arts and scarres,
    And snatch from each a crowne?

---

[1] Lovelace refers, it may be presumed, to an edition of *Achilles Tatius*, in which the Greek text was printed with a Latin translation.

[2] " *Pallas Armata.* The Gentlemen's Armorie. Wherein the

II.

Wouldst be a wonder ? Such a one,
 As should win with a looke ?
A bishop in a garison,
 And conquer by the booke ?

III.

Take then this mathematick shield,
 And henceforth by its rules
Be able to dispute ith' field,
 And combate in the schooles.

---

right and genuine use of the Rapier and of the Sword, as well
against the right handed as against the left handed man ' is dis-
played.' [By G. A.] London, 1639, 8vo. With several illus-
trative woodcuts." The lines, as originally printed in *Pallas
Armata*, vary from those subsequently admitted into *Lucasta*.
They are as follow :—

TO THE READER.

Harke, reader, would'st be learn'd ith' warres,
 A *captaine* in a gowne ?
Strike a league with bookes and starres,
 And weave of both the crowne?

Would'st be a wonder? Such a one
 As would winne with a looke?
A schollar in a garrison ?
 And conquer by the booke ?

Take then this mathematick shield,
 And henceforth by its rules,
Be able to dispute ith' field,
 And combate in the schooles.

Whil'st peacefull learning once agen
 And th' souldier do concorde,
As that he fights now with her penne,
 And she writes with his sword.
 RICH. LOVELACE, *A. Glouces. Oxon.*

IV.

Whilst peaceful learning once againe
And the souldier so concord,
As that he fights now with her penne,
And she writes with his sword.

TO FLETCHER REVIV'D.[1]

OW have I bin religious? what strange good
Has scap't me, that I never understood?
Have I hel-guarded Hæresie o'rthrowne?
Heald wounded states? made kings and
    kingdoms one?
That *Fate* should be so merciful to me,
To let me live t' have said I have read thee.

Faire star, ascend! the joy! the life! the light
Of this tempestuous age, this darke worlds sight!
Oh, from thy crowne of glory dart one flame
May strike a sacred reverence, whilest thy name
(Like holy flamens to their god of day)
We bowing, sing; and whilst we praise, we pray.

Bright spirit! whose æternal motion
Of wit, like Time, stil in it selfe did run,

---

[1] Fletcher the dramatist fell a victim to the plague of 1625.
See Aubrey's *Lives*, vol. 2, part i. p. 352. The verses here republished were originally prefixed to the first collected edition of
Beaumont and Fletcher's *Tragedies and Comedies*, 1647, folio. It
is scarcely necessary to remind the reader that Lovelace was only
a child when Fletcher died.

Binding all others in it, and did give
Commission, how far this or that shal live ;
Like *Destiny* of poems who, as she
Signes death to all, her selfe can never dye.

And now thy purple-robed Tragedy,[1]
In her imbroider'd buskins, cals mine eye,
Where the brave Ætius we see betray'd,
T' obey his death, whom thousand lives obey'd ;
Whilst that the mighty foole his scepter breakes,
And through his gen'rals wounds his own doome speakes,
Weaving thus richly *Valentinian*,
The costliest monarch with the cheapest man.

Souldiers may here to their old glories adde,
The *Lover* love, and be with reason *mad :*[2]
Not, as of old, Alcides furious,[3]
Who wilder then his bull did teare the house
(Hurling his language with the canvas stone):
Twas thought the monster ror'd the sob'rer tone.

But ah ! when thou thy sorrow didst inspire
With passions, blacke as is her darke attire,

---

[1] *Valentinian, a Tragedy.* First printed in the folio of 1647.
[2] *The Mad Lover.* Also first printed in the folio of 1647.
[3] An allusion to the *Hercules Furens* of Euripides. Lovelace had, no doubt, some tincture of Greek scholarship (See Wood's *Ath. Ox.* ii. 466); but as to the extent of his acquirements in this direction, it is hard to speak with confidence. Among the books of Mr. Thomas Jolley, dispersed in 1853, was a copy of Clenardus *Institutiones Græcæ Linguæ*, Lugd. Batav. 1626, 8vo., on the title of which was " Richard Lovelace, 1630, March 5," supposed to be the autograph of the poet when a schoolboy.

Virgins as sufferers have wept to see
So white a soule, so red a crueltie ;
That thou hast griev'd, and with unthought redresse
Dri'd their wet eyes who now thy mercy blesse ;
Yet, loth to lose thy watry jewell, when
Joy wip't it off, laughter straight sprung't agen.

Now ruddy cheeked Mirth with rosie wings[1]
Fans ev'ry brow with gladnesse, whilst she sings
Delight to all, and the whole theatre
A festivall in heaven doth appeare :
Nothing but pleasure, love ; and (like the morne)
Each face a gen'ral smiling doth adorne.

Heare ye, foul speakers, that pronounce the aire
Of stewes and shores,[2] I will informe you where
And how to cloath aright your wanton wit,
Without her nasty bawd attending it :[3]
View here a loose thought sayd with such a grace,
Minerva might have spoke in Venus face ;
So well disguis'd, that 'twas conceiv'd by none
But Cupid had Diana's linnen on ;
And all his naked parts so vail'd, th' expresse
The shape with clowding the uncomlinesse ;
That if this Reformation, which we
Receiv'd, had not been buried with thee,

---

[1] In the margin of the copy of 1647, against these lines is written—" *Comedies: The Spanish Curate, The Humorous Lieu-tenant, The Tamer Tamed, The Little French Lawyer.*"

[2] Sewers.

[3] *The Custome of the Countrey*—Marginal note in the copy of 1647.

The stage (as this worke) might have liv'd and lov'd
Her lines, the austere Skarlet [1] had approv'd :
And th' actors wisely been from that offence
As cleare, as they are now from audience. [2]

Thus with thy Genius did the scœne expire, [3]
Wanting thy active and correcting fire,
That now (to spread a darknesse over all)
Nothing remaines but Poesie to fall :
And though from these thy Embers we receive
Some warmth, so much as may be said, we live ;
That we dare praise thee blushlesse, in the head
Of the best piece Hermes to Love [4] e're read ;
That we rejoyce and glory in thy wit,
And feast each other with remembring it ;
That we dare speak thy thought, thy acts recite :
Yet all men henceforth be afraid to write.

---

[1] Query, *Laud.*

[2] These lines refer to the prohibition published by the Parliament against the performance of stage-plays and interludes. The first ordinance appeared in 1642, but that not being found effectual, a more stringent measure was enacted in 1647, directing, under the heaviest penalties, the total and immediate abolition of theatricals.

[3] *i. e.* The scenic drama. The original meaning of *scene* was a wooden stage for the representation of plays, &c., and it is here used therefore in its primitive sense.

[4] In the old mythology of Greece, Cupid is the pupil of Mercury or Hermes; or, in other words, *Love* is instructed by *Eloquence* and *Wit.*

UCASTA.

Posthume

POEMS

OF

Richard Lovelace Esq;

Those Honours come too late,
That on our Ashes waite.
> Mart. lib. 1. Epig. 26.

LONDON.

Printed by *William Godbid* for
Clement Darby.

1 6 5 9.

THE DEDICATION.

TO THE RIGHT HONORABLE JOHN LOVELACE, ESQUIRE.[1]

Sir,

LUCASTA (fair, but hapless maid!)
    Once flourisht underneath the shade
    Of your illustrious Mother; now,
    An orphan grown, she bows to you!
To you, her vertues' noble heir;
Oh may she find protection there!
Nor let her welcome be the less,
'Cause a rough hand makes her address:
One (to whom foes the Muses are)
Born and bred up in rugged war:

---

[1] This gentleman was the eldest son of John, second Lord
Lovelace of Hurley, co. Berks, by Anne, daughter of Thomas,
Earl of Cleveland. The first part of *Lucasta* was inscribed by
the poet himself to Lady Lovelace, his mother.

For, conscious how unfit I am,
I only have pronounc'd her name
To waken pity in your brest,
And leave her tears to plead the rest.

Sir,

Your most obedient

Servant and kinsman

Dudley Posthumus-Lovelace.

POEMS.

TO LVCASTA.

HER RESERVED LOOKS.

LUCASTA, frown, and let me die,
    But smile, and see, I live ;
    The sad indifference of your eye
    Both kills and doth reprieve.
You hide our fate within its screen ;
    We feel our judgment, ere we hear.
So in one picture I have seen
    An angel here, the devil there.

LUCASTA LAUGHING.

HARK, how she laughs aloud,
    Although the world put on its shrowd :
Wept at by the fantastic crowd,
    Who cry : one drop, let fall
From her, might save the universal ball.
    She laughs again
    At our ridiculous pain ;
And at our merry misery
    She laughs, until she cry.

Sages, forbear
That ill-contrived tear,
Although your fear
Doth barricado hope from your soft ear.
That which still makes her mirth to flow,
Is our sinister-handed woe,
Which downwards on its head doth go,
And, ere that it is sown, doth grow.
This makes her spleen contract,
And her just pleasure feast:
For the unjustest act
Is still the pleasant'st jest.

NIGHT.

TO LUCASTA.

IGHT! loathed jaylor of the lock'd up sun,
And tyrant-turnkey on committed day,
Bright eyes lye fettered in thy dungeon,
And Heaven it self doth thy dark wards
obey.
Thou dost arise our living hell;
With thee grones, terrors, furies dwell;
Until *Lucasta* doth awake,
And with her beams these heavy chains off shake.

Behold! with opening her almighty lid,
Bright eyes break rowling, and with lustre spread,
And captive day his chariot mounted is;

Night to her proper hell is beat,
And screwed to her ebon seat;
Till th' Earth with play oppressed lies,
And drawes again the curtains of her eyes.

But, bondslave, I know neither day nor night;
 Whether she murth'ring sleep, or saving wake;
Now broyl'd ith' zone of her reflected light,
 Then frose, my isicles, not sinews shake.
  Smile then, new Nature, your soft blast
  Doth melt our ice, and fires waste;
Whil'st the scorch'd shiv'ring world new born
Now feels it all the day one rising morn.

LOVE INTHRON'D.

ODE.

I.

NTROTH, I do my self perswade,
 That the wilde boy is grown a man,
And all his childishnesse off laid,
 E're since *Lucasta* did his fires fan;
  H' has left his apish jigs,
  And whipping hearts like gigs:
For t' other day I heard him swear,
That beauty should be crown'd in honours chair.

II.

With what a true and heavenly state
 He doth his glorious darts dispence,
Now cleans'd from falshood, blood and hate,
 And newly tipt with innocence!

Love Justice is become,
   And doth the cruel doome ;
  Reversed is the old decree ;
Behold ! he sits inthron'd with majestic.

III.

Inthroned in *Lucasta's* eye,
   He doth our faith and hearts survey ;
Then measures them by sympathy,
    And each to th' others breast convey ;
     Whilst to his altars now
     The frozen vestals bow,
   And strickt Diana too doth go
A-hunting with his fear'd, exchanged bow.

IV.

Th' imbracing seas and ambient air
   Now in his holy fires burn ;
Fish couple, birds and beasts in pair
   Do their own sacrifices turn.
    This is a miracle,
    That might religion swell ;
  But she, that these and their god awes,
Her crowned self submits to her own laws.

HER MUFFE.

I.

'TWAS not for some calm blessing to deceive,
   Thou didst thy polish'd hands in shagg'd
     furs weave ;
   It were no blessing thus obtain'd :
Thou rather would'st a curse have gain'd,
Then let thy warm driven snow be ever stain'd.

II.

Not that you feared the discolo'ring cold
Might alchymize their silver into gold;
   Nor could your <u>ten white nuns</u> so sin,
   That you should thus pennance them in,
Each in her coarse hair smock of discipline.

III.

Nor, Hero-like who, on their crest still wore
A lyon, panther, leopard, or a bore,
   To looke their enemies in their herse,
   Thou would'st thy hand should deeper pierce,
And, in its softness rough, appear more fierce.

IV.

No, no, *Lucasta*, destiny decreed,
That beasts to thee a sacrifice should bleed,
   And strip themselves to make you gay:
   For ne'r yet herald did display
A coat, where *sables* upon *ermin* lay.

V.

This for lay-lovers, that must stand at dore,
Salute the threshold, and admire no more;
   But I, in my invention tough,
   Rate not this outward bliss enough,
But still contemplate must the hidden muffe.

A BLACK PATCH[1] ON LUCASTA'S FACE.

DULL as I was, to think that a court fly
   Presum'd so neer her eye;
   When 'twas th' industrious bee
   Mistook her glorious face for paradise,
To summe up all his chymistry of spice;
   With a brave pride and honour led,
   Neer both her suns he makes his bed,
And, though a spark, struggles to rise as red.

---

[1] The following is a poet's lecture to the ladies of his time on the long prevailing practice of wearing patches, in which it seems that Lucasta acquiesced:—

BLACK PATCHES.

Vanitas Vanitatum.

LADIES turn conjurers, and can impart
The hidden mystery of the black art,
Black artificial patches do betray;
They more affect the works of night than day.
The creature strives the Creator to disgrace,
By patching that which is a perfect face:
A little stain upon the purest dye
Is both offensive to the heart and eye.
Defile not then with spots that face of snow,
Where the wise God His workmanship doth show,
The light of nature and the light of grace
Is the complexion for a lady's face.
   Flamma sine Fumo, by R. Watkyns, 1662, p. 81.

In a poem entitled *The Bursse of Reformation,* in praise of the New Exchange, printed in *Wit Restored,* 1658, patches are enumerated among the wares of all sorts to be procured there:—

   " Heer patches are of every cut,
     For pimples and for scars."

Then æmulates the gay
Daughter of day;
Acts the romantick phœnix' fate,
When now, with all his sweets lay'd out in state,
Lucasta scatters but one heat,
And all the aromatick pills do sweat,
And gums calcin'd themselves to powder beat,
Which a fresh gale of air
Conveys into her hair;
Then chaft, he's set on fire,
And in these holy flames doth glad expire;
And that black marble tablet there
So neer her cither sphere
Was plac'd; nor foyl, nor ornament,
But the sweet little bee's large monument.

ANOTHER.

I.

AS I beheld a winter's evening air,
Curl'd in her court-false-locks of living hair,
Butter'd with jessamine the sun left there.

They were also used for rheum, as appears from a passage in
Westward Hoe, 1607 :—

"*Judith.* I am so troubled with the rheum too. Mouse, what's
good for it?

Honey. How often I have told you you must get a patch."

WEBSTER's *Works*, ed. Hazlitt, i. 87. See DURFEY's *Pills
to Purge Melancholy*, v. 197.

" Mrs. Pepys wore patches, and so did my Lady Sandwich and
her daughter."—*Diary*, 30 Aug. and 20 Oct. 1660.

II.

Galliard and clinquant she appear'd to give,
A serenade or ball to us that grieve,
And teach us *a la mode* more gently live.

III.

But as a Moor, who to her cheeks prefers
White spots, t' allure her black idolaters,
Me thought she look'd all ore-bepatch'd with stars.

IV.

Like the dark front of some Ethiopian queen,
Vailed all ore with gems of red, blew, green,
Whose ugly night seem'd masked with days skreen.

V.

Whilst the fond people offer'd sacrifice
To saphyrs, 'stead of veins and arteries,
And bow'd unto the diamonds, not her eyes.

VI.

Behold *Lucasta's* face, how't glows like noon !
A sun intire is her complexion,
And form'd of one whole constellation.

VII.

So gently shining, so serene, so cleer,
Her look doth universal Nature cheer ;
Only a cloud or two hangs here and there.

TO LUCASTA.

I.

LAUGH and sing, but cannot tell
Whether the folly on't sounds well;
    But then I groan,
    Methinks, in tune;
Whilst grief, despair and fear dance to the air
    Of my despised prayer.

II.

A pretty antick love does this,
Then strikes a galliard with a kiss;
    As in the end
    The chords they rend;
So you but with a touch from your fair hand
    Turn all to saraband.

TO LUCASTA.

I.

LIKE to the sent'nel stars, I watch all night;
    For still the grand round of your light
    And glorious breast
Awake[1] in me an east:
Nor will my rolling eyes ere know a west.

---

[1] Original has *awakes*.

II.

Now on my down I'm toss'd as on a wave,
 And my repose is made my grave ;
   Fluttering I lye,
   Do beat my self and dye,
But for a resurrection from your eye.

III.

Ah, my fair murdresse ! dost thou cruelly heal
 With various pains to make me well ?
   Then let me be
   Thy cut anatomie,
And in each mangled part my heart you'l see.

LUCASTA AT THE BATH.

I.

' TH' autumn of a summer's day,
 When all the winds got leave to play,
 Lucasta, that fair ship, is lanch'd,
 And from its crust this almond blanch'd.

II.

Blow then, unruly northwind, blow ,
'Till in their holds your eyes you stow ;
And swell your cheeks, bequeath chill death ;
See ! she hath smil'd thee out of breath.

III.

Court, gentle zephyr, court and fan
Her softer breast's carnation wan ;
Your charming rhethorick of down
Flyes scatter'd from before her frown.

IV.

Say, my white water-lilly, say,
How is't those warm streams break away,
Cut by thy chast cold breast, which dwells
Amidst them arm'd in isicles?

V.

And the hot floods, more raging grown,
In flames of thee then in their own,
In their distempers wildly glow,
And kisse thy pillar of fix'd snow.

VI.

No sulphur, through whose each blew vein
The thick and lazy currents strein,
Can cure the smarting nor the fell
Blisters of love, wherewith they swell.

VII.

These great physicians of the blind,
The lame, and fatal blains of Inde
In every drop themselves now see
Speckled with a new leprosie.

VIII.

As sick drinks are with old wine dash'd,
Foul waters too with spirits wash'd,
Thou greiv'd, perchance, one tear let'st fall,
Which straight did purifie them all.

IX.

And now is cleans'd enough the flood,
Which since runs cleare as doth thy blood;
Of the wet pearls uncrown thy hair,
And mantle thee with ermin air.

X.

Lucasta, hail ! fair conqueresse
Of fire, air, earth and seas !
Thou whom all kneel to, yet even thou
Wilt unto love, thy captive, bow.

THE ANT.[1]

I.

FORBEAR, thou great good husband, little
    ant ;
    A little respite from thy flood of sweat !
Thou, thine own horse and cart under this
    plant,
Thy spacious tent, fan thy prodigious heat ;
Down with thy double load of that one grain !
It is a granarie for all thy train.

---

[1] A writer in *Censura Literaria*, x. 292 (first edit.)—the late
E. V. Utterson, Esq.—highly praises this little poem, and says
that it is not unworthy of Cowper. I think it highly probable
that the translation from Martial (lib. vi. Ep. 15), at the end
of the present volume, was executed prior to the composition of
these lines; and that the latter were suggested by the former.
Compare the beautiful description of the ant in the *Proverbs of
Solomon :*—" Go to the ant, thou sluggard; consider her ways
and be wise: which having no guide, overseer, or ruler, pro-
videth her meat in the summer, and gathereth her food in the
harvest.—*Proverbs*, vi. 6-8.

In the poems of John Cleveland, 1669, is a piece entitled "Fus-
cara, or the Bee Errant," which is of a somewhat similar character,
and is by no means a contemptible production, though spoiled by

II.

Cease, large example of wise thrift, awhile
(For thy example is become our law),
And teach thy frowns a seasonable smile :
So Cato sometimes the nak'd Florals saw.[1]
And thou, almighty foe, lay by thy sting,
Whilst thy unpay'd musicians, crickets, sing.

III.

Lucasta, she that holy makes the day,
And 'stills new life in fields of fueillemort,[2]
Hath back restor'd their verdure with one ray,
And with her eye bid all to play and sport,
Ant, to work still ! age will thee truant call ;
And to save now, th'art worse than prodigal.

IV.

Austere and cynick ! not one hour t' allow,
To lose with pleasure, what thou gotst with pain ;
But drive on sacred festivals thy plow,
Tearing high-ways with thy ore-charged wain.
Not all thy life-time one poor minute live,
And thy ore-labour'd bulk with mirth relieve ?

---

that *lues alchymistica* which disfigures so much of the poetry of Cleveland's time. The abilities of Cleveland as a writer seem to have been underrated by posterity, in proportion to the undue praise lavished upon him by his contemporaries.

[1] The Floralia, games antiently celebrated at Rome in honour of Flora.

[2] Here used for *dead or faded vegetation*, but strictly it means *dead or faded leaf*. *Filemort* is another form of the same word.

v.

Look up then, miserable ant, and spie
   Thy fatal foes, for breaking of their[1] law,
Hov'ring above thee: Madam *Margaret Pie:*
   And her fierce servant, meagre Sir *John Daw:*
Thy self and storehouse now they do store up,
And thy whole harvest too within their crop.

vi.

Thus we unt[h]rifty thrive within earth's tomb
   For some more rav'nous and ambitious jaw:
The grain in th' ant's, the ant[2] in the pie's womb,
   The pie in th' hawk's, the hawk[3] ith' eagle's maw.
So scattering to hord 'gainst a long day,
Thinking to save all, we cast all away.

SONG.

I.

STRIVE not, vain lover, to be fine;
   Thy silk's the silk-worm's, and not thine:
   You lessen to a fly your mistriss' thought,
   To think it may be in a cobweb caught.
What, though her thin transparent lawn
   Thy heart in a strong net hath drawn:
Not all the arms the god of fire ere made
Can the soft bulwarks of nak'd love invade.

---

[1] Original has *her.*
[2] Original reads *ants.*
[3] Original reads *hawks.*

II.

Be truly fine, then, and yourself dress
In her fair soul's immac'late glass.
Then by reflection you may have the bliss
Perhaps to see what a true fineness is;
　　When all your gawderies will fit
　　Those only that are poor in wit.
She that a clinquant outside doth adore,
Dotes on a gilded statue and no more.

IN ALLUSION TO THE FRENCH SONG.

N' ENTENDEZ VOUS PAS CE LANGUAGE.

Chorus.

THEN *understand you not (fair choice)*
　This language without tongue or voice?

I.

How often have my tears
Invaded your soft ears,
And dropp'd their silent chimes
A thousand thousand times?
Whilst echo did your eyes,
And sweetly sympathize;
But that the wary lid
Their sluces did forbid.

Cho.　*Then understand you not (fair choice)*
　　This language without tongue or voice!

II.

My arms did plead my wound,
Each in the other bound ;
Volleys of sighs did crowd,
And ring my griefs alowd ;
Grones, like a canon-ball,
Batter'd the marble wall,
That the kind neighb'ring grove
Did mutiny for love.

Cho. *Then understand you not (fair choice)*
   This language without tongue or voice?

III.

The rheth'rick of my hand
Woo'd you to understand ;
Nay, in our silent walk
My very feet would talk ;
My knees were eloquent,
And spake the love I meant ;
But deaf unto that ayr,
They, bent, would fall in prayer.

Cho. *Yet understand you not (fair choice)*
   This language without tongue or voice?

IV.

No? Know, then, I would melt
On every limb I felt,
And on each naked part
Spread my expanded heart,
That not a vein of thee
But should be fill'd with mee.

Whilst on thine own down, I
Would tumble, pant, and dye.

Cho.   *You understand not this (fair choice);*
      This language wants both tongue and voice.

COURANTE[1] MONSIEUR.

HAT frown, Aminta, now hath drown'd
    Thy bright front's pow'r, and crown'd
        Me that was bound.
No, no, deceived cruel, no!
      Love's fiery darts,
Till tipt with kisses, never kindle hearts.

Adieu, weak beauteous tyrant, see!
    Thy angry flames meant me,[2]
        Retort on thee:
For know, it is decreed, proud fair,
      I ne'r must dye
By any scorching, but a melting, eye.

---

[1] *Courante* was a favourite dance and dance-tune.   It is still known under the same name.

[2] *i. e. that* meant me, which was intended for me.

A LOOSE SARABAND.

I.

NAY, prethee, dear, draw nigher,
  Yet closer, nigher yet;
  Here is a double fire,
    A dry one and a wet.
True lasting heavenly fuel
Puts out the vestal jewel,
When once we twining marry
Mad love with wild canary.

II.

Off with that crowned Venice,[1]
  'Till all the house doth flame,
Wee'l quench it straight in Rhenish,
  Or what we must not name.
Milk lightning still asswageth;
So when our fury rageth,
As th' only means to cross it,
Wee'l drown it in love's posset.

III.

Love never was well-willer
  Unto my nag or mee,
Ne'r watter'd us ith' cellar,
  But the cheap buttery.
At th' head of his own barrells,
Where broach'd are all his quarrels,

---

[1] *Qu.* a crowned goblet of Venice glass.

Should a true noble master
Still make his guest his taster.

IV.

See, all the world how't staggers,
   More ugly drunk then we,
As if far gone in daggers
   And blood it seem'd to be.
We drink our glass of roses,
Which nought but sweets discloses :
Then in our loyal chamber
Refresh us with love's amber.

V.

Now tell me, thou fair cripple,
   That dumb canst scarcely see
Th' almightinesse of tipple,
   And th' ods 'twixt thee and thee,
What of Elizium's missing,
Still drinking and still kissing ;
Adoring plump October ;
Lord ! what is man, and[1] sober ?

VI.

Now, is there such a trifle
   As honour, the fools gyant,
What is there left to rifle,
   When wine makes all parts plyant ?
Let others glory follow,
In their false riches wallow,
And with their grief be merry :
Leave me but love and sherry.

---

[1] *i. e.* if.

THE FALCON.

AIR Princesse of the spacious air,
That hast vouchsaf'd acquaintance here,
With us are quarter'd below stairs,
That can reach heav'n with nought but
  pray'rs;
Who, when our activ'st wings we try,
Advance a foot into the sky.

Bright heir t' th' bird imperial,
From whose avenging penons fall
Thunder and lightning twisted spun!
Brave cousin-german to the Sun!
That didst forsake thy throne and sphere,
To be an humble pris'ner here;
And for a pirch of her soft hand,
Resign the royal woods' command.

How often would'st thou shoot heav'ns ark,
Then mount thy self into a lark;
And after our short faint eyes call,
When now a fly, now nought at all!
Then stoop so swift unto our sence,
As thou wert sent intelligence!

Free beauteous slave, thy happy feet
In silver fetters vervails[1] meet,
And trample on that noble wrist,
The gods have kneel'd in vain t' have kist.

---

[1] *i. e. vervels.* See Halliwell's *Dictionary of Archaic and Provincial Words,* art. *vervel.*

But gaze not, bold deceived spye,
Too much oth' lustre of her eye ;
The Sun thou dost out stare, alas !
Winks at the glory of her face.

Be safe then in thy velvet helm,
Her looks are calms that do orewhelm,
Then the Arabian bird more blest,
Chafe in the spicery of her breast,
And loose you in her breath a wind
Sow'rs the delicious gales of Inde.

But now a quill from thine own wing
I pluck, thy lofty fate to sing ;
Whilst we behold the various fight
With mingled pleasure and affright ;
The humbler hinds do fall to pray'r,
As when an army's seen i' th' air,
And the prophetick spannels run,
And howle thy epicedium.

The heron mounted doth appear
On his own Peg'sus a lanceer,
And seems, on earth when he doth but,
A proper halberdier on foot ;
Secure i' th' moore, about to sup,
The dogs have beat his quarters up.

And now he takes the open air,
Drawes up his wings with tactick care ;
Whilst th' expert falcon swift doth climbe
In subtle mazes serpentine ;
And to advantage closely twin'd
She gets the upper sky and wind,

N

Where she dissembles to invade,
And lies a pol'tick ambuscade.

The hedg'd-in heron, whom the foe
Awaits above, and dogs below,
In his fortification lies,
And makes him ready for surprize;
When roused with a shrill alarm,
Was shouted from beneath : they arm.

The falcon charges at first view
With her brigade of talons, through
Whose shoots, the wary heron beat
With a well counterwheel'd retreat.
But the bold gen'ral, never lost,
Hath won again her airy post;
Who, wild in this affront, now fryes,
Then gives a volley of her eyes.

The desp'rate heron now contracts
In one design all former facts ;
Noble, he is resolv'd to fall,
His and his en'mies funerall,
And (to be rid of her) to dy,
A publick martyr of the sky.

When now he turns his last to wreak
The palizadoes of his beak,
The raging foe impatient,
Wrack'd with revenge, and fury rent,
Swift as the thunderbolt he strikes
Too sure upon the stand of pikes ;

There she his naked breast doth hit,
And on the case of rapiers's split.

But ev'n in her expiring pangs
The heron's pounc'd within her phangs,
And so above she stoops to rise, ·
A trophee and a sacrifice ;
Whilst her own bells in the sad fall
Ring out the double funerall.

Ah, victory, unhap'ly wonne !
Weeping and red is set the Sun ;
Whilst the whole field floats in one tear,
And all the air doth mourning wear.
Close-hooded all thy kindred come
To pay their vows upon thy tombe ;
The hobby[1] and the musket[2] too
Do march to take their last adieu.

The lanner[3] and the lanneret[4]
Thy colours bear as banneret ;

---

[1] A kind of falcon.   It is the *falco subbuteo* of Linnæus.
Lyly, in his *Euphues* (1579, fol. 28), makes Lucilla say—"No
birde can looke agains the Sunne, but those that bee bredde
of the eagle, neyther any hawke soare so hie as the broode of
the hobbie."
        "Then rouse thee, muse, each little hobby plies
        At scarabes and painted butterflies."
                WITHER's *Abuses Stript and Whipt*, 1613.
[2] The young male sparrow-hawk.
[3] The *falco luniurius* of Linnæus.
[4] The female of the *lanner*. Latham (Faulconrie, lib. ii. chap.
v. ed. 1658), explains the difference between the *lanner* and the
goshawk.

The *goshawk* and her *tercel*[1] rows'd
With tears attend thee as new bows'd,
All these are in their dark array,
Led by the various herald-jay.

But thy eternal name shall live
Whilst quills from ashes fame reprieve,
Whilst open stands renown's wide dore,
And wings are left on which to soar;
Doctor robbin, the prelate pye,
And the poetick swan, shall dye,
Only to sing thy elegic.

LOVE MADE IN THE FIRST AGE.

TO CHLORIS.

I.

IN the nativity of time,
   Chloris! it was not thought a crime
      In direct Hebrew for to woe.
Now wee make love, as all on fire,
Ring retrograde our lowd desire,
      And court in English backward too.

II.

Thrice happy was that golden age,
When complement was constru'd rage,

---

[1] Here used for the female of the goshawk. *Tiercel* and *tassel* are other forms of the same word. See Strutt's *Sports and Pastimes*, ed. Hone, 1845, p. 37.

And fine words in the center hid ;
When cursed *no* stain'd no maid's blisse,
And all discourse was summ'd in *yes*,
And nought forbad, but to forbid.

III.[1]

Love then unstinted love did sip,
And cherries pluck'd fresh from the lip,
On cheeks and roses free he fed ;
Lasses, like Autumne plums, did drop,
And lads indifferently did crop
A flower and a maiden-head.

IV.

Then unconfined each did tipple
Wine from the bunch, milk from the nipple ;
Paps tractable as udders were.
Then equally the wholsome jellies
Were squeez'd from olive-trees and bellies :
Nor suits of trespasse did they fear.

V.

A fragrant bank of strawberries,
Diaper'd with violets' eyes,
Was table, table-cloth and fare ;
No palace to the clouds did swell,
Each humble princesse then did dwell
In the Piazza of her hair.

VI.

Both broken faith and th' cause of it,
All-damning gold, was damn'd to th' pit ;

---

[1] This and the succeeding stanza are omitted by Mr. Singer
in his reprint.

Their troth seal'd with a clasp and kisse,
Lasted until that extreem day,
In which they smil'd their souls away,
    And in each other breath'd new blisse.

VII.

Because no fault, there was no tear;
No groue did grate the granting ear,
    No false foul breath, their del'cat smell.
No serpent kiss poyson'd the tast,
Each touch was naturally chast,
    And their mere Sense a Miracle.

VIII.

Naked as their own innocence,
And unembroyder'd from offence,
    They went, above poor riches, gay;
On softer than the cignet's down,
In beds they tumbled off their own:
    For each within the other lay.

IX.

Thus did they live: thus did they love,
Repeating only joyes above,
    And angels were but with cloaths on,
Which they would put off cheerfully,
To bathe them in the Galaxie,
    Then gird them with the heavenly zone.

X.

Now, Chloris! miserably crave
The offer'd blisse you would not have,
    Which evermore I must deny:
Whilst ravish'd with these noble dreams,
And crowned with mine own soft beams,
    Injoying of my self I lye.

TO A LADY WITH CHILD THAT ASK'D
AN OLD SHIRT.[1]

ND why an honour'd ragged shirt, that shows,
Like tatter'd ensigns, all its bodie's blows?
Should it be swathed in a vest so dire,
It were enough to set the child on fire;
Dishevell'd queen[s] should strip them of their hair,
And in it mantle the new rising heir:
Nor do I know ought worth to wrap it in,
Except my parchment upper-coat of skin;
And then expect no end of its chast tears,
That first was rowl'd in down, now furs of bears.

But since to ladies 't hath a custome been
Linnen to send, that travail and lye in;
To the nine sempstresses, my former friends,
I su'd; but they had nought but shreds and ends.
At last, the jolli'st of the three times three
Rent th' apron from her smock, and gave it me;
'Twas soft and gentle, subt'ly spun, no doubt;
Pardon my boldnese, madam; *here's the clout.*

---

[1] A portion of this little poem is quoted in Brand's *Popular Antiquities* (edit. 1849, ii. 70), as an illustration of the custom to which it refers. No second example of such an usage seems to have been known to Brand and his editors.

SONG.

I.

IN mine one monument I lye,
   And in my self am buried;
Sure, the quick lightning of her eye
   Melted my soul ith' scabberd dead;
And now like some pale ghost I walk,
And with another's spirit talk.

II.

Nor can her beams a heat convey,
   That may my frozen bosome warm,
Unless her smiles have pow'r, as they,
   That a cross charm can countercharm.
But this is such a pleasing pain,
I'm loth to be alive again.

ANOTHER.

I DID believe I was in heav'n,
When first the heav'n her self was giv'n,
That in my heart her beams did passe
As some the sun keep in a glasse,
So that her beauties thorow me
Did hurt my rival-enemy.
But fate, alas! decreed it so,
That I was engine to my woe:
For, as a corner'd christal spot,
My heart diaphanous was not;
But solid stuffe, where her eye flings
Quick fire upon the catching strings:

Yet, as at triumphs in the night,
You see the Prince's Arms in light,
So, when I once was set on flame,
I burnt all ore the letters of her name.

ODE.

I.

YOU are deceiv'd; I sooner may, dull fair,
 Seat a dark Moor in Cassiopea's[1] chair,
  Or on the glow-worm's uselesse light
  Bestow the watching flames of night,
 Or give the rose's breath
 To executed death,
   Ere the bright hiew
   Of verse to you;
It is just Heaven on beauty stamps a fame,
And we, alas! its triumphs but proclaim.

II.

What chains but are too light for me, should I
Say that Lucasta in strange arms could lie?

---

[1] The constellation so called. In old drawings Cassiopeia is represented as a woman sitting in a chair with a branch in her hand, and hence the allusion here. Dixon, in his *Canidia*, 1683, part i. p. 35, makes his witches say:—

 "We put on Berenice's hair,
  And sit in Cassiopeia's chair."

Randolph couples it with "Ariadne's Crowne" in the following passage:—

 "Shine forth a constellation, full and bright,
 Bless the poor heavens with more majestick light,
 Who in requitall shall present you there
 Ariadne's Crowne and *Cassiopeia's Chayr.*"
       Poems, ed. 1640, p. 14.

Or that Castara[1] were impure ;
Or Saccarisa's[2] faith unsure ?
    That Chloris' love, as hair,
    Embrac'd each en'mies air ;
      That all their good
      Ran in their blood?
'Tis the same wrong th' unworthy to inthrone,
As from her proper sphere t' have vertue thrown.

III.

That strange force on the ignoble hath renown ;
As *Aurum Fulminans*, it blows vice down.
    'Twere better (heavy one) to crawl
    Forgot, then raised, trod on [to] fall.
      All your defections now
      Are not writ on your brow ;
        Odes to faults give
        A shame must live.
When a fat mist we view, we coughing run ;
But, that once meteor drawn, all cry : undone.

IV.

How bright the fair Paulina[3] did appear,
When hid in jewels she did seem a star !
    But who could soberly behold
    A wicked owl in cloath of gold,

---

[1] William Habington published his poems under the name of *Castara*, a fictitious appellation signifying the daughter of Lord Powis. This lady was eventually his wife. The first edition of *Castara* appeared in 1634, the second in 1635, and the third in 1640.

[2] Waller's *Sacharissa, i. e.* Lady Dorothy Sydney.

[3] Lollia Paulina, who first married Memmius Regulus, and

Or the ridiculous Ape
In sacred Vesta's shape?
So doth agree
Just praise with thee:
For since thy birth gave thee no beauty, know,
No poets pencil must or can do so.

THE DUELL.

I.

LOVE drunk, the other day, knockt at my
brest,
But I, alas! was not within.
My man, my ear, told me he came t' attest,
That without cause h'd boxed him,
And battered the windows of mine eyes,
And took my heart for one of's nunneries.

II.

I wondred at the outrage safe return'd,
And stormed at the base affront;
And by a friend of mine, bold faith, that burn'd,
I called him to a strict accompt.
He said that, by the law, the challeng'd might
Take the advantage both of arms and fight.

III.

Two darts of equal length and points he sent,
And nobly gave the choyce to me,

---

subsequently the Emperor Caligula, from both of whom she was
divorced. She inherited from her father enormous wealth.

Which I not weigh'd, young and indifferent,
 Now full of nought but victorie.
So we both met in one of's mother's groves,
The time, at the first murm'ring of her doves.

IV.

I stript myself naked all o're, as he :
 For so I was best arm'd, when bare.
His first pass did my liver rase : yet I
 Made home a falsify [1] too neer :
For when my arm to its true distance came,
I nothing touch'd but a fantastick flame.

V.

This, this is love we daily quarrel so,
 An idle Don-Quichoterie :
We whip our selves with our own twisted wo,
 And wound the ayre for a fly.
The only way t' undo this enemy
Is to laugh at the boy, and he will cry.

CUPID FAR GONE.

I.

WHAT, so beyond all madnesse is the elf,
 Now he hath got out of himself !
 His fatal enemy the Bee,
 Nor his deceiv'd artillerie,
His shackles, nor the roses bough
Ne'r half so netled him, as he is now.

---

[1] " To falsify a thrust," says Phillips (*World of Words*, ed. 1706, art. *falsify*), " is to make a feigned pass." Lovelace here employs the word as a substantive rather awkwardly ; but the meaning is, no doubt, the same.

II.[1]

See! at's own mother he is offering;
  His finger now fits any ring;
  Old Cybele he would enjoy,
  And now the girl, and now the boy.
  He proffers Jove a back caresse,
And all his love in the antipodes.

III.

Jealous of his chast Psyche, raging he
  Quarrels with[2] student Mercurie,
  And with a proud submissive breath
  Offers to change his darts with Death.
  He strikes at the bright eye of day,
And Juno tumbles in her milky way.

IV.

The dear sweet secrets of the gods he tells,
  And with loath'd hate lov'd heaven he swells;
    Now, like a fury, he belies
    Myriads of pure virginities,
  And swears, with this false frenzy hurl'd,
There's not a vertuous she in all the world.

V.

Olympus he renownces, then descends,
  And makes a friendship with the fiends;
    Bids Charon be no more a slave,
    He Argos rigg'd with stars shall have,
  And triple Cerberus from below
Must leash'd t' himself with him a hunting go.

---

[1] This stanza was suppressed by Mr. Singer.
[2] Original reads *the.*

A MOCK SONG.

I.

NOW Whitehall's in the grave,
　　And our head is our slave,
　　The bright pearl in his close shell of oyster;
　　Now the miter is lost,
　　The proud Prælates, too, crost,
And all Rome's confin'd to a cloister.
He, that Tarquin was styl'd,
　　Our white land's exil'd,
　　Yea, undefil'd;
Not a court ape's left to confute us;
　　Then let your voyces rise high,
　　As your colours did flye,
　　And flour'shing cry:
Long live the brave Oliver-Brutus.[1]

II.

　　Now the sun is unarm'd,
　　And the moon by us charm'd,
All the stars dissolv'd to a jelly;
　　Now the thighs of the Crown
　　And the arms are lopp'd down,
And the body is all but a belly.
　　Let the Commons go on,
　　The town is our own,
　　We'l rule alone:

---

[1] Cromwell.

For the Knights have yielded their spent-gorge;
　　And an order is tane
　　With *HONY SOIT* profane,
　　　Shout forth amain:
For our Dragon hath vanquish'd the St. George.

A FLY CAUGHT IN A COBWEB.

SMALL type of great ones, that do hum
　　Within this whole world's narrow room,
　　That with a busie hollow noise
　　Catch at the people's vainer voice,
And with spread sails play with their breath,
Whose very hails new christen death.
Poor Fly, caught in an airy net,
Thy wings have fetter'd now thy feet;
Where, like a Lyon in a toyl,
Howere thou keep'st a noble coyl,
And beat'st thy gen'rous breast, that o're
The plains thy fatal buzzes rore,
Till thy all-bellyd foe (round elf [1])
Hath quarter'd thee within himself.

　　Was it not better once to play
I' th' light of a majestick ray,
Where, though too neer and bold, the fire
Might sindge thy upper down attire,
And thou i' th' storm to loose an eye,
A wing, or a self-trapping thigh:

---

[1] The spider.

Yet hadst thou fal'n like him, whose coil
Made fishes in the sea to broyl,
When now th'ast scap'd the noble flame ;
Trapp'd basely in a slimy frame,
And free of air, thou art become
Slave to the spawn of mud and lome ?

Nor is't enough thy self do's dresse
To thy swoln lord a num'rous messe,
And by degrees thy thin veins bleed,
And piecemeal dost his poyson feed ;
But now devour'd, art like to be
A net spun for thy familie,
And, straight expanded in the air,
Hang'st for thy issue too a snare.
Strange witty death and cruel ill
That, killing thee, thou thine dost kill !
Like pies, in whose entombed ark
All fowl crowd downward to a lark,
Thou art thine en'mies' sepulcher,
And in thee buriest, too, thine heir.

Yet Fates a glory have reserv'd
For one so highly hath deserv'd.
As the rhinoceros doth dy
Under his castle-enemy,
As through the cranes trunk throat doth speed,
The aspe doth on his feeder feed ;
Fall yet triumphant in thy woe,
Bound with the entrails of thy foe.

A FLY ABOUT A GLASSE OF BURNT CLARET.

I.

ORBEAR this liquid fire, Fly,
It is more fatal then the dry,
That singly, but embracing, wounds ;
And this at once both burns and drowns.

II.

The salamander, that in heat
And flames doth cool his monstrous sweat,
Whose fan a glowing cake is said,
Of this red furnace is afraid.

III.

Viewing the ruby-christal shine,
Thou tak'st it for heaven-christalline ;
Anon thou wilt be taught to groan :
'Tis an ascended Acheron.

IV.

A snow-ball heart in it let fall,
And take it out a fire-ball ;
An icy breast in it betray'd
Breaks a destructive wild granade.

V.

'Tis this makes Venus altars shine,
This kindles frosty Hymen's pine ;
When the boy grows old in his desires,
This flambeau doth new light his fires.

o

VI.

Though the cold hermit ever wail,
Whose sighs do freeze, and tears drop hail,
Once having pass'd this, will ne'r
Another flaming purging fear.

VII.

The vestal drinking this doth burn
Now more than in her fun'ral urn ;
Her fires, that with the sun kept race,
Are now extinguish'd by her face.

VIII.

The chymist, that himself doth still,[1]
Let him but tast this limbecks [2] bill,

---

[1] *i. e.* distil.

[2] Lovelace was by no means peculiar in the fondness which he has shown in this poem and elsewhere for figures drawn from the language of alchemy.

" Retire into thy grove of eglantine,
   Where I will all those ravished sweets distill
   Through Love's alembic, and with chemic skill
   From the mix'd mass one sovereign balm derive."
                    CAREW'S *Poems* (1640), ed. 1772, p. 77.
        " ———I will try
   From the warm limbeck of my eye,
   In such a method to distil
   Tears on thy marble nature———"
            SHIRLEY'S *Poems* (Works by Dyce, vi. 407).
   " Nature's Confectioner, the *Bee*,
   Whose suckers are moist *Alchymie*,
   The still of his refining Mould,
   Minting the garden into gold."
                CLEVELAND'S *Poems*, ed. 1669, p. 4.
   " Fisher is here with purple wing,
   Who brings me to the Spring-head, where
   Crystall is Lymbeckt all the year."
            LORD WESTMORELAND'S *Otia Sacra*, 1648, p. 137

And prove this sublimated bowl,
He'll swear it will calcine a soul.

IX.

Noble, and brave! now thou dost know
The false prepared decks below,
Dost thou the fatal liquor sup,
One drop, alas! thy barque blowes up.

X.

What airy country hast to save,
Whose plagues thou'lt bury in thy grave?
For even now thou seem'st to us
On this gulphs brink a Curtius.

XI.

And now th' art faln (magnanimous Fly)
In, where thine Ocean doth fry,
Like the Sun's son, who blush'd the flood
To a complexion of blood.

XII.

Yet, see! my glad auricular
Redeems thee (though dissolv'd) a star,
Flaggy[1] thy wings, and scorch'd thy thighs,
Thou ly'st a double sacrifice.

---

[1] *Weak.* The word was once not very uncommon in writings. Bacon, Spenser, &c. use it ; but it is now, I believe, confined to Somersetshire and the bordering counties.

" *Luke.*   A south wind
Shall sooner soften marble, and the rain,
That slides down gently from his flaggy wings,
O'erflow the Alps."
           MASSINGER's *City Madam,* 1658.

XIII.

And now my warning, cooling breath
Shall a new life afford in death ;
See ! in the hospital of my hand
Already cur'd, thou fierce do'st stand.

XIV.

Burnt insect ! dost thou reaspire
The moist-hot-glasse and liquid fire ?
I see 'tis such a pleasing pain,
Thou would'st be scorch'd and drown'd again.

FEMALE GLORY.

MONGST the worlds wonders, there doth
yet remain
One greater than the rest, that's all those
o're again,
And her own self beside : A Lady, whose soft breast
Is with vast honours soul and virtues life possest.
Fair as original light first from the chaos shot,
When day in virgin-beams triumph'd, and night was not,
And as that breath infus'd in the new-breather good,
When ill unknown was dumb, and bad not understood ;
Chearful, as that aspect at this world's finishing,
When cherubims clapp'd wings, and th' sons of Heaven
did sing ;
Chast as th' Arabian bird, who all the ayr denyes,[1]
And ev'n in flames expires, when with her selfe she lyes.

---

[1] The Phœnix.

Oh ! she's as kind as drops of new faln April showers,
That on each gentle breast spring fresh perfuming
     flowers ;
She's constant, gen'rous, fixt ; she's calm, she is the all
We can of vertue, honour, faith, or glory call,
And she is (whom I thus transmit to endless fame)
Mistresse oth' world and me, and LAURA is her name.

A DIALOGUE.

LUTE AND VOICE.

L.   ING, Laura, sing, whilst silent are the
        sphears,
        And all the eyes of Heaven are turn'd
        to ears.

V. Touch thy dead wood, and make each living tree
    Unchain its feet, take arms, and follow thee.

Chorus.

L. Sing.   *V.* Touch. O Touch.   *L.* O Sing.
Both. It is the souls, souls sole offering.

V. Touch the divinity of thy chords, and make
    Each heart string tremble, and each sinew shake.

L. Whilst with your voyce you rarifie the air,
    None but an host of angels hover here.

Chorus.   Sing, Touch, &c.

V. Touch thy soft lute, and in each gentle thread
    The lyon and the panther captive lead.

L. Sing, and in heav'n inthrone deposed love,
  Whilst angels dance, and fiends in order move.

Double Chorus.

What sacred charm may this then be
  In harmonic,
That thus can make the angels wild,
  The devils mild,
And teach[1] low hell to heav'n to swell,
And the high heav'n to stoop to hell?

A MOCK CHARON.

DIALOGUE.

Cha. W.

W. CHARON! thou slave! thou fooll! thou
  cavaleer![2]

Cha. A slave! a fool! what traitor's
  voice I hear?

W. Come bring thy boat. *Ch.* No, sir. *W.* No!
  sirrah, why?

Cha. The blest will disagree, and fiends will mutiny
  At thy, at thy [un]numbred treachery.

W. Villain, I have a pass which who disdains,
  I will sequester the Elizian plains.

---

[1] Original and Singer read *reach.*

[2] This word is used here merely to denote a *gallant,* a *fellow.*
From being in its primitive sense a most honourable appellation,
it became, during and after the civil war between Charles and
the Parliament, a term of equivocal import.

Cha. Woes me, ye gentle shades! where shall I dwell?
He's come! It is not safe to be in hell.

Chorus.

Thus man, his honor lost, falls on these shelves;
Furies and fiends are still true to themselves.

Cha. You must, lost fool, come in. *W.* Oh, let me in!
But now I fear thy boat will sink with my ore-weighty
sin.
Where, courteous Charon, am I now? *Cha.* Vile
rant![1]
At the gates of thy supreme Judge Rhadamant.

Double Chorus of Divels.

Welcome to rape, to theft, to perjurie,
To all the ills thou wert, we canot hope to be;
Oh, pitty us condemned! Oh, cease to wooe,
And softly, softly breath, least you infect us too.

THE TOAD AND SPYDER.

A DUELL.

UPON a day, when the Dog-star
Unto the world proclaim'd a war,
And poyson bark'd from his black throat,
And from his jaws infection shot,
Under a deadly hen-bane shade
With slime infernal mists are made,

---

[1] Here equivalent to *ranter*, and used for the sake of the metre.

Met the two dreaded enemies,
Having their weapons in their eyes.

First from his den rolls forth that load
Of spite and hate, the speckl'd toad,
And from his chaps a foam doth spawn,
Such as the loathed three heads yawn;
Defies his foe with a fell spit,
To wade through death to meet with it;
Then in his self the lymbeck turns,
And his elixir'd poyson urns.
Arachne, once the fear oth' maid[1]
Cœlestial, thus unto her pray'd:
Heaven's blew-ey'd daughter, thine own mother!
The Python-killing Sun's thy brother.
Oh! thou, from gods that didst descend,
With a poor virgin to contend,
Shall seed of earth and hell ere be
A rival in thy victorie?
Pallas assents: for now long time
And pity had clean rins'd her crime;
When straight she doth with active fire
Her many legged foe inspire.
Have you not seen a charact[2] lie
A great cathedral in the sea,

---

[1] It will be seen that this poem partly turns on the mythological tale of Arachne and Minerva, and the metamorphosis of the former by the angry goddess into a spider (ἀράχνη).

[2] *i. e. carak*, or *carrick*, as the word is variously spelled. This large kind of ship was much used by the Greeks and Venetians during the middle ages, and also by other nations.

Under whose Babylonian walls
A small thin frigot almshouse stalls ?
So in his slime the toad doth float
And th' spyder by, but seems his boat.
And now the naumachie [1] begins ;
Close to the surface her self spins :
Arachne, when her foe lets flye
A broad-side of his breath too high,
That's over-shot, the wisely-stout,
Advised maid doth tack about ;
And now her pitchy barque doth sweat,
Chaf'd in her own black fury wet ;
Lasie and cold before, she brings
New fires to her contracted stings,
And with discolour'd spumes doth blast
The herbs that to their center hast.
Now to the neighb'ring henbane top
Arachne hath her self wound up,
And thence, from its dilated leaves,
By her own cordage downwards weaves,
And doth her town of foe attack,[2]
And storms the rampiers [3] of his back ;
Which taken in her colours spread,
March to th' citadel of's head.

---

[1] The poet rather awkwardly sustains his simile, and employs, in expressing a contest between the toad and the spider, a term signifying a naval battle, or, at least, a fight between two ships.

[2] Lovelace's fondness for military similitudes is constantly standing in the way, and marring his attempts at poetical imagery.

[3] A form of *rampart*, sanctioned by Dryden.

Now as in witty torturing Spain,
The brain is vext to vex the brain,
Where hereticks bare heads are arm'd
In a close helm, and in it charm'd
An overgrown and meagre rat,
That peece-meal nibbles himself fat;
So on the toads blew-cheequer'd scull
The spider gluttons her self full.
And vomiting her Stygian seeds,
Her poyson on his poyson feeds.
Thus the invenom'd toad, now grown
Big with more poyson than his own,
Doth gather all his pow'rs, and shakes
His stormer in's disgorged lakes;
And wounded now, apace crawls on
To his next plantane surgeon,[1]
With whose rich balm no sooner drest,
But purged is his sick swoln breast;
And as a glorious combatant,
That only rests awhile to pant,
Then with repeated strength and scars,
That smarting fire him new to wars,
Deals blows that thick themselves prevent,
As they would gain the time he spent.

So the disdaining angry toad,
That calls but a thin useless load,
His fatal feared self comes back
With unknown venome fill'd to crack.

---

[1] Medicinal herb or plant.

Th' amased spider, now untwin'd,
Hath crept up, and her self new lin'd
With fresh salt foams and mists, that blast
The ambient air as they past.
And now me thinks a Sphynx's wing
I pluck, and do not write, but sting ;
With their black blood my pale inks blent,[1]
Gall's but a faint ingredient.
The pol'tick toad doth now withdraw,
Warn'd, higher in *campaniá.*[2]
There wisely doth, intrenched deep,
His body in a body keep,
And leaves a wide and open pass
T' invite the foe up to his jaws,
Which there within a foggy blind
With fourscore fire-arms were lin'd.
The gen'rous active spider doubts
More ambuscadoes than redoubts ;
So within shot she doth pickear,[3]
Now gall's the flank, and now the rear ;
As that [4] the toad in's own dispite
Must change the manner of his fight,
Who, like a glorious general,
With one home-charge lets fly at all.

---

[1] Blended.
[2] *Campania* may signify, in the present passage, either a field or the country generally, or a plain. It is a clumsy expression.
[3] In the sense in which it is here used this word seems to be peculiar to Lovelace. *To pickear,* or *pickeer,* means *to skirmish.*
[4] So that.

Chaf'd with a fourfold ven'mous foam
Of scorn, revenge, his foes and 's own,
He seats him in his loathed chair,
New-made him by each mornings air,
With glowing eyes he doth survey
Th' undaunted hoast he calls his prey;
Then his dark spume he gred'ly laps,
And shows the foe his grave, his chaps.

Whilst the quick wary Amazon
Of 'vantage takes occasion,
And with her troop of leggs carreers
In a full speed with all her speers.
Down (as some mountain on a mouse)
On her small cot he flings his house;
Without the poyson of the elf,
The toad had like t' have burst himself:
For sage Arachne with good heed
Had stopt herself upon full speed,
And, 's body now disorder'd, on
She falls to execution.
The passive toad now only can
Contemn and suffer.   Here began
The wronged maids ingenious rage,
Which his heart venome must asswage.
One eye she hath spet out, strange smother,
When one flame doth put out another,
And one eye wittily spar'd, that he
Might but behold his miserie.
She on each spot a wound doth print,
And each speck hath a sting within't;

Till he but one new blister is,
And swells his own periphrasis.
Then fainting, sick, and yellow-pale,
She baths him with her sulph'rous stale ;
Thus slacked is her Stygian fire,
And she vouchsafes now to retire.
Anon the toad begins to pant,
Bethinks him of th' almighty plant,
And lest he peece-meal should be sped,
Wisely doth finish himself dead.
Whilst the gay girl, as was her fate,
Doth wanton and luxuriate,
And crowns her conqu'ring head all or
With fatal leaves of hellebore.
Not guessing at the pretious aid
Was lent her by the heavenly maid.
The neer expiring toad now rowls
Himself in lazy bloody scrowls,
To th' sov'raign salve of all his ills,
That only life and health distills.
But loe ! a terror above all,
That ever yet did him befall !

Pallas, still mindful of her foe,
(Whilst they did with each fires glow)
Had to the place the spiders lar
Dispath'd before the ev'nings star.
He learned was in Natures laws,
Of all her foliage knew the cause,
And 'mongst the rest in his choice want
Unplanted had this plantane plant.

The all-confounded toad doth see
His life fled with his remedie,
And in a glorious despair
First burst himself, and next the air;
Then with a dismal horred yell
Beats down his loathsome breath to hell.

But what inestimable bliss
This to the sated virgin is,
Who, as before of her fiend foe,
Now full is of her goddess too!
She from her fertile womb hath spun
Her stateliest pavillion,
Whilst all her silken flags display,
And her triumphant banners play;
Where Pallas she ith' midst doth praise,
And counterfeits her brothers rayes,
Nor will she her dear lar forget,
Victorious by his benefit,
Whose roof inchanted she doth free
From haunting gnat and goblin bee,
Who, trapp'd in her prepared toyle,
To their destruction keep a coyle.

Then she unlocks the toad's dire head,
Within whose cell is treasured
That pretious stone, which she doth call
A noble recompence for all,
And to her lar doth it present,
Of his fair aid a monument.

THE SNAYL.

ISE emblem of our politick world,
Sage Snayl, within thine own self curl'd,
Instruct me softly to make hast,
Whilst these my feet go slowly fast.

Compendious Snayl! thou seem'st to me
Large Euclid's strict epitome;
And in each diagram dost fling
Thee from the point unto the ring.
A figure now triangulare,
An oval now, and now a square,
And then a serpentine, dost crawl,
Now a straight line, now crook'd, now all.

Preventing[1] rival of the day,
Th' art up and openest thy ray;
And ere the morn cradles the moon,[2]
Th' art broke into a beauteous noon.
Then, when the Sun sups in the deep,
Thy silver horns o're Cinthia's peep;
And thou, from thine own liquid bed,
New Phœbus, heav'st thy pleasant head.

---

[1] Anticipating, forerunning.

[2] It can scarcely be requisite to mention that Lovelace refers to the gradual evanescence of the moon before the growing daylight. It is well known that the lunar orb is, at certain times, visible sometime even after sunrise.

Who shall a name for thee create,
Deep riddle of mysterious state ?
Bold Nature, that gives common birth
To all products of seas and earth,
Of thee, as earth-quakes, is afraid,
Nor will thy dire deliv'ry aid.

Thou, thine own daughter, then, and sire,
That son and mother art intire,
That big still with thy self dost go,
And liv'st an aged embrio ;
That like the cubbs of India,
Thou from thy self a while dost play ;
But frighted with a dog or gun,
In thine own belly thou dost run,
And as thy house was thine own womb,
So thine own womb concludes thy tomb.

But now I must (analys'd king)
Thy oeconomick virtues sing ;
Thou great stay'd husband still within,
Thou thee that's thine dost discipline ;
And when thou art to progress bent,
Thou mov'st thy self and tenement,
As warlike Scythians travayl'd, you
Remove your men and city too ;
Then, after a sad dearth and rain,
Thou scatterest thy silver train ;
And when the trees grow nak'd and old,
Thou cloathest them with cloth of gold,
Which from thy bowels thou dost spin,
And draw from the rich mines within.

Now hast thou chang'd thee, saint, and made
Thy self a fane that's cupula'd;
And in thy wreathed cloister thou
Walkest thine own gray fryer too;
Strickt and lock'd up, th'art hood all ore,
And ne'r eliminat'st thy dore.
On sallads thou dost feed severe,
And 'stead of beads thou drop'st a tear,
And when to rest each calls the bell,
Thou sleep'st within thy marble cell,
Where, in dark contemplation plac'd,
The sweets of Nature thou dost tast,
Who now with time thy days resolve,
And in a jelly thee dissolve,
Like a shot star, which doth repair
Upward, and rarifie the air.

ANOTHER.

THE Centaur, Syren, I foregoe;
    Those have been sung, and lowdly too:
    Nor of the mixed Sphynx Ile write,
    Nor the renown'd Hermaphrodite.
Behold! this huddle doth appear
Of horses, coach and charioteer,
That moveth him by traverse law,
And doth himself both drive and draw;
Then, when the Sunn the south doth winne,
He baits him hot in his own inne.

I heard a grave and austere clark
Resolv'd him pilot both and barque;
That, like the fam'd ship of *Trevere*,
Did on the shore himself lavere:
Yet the authentick do beleeve,
Who keep their judgement in their sleeve,
That he is his own double man,
And sick still carries his sedan:
Or that like dames i'th land of Luyck,
He wears his everlasting huyck.[1]
But banisht, I admire his fate,
Since neither ostracisme of state,
Nor a perpetual exile,
Can force this virtue, change his soyl:
For, wheresoever he doth go,
He wanders with his country too.

---

[1] *i. q. huke.* "Huke," says Minshen, "is a mantle such as women use in Spaine, Germanie, and the Low Countries, when they goe abroad." Lovelace clearly adopts the word for the sake of the metre; otherwise he might have chosen a better one.

THE TRIUMPHS OF PHILAMORE AND AMORET.

TO THE NOBLEST OF OUR YOUTH AND BEST OF FRIENDS, CHARLES COTTON, Esquire.[1]

BEING AT BERISFORD, AT HIS HOUSE IN STAFFORD-SHIRE. FROM LONDON.

A POEM.

SIR, your sad absence I complain, as earth
Her long-hid spring, that gave her verdures birth,
Who now her cheerful aromatick head
Shrinks in her cold and dismal widow'd bed;
Whilst the false sun her lover doth him move
Below, and to th' antipodes make love.

What fate was mine, when in mine obscure cave
(Shut up almost close prisoner in a grave)
Your beams could reach me through this vault of night,
And canton the dark dungeon with light!
Whence me (as gen'rous Spahys) you unbound,
Whilst I now know my self both free and crown'd.

---

[1] Charles Cotton the younger, Walton's friend. He was born on the 28th of April, 1630. He married, in 1656, Isabella, daughter of Sir Thomas Hutchinson, of Owthorp, co. Notts, Knight. See Walton's *Angler*, ed. 1760, where a life of Cotton, compiled from the notes of the laborious Oldys, will be found. The poet died in 1687, and, two years later, his miscellaneous verses were printed in an octavo volume.

But as at Meccha's tombe, the devout blind
Pilgrim (great husband of his sight and mind)
Pays to no other object this chast prise,
Then with hot earth anoynts out both his eyes:
So having seen your dazling glories store,
It is enough, and sin for to see more.

Or, do you thus those pretious rayes withdraw
To whet my dull beams, keep my bold in aw?
Or, are you gentle and compassionate,
You will not reach me Regulus his fate?
Brave prince! who, eagle-ey'd of eagle kind,
Wert blindly damn'd to look thine own self blind!

But oh, return those fires, too cruel-nice!
For whilst you fear me cindars, see, I'm ice!
A nummed speaking clod and mine own show,[1]
My self congeal'd, a man cut out in snow:
Return those living fires. Thou, who that vast
Double advantage from one-ey'd Heav'n hast,
Look with one sun, though 't but obliquely be,
And if not shine, vouchsafe to wink on me.

Perceive you not a gentle, gliding heat,
And quick'ning warmth, that makes the statua sweat;
As rev'rend Ducaleon's black-flung stone,
Whose rough outside softens to skin, anon
Each crusty vein with wet red is suppli'd,
Whilst nought of stone but in its heart doth 'bide.

So from the rugged north, where your soft stay
Hath stampt them a meridian and kind day;

---

[1] *i. e.* the shadow of myself.

Where now each *a la mode* inhabitant
Himself and 's manners both do pay you rent,
And 'bout your house (your pallace) doth resort,
And 'spite of fate and war creates a court.

So from the taught north, when you shall return,
To glad those looks that ever since did mourn,
When men uncloathed of themselves you'l see,
Then start new made, fit, what they ought to be;
Hast! hast! you, that your eyes on rare sights feed:
For thus the golden triumph is decreed.

The twice-born god, still gay and ever young,
With ivic crown'd, first leads the glorious throng:
He Ariadne's starry coronet
Designs for th' brighter beams of Amoret;
Then doth he broach his throne, and singing quaff
Unto her health his pipe of god-head off.

Him follow the recanting, vexing Nine
Who, wise, now sing thy lasting fame in wine;
Whilst Phœbus, not from th' east, your feast t' adorn,
But from th' inspir'd Canaries, rose this morn.

Now you are come, winds in their caverns sit,
And nothing breaths, but new-inlarged wit.
Hark! One proclaims it piacle[1] to be sad,
And th' people call 't religion to be mad.

---

[1] A crime, from the Latin *piaculum* which, from meaning properly *an atonement*, was afterwards used to express *what required* an atonement, *i. e.* an offence or sin.

But now, as at a coronation,
When noyse, the guard, and trumpets are oreblown,
The silent commons mark their princes way,
And with still reverence both look and pray;
So they amaz'd expecting do adore,
And count the rest but pageantry before.

Behold! an hoast of virgins, pure as th' air
In her first face,[1] ere mists durst vayl her hair:
Their snowy vests, white as their whiter skin,
Or their far chaster whiter thoughts within:
Roses they breath'd and strew'd, as if the fine
Heaven did to earth his wreath of swets resign;
They sang aloud: "*Thrice, oh thrice happy, they*
That can, like these, in love both yield and sway."

Next herald Fame (a purple clowd her bears),
In an imbroider'd coat of eyes and ears,
Proclaims the triumph, and these lovers glory,
Then in a book of steel records the story.

And now a youth of more than god-like form
Did th' inward minds of the dumb throng alarm;
All nak'd, each part betray'd unto the eye,
Chastly: for neither sex ow'd he or she.
And this was heav'nly love. By his bright hand,
A boy of worse than earthly stuff did stand;
His bow broke, his fires out, and his wings clipt,
And the black slave from all his false flames stript;

---

[1] The sky in the early part of the morning, before it is clouded
by mists.

Whose eyes were new-restor'd but to confesse
This day's bright blisse, and his own wretchednesse;
Who, swell'd with envy, bursting with disdain,
Did cry to cry, and weep them out again.

And now what heav'n must I invade, what sphere
Rifle of all her stars, t' inthrone her there?
No! Phœbus, by thy boys[1] fate we beware
Th' unruly flames o'th' firebrand, thy carr;
Although, she there once plac'd, thou, Sun, shouldst see
Thy day both nobler governed and thee.
Drive on, Bootes, thy cold heavy wayn,
Then grease thy wheels with amber in the main,
And Neptune, thou to thy false Thetis gallop,
Appollo's set within thy bed of scallop:
Whilst Amoret, on the reconciled winds
Mounted, and drawn by six cælestial minds,
She armed was with innocence and fire,
That did not burn: for it was chast desire;
Whilst a new light doth gild the standers by.
Behold! it was a day shot from her eye;
Chafing perfumes oth' East did throng and sweat,
But by her breath they melting back were beat.
A crown of yet-nere-lighted stars she wore,
In her soft hand a bleeding heart she bore,
And round her lay of broken millions more;[2]

---

[1] Phaeton.

[2] Original reads, *of millions broken more.* The above is certainly preferable; but the reader may judge for himself. It should be borne in mind that the second part of *Lucasta* was not even printed during the poet's life. If he had survived to re-

Then a wing'd crier thrice aloud did call :
Let Fame proclaim this one great prise for all.

By her a lady that might be call'd fair,
And justly, but that Amoret was there,
Was pris'ner led ; th' unvalewed robe she wore
Made infinite lay lovers to adore,
Who vainly tempt her rescue (madly bold)
Chained in sixteen thousand links of gold ;
Chrysetta thus (loaden with treasures) slave
Did strow the pass with pearls, and her way pave.

But loe ! the glorious cause of all this high
True heav'nly state, brave Philamore, draws nigh,
Who, not himself, more seems himself to be,
And with a sacred extasie doth see !
Fix'd and unmov'd on 's pillars he doth stay,
And joy transforms him his own statua ;
Nor hath he pow'r to breath [n]or strength to greet
The gentle offers of his Amoret,
Who now amaz'd at 's noble breast doth knock,
And with a kiss his gen'rous heart unlock ;
Whilst she and the whole pomp doth enter there,
Whence her nor Time nor Fate shall ever tear.
But whether am I hurl'd ? ho ! back ! awake
From thy glad trance : to thine old sorrow take !
Thus, after view of all the Indies store,
The slave returns unto his chain and oar ;

publish the first portion, and to revise the second, perhaps we
should have had a better text.

Thus poets, who all night in blest heav'ns dwell,
Are call'd next morn to their true living hell;
So I unthrifty, to myself untrue,
Rise cloath'd with real wants, 'cause wanting you,
And what substantial riches I possesse,
I must to these unvalued dreams confesse.

But all our clowds shall be oreblown, when thee
In our horizon bright once more we see;
When thy dear presence shall our souls new-dress,
And spring an universal cheerfulnesse;
When we shall be orewhelm'd in joy, like they
That change their night for a vast half-year's day.

Then shall the wretched few, that do repine,
See and recant their blasphemies in wine;
Then shall they grieve, that thought I've sung too free,
High and aloud of thy true worth and thee,
And their fowl heresies and lips submit
To th' all-forgiving breath of Amoret;
And me alone their angers object call,
That from my height so miserably did fall;
And crie out my invention thin and poor,
Who have said nought, since I could say no more.

ADVICE TO MY BEST BROTHER, COLL:
FRANCIS LOVELACE.[1]

FRANK, wil't live unhandsomely? trust not
    too far
Thy self to waving seas: for what thy star,
Calculated by sure event, must be,
Look in the glassy-epithete,[2] and see.

Yet settle here your rest, and take your state,
And in calm halcyon's nest ev'n build your fate;
Prethee lye down securely, Frank, and keep
With as much no noyse the inconstant deep

---

[1] One of the younger brothers of the poet. In the year of
the Restoration he filled the office of Recorder of Canterbury,
and in that capacity delivered the address of the city to Charles
II. on his passage through the place. This speech was printed
in 1660, 4to, three leaves. The following extracts from the
Calendars of State Papers (Domestic Series, 1660-1, page 139),
throw a little additional light on the history of this person:—

"1660, July 1.—Petition of Fras. Lovelace, Recorder of Canterbury, to the King, for the stewardship of the liberties of St.
Augustine, near Canterbury, for himself and his son Goldwell.
Has suffered sequestration, imprisonment, and loss of office, for
his loyalty. *With a note of the requested grant for Fras. Lovelace.*

"Grant to Fras. Lovelace, of the office of chief steward of the
Liberties of the late monastery of St. Augustine, near Canterbury."

[2] Unless the poet is advising his brother, before the latter
ventures on a long sea voyage, to look in the crystal, or beryl,
so popular at that time, in order to read his fortune, I must con-
fess my ignorance of the meaning of "glassy-epithete." See,
for an account of the beryl, Aubrey's *Miscellanies*, edit. 1857,
p. 154.

As its inhabitants; nay, stedfast stand,
As if discover'd were a New-found-land,
Fit for plantation here. Dream, dream still,
Lull'd in Dione's cradle; dream, untill
Horrour awake your sense, and you now find
Your self a bubbled pastime for the wind;
And in loose Thetis blankets torn and tost.
Frank, to undo thy self why art at cost?

Nor be too confident, fix'd on the shore:
For even that too borrows from the store
Of her rich neighbour, since now wisest know
(And this to Galileo's judgement ow),
The palsie earth it self is every jot
As frail, inconstant, waveing, as that blot
We lay upon the deep, that sometimes lies
Chang'd, you would think, with 's botoms properties;
But this eternal, strange Ixion's wheel
Of giddy earth ne'er whirling leaves to reel,
Till all things are inverted, till they are
Turn'd to that antick confus'd state they were.

Who loves the golden mean, doth safely want
A cobwebb'd cot and wrongs entail'd upon't;
He richly needs a pallace for to breed
Vipers and moths, that on their feeder feed;
The toy that we (too true) a mistress call,
Whose looking-glass and feather weighs up all;
And cloaths which larks would play with in the sun,
That mock him in the night, when 's course is run.

To rear an edifice by art so high,
That envy should not reach it with her eye,

Nay, with a thought comenceer it. Wouldst thou know,
How such a structure should be raisd, build low.
The blust'ring winds invisible rough stroak
More often shakes the stubborn'st, prop'rest oak ;
And in proud turrets we behold withal,
'Tis the imperial top declines to fall :
Nor does Heav'n's lightning strike the humble vales,
But high-aspiring mounts batters and scales.

A breast of proof defies all shocks of Fate,
Fears in the best, hopes in the worser state ;
Heaven forbid that, as of old, time ever
Flourish'd in spring so contrary, now never.
That mighty breath, which blew foul Winter hither,
Can eas'ly puffe it to a fairer weather.
Why dost despair then, Frank ? Æolus has
A Zephyrus as well as Boreas.

'Tis a false sequel, solœcisme 'gainst those
Precepts by fortune giv'n us, to suppose
That, 'cause it is now ill, 't will ere be so ;
Apollo doth not always bend his bow ;
But oft, uncrowned of his beams divine,
.With his soft harp awakes the sleeping Nine.

In strictest things magnanimous appear,
Greater in hope, howere thy fate, then[1] fear :
Draw all your sails in quickly, though no storm
Threaten your ruine with a sad alarm ;
For tell me how they differ. tell me, pray,
A cloudy tempest and a too fair day ?

---

[1] Than.

PARIS'S SECOND JUDGEMENT,

UPON THE THREE DAUGHTERS OF MY DEAR BROTHER MR. R. CÆSAR.[1]

BEHOLD! three sister-wonders, in whom
    met,
  Distinct and chast, the splendrous[2] counter-
    feit[3]
Of Juno, Venus and the warlike Maid,
Each in their three divinities array'd;
The majesty and state of Heav'ns great Queen,
And when she treats the gods, her noble meen;
The sweet victorious beauties and desires
O' th' sea-born princess, empresse too of fires;
The sacred arts and glorious lawrels torn
From the fair brow o' th' goddesse father-born;
All these were quarter'd in each snowy coat,
With canton'd[4] honours of their own, to boot.
Paris, by fate new-wak'd from his dead cell,
Is charg'd to give his doom impossible.

---

[1] Second son of Sir John Cæsar, Knt., who was the second surviving son of Sir Julius Cæsar, Knt., Master of the Rolls. Mr. Robert Cæsar married the poet's sister Johanna, by whom he had three daughters, co-heirs—Anne, Juliana, and Johanna. These are the ladies commemorated in the text.—See LODGE's *Life of Sir Julius Cæsar*, 1827, p. 54.

[2] Original reads *splendors.*

[3] This word is here used to signify simply *resemblance* or *copy.*

[4] *i. e.* quartered. *Canton,* in heraldry, is a square space at one of the corners of a shield of arms.

He views in each the brav'ry[1] of all Ide ;
Whilst one, as once three, doth his soul divide.
Then sighs so equally they're glorious all :
What pity the whole world is but one ball!

PEINTURE.

A PANEGYRICK TO THE BEST PICTURE OF FRIENDSHIP,

MR. PET. LILLY.

F Pliny, Lord High Treasurer of all[2]
Natures exchequer shuffled in this our ball,[3]
Peinture her richer rival did admire,
And cry'd she wrought with more almighty
fire,
That judg'd the unnumber'd issue of her scrowl,
Infinite and various as her mother soul,
That contemplation into matter brought,
Body'd Ideas, and could form a thought.
Why do I pause to couch the cataract,[4]
And the grosse pearls from our dull eyes abstract,

---

[1] Bravery here means, as it often does in writers of and before the time of Lovelace, *a beautiful or fine spectacle*, or simply *beauty*. *Brave* in the sense of *fine* (gaudy or gallant) is still in use.

[2] An allusion is, of course, intended to Pliny's *Natural History* which, through Holland's translation, became popular in England after 1601.

[3] *i. e.* in our globe.

[4] A term borrowed from the medical, or rather surgical, vocabulary. "To couch a cataract" (*i. e.* in the eye) is to remove it by surgical process.

That, pow'rful Lilly, now awaken'd we
This new creation may behold by thee?

To thy victorious pencil all, that eyes
And minds can reach, do bow. The deities
Bold Poets first but feign'd, you do and make,
And from your awe they our devotion take.
Your beauteous pallet first defin'd Love's Queen,
And made her in her heav'nly colours seen ;
You strung the bow of the Bandite her son,[1]
And tipp'd his arrowes with religion.
Neptune as unknown as his fish might dwell,
But that you seat him in his throne of shell.
The thunderers artillery and brand,
You fancied Rome in his fantastick hand ;
And the pale frights, the pains, and fears of hell
First from your sullen melancholy fell.
Who cleft th' infernal dog's loath'd head in three,
And spun out Hydra's fifty necks ? by thee
As prepossess'd w' enjoy th' Elizian plain,
Which but before was flatter'd[2] in our brain.
Who ere yet view'd airs child invisible,
A hollow voice, but in thy subtile skill?
Faint stamm'ring Eccho you so draw, that we
The very repercussion do see.
Cheat-*hocus-pocus*-Nature an assay[3]
O' th' spring affords us : præsto, and away![4]

---

[1] An allusion to Lely's pictures of Venus and Cupid.
[2] Falsely portrayed.
[3] A glimpse.
[4] Some picture by Lely, in which the painter introduced a

You all the year do chain her and her fruits,
Roots to their beds, and flowers to their roots.
Have not mine eyes feasted i' th' frozen Zone
Upon a fresh new-grown collation
Of apples, unknown sweets, that seem'd to me
Hanging to tempt as on the fatal tree,
So delicately limn'd I vow'd to try
My[1] appetite impos'd upon my eye?[2]

    You, sir, alone, fame, and all-conqu'ring rime,
File[3] the set teeth of all-devouring time.
When beauty once thy vertuous paint hath on,
Age needs not call her to vermilion;
Her beams nere shed or change like th' hair of day,[4]
She scatters fresh her everlasting ray.
Nay, from her ashes her fair virgin fire
Ascends, that doth new massacres conspire,
Whilst we wipe off the num'rous score of years,
And do behold our grandsire[s] as our peers;

---

spring landscape, is meant. The poet feigns the copy of Nature
to be so close that one might suppose the Spring had set in before the usual time. The canvass is removed, and the illusion is
dispelled. " Præsto, 'tis away," would be a preferable reading.

  [1] *i. e.* if my appetite, &c. Lovelace's style is elliptical to an
almost unexampled degree.

  [2] The same story, with variations, has been told over and over
again since the time of Zeuxis.

  [3] Original edition has *files.*

  [4] *Hair* is here used in what has become quite an obsolete
sense. The meaning is outward form, nature, or character.
The word used to be by no means uncommon; but it is now, as
was before remarked, out of fashion; and, indeed, I do not think
that it is found even in any old writer used exactly in the way
in which Lovelace has employed it.

With the first father of our house compare
We do the features of our new-born heir:
For though each coppied a son, they all
Meet in thy first and true original.

    Sacred! luxurious! what princesse not
But comes to you to have her self begot?
As, when first man was kneaded, from his side
Is born to's hand a ready-made-up bride.
He husband to his issue then doth play,
And for more wives remove the obstructed way:
So by your art you spring up in two noons
What could not else be form'd by fifteen suns;
Thy skill doth an'mate the prolifick flood,
And thy red oyl assimilates to blood.

    Where then, when all the world pays its respect,
Lies our transalpine barbarous neglect?
When the chast hands of pow'rful Titian
Had drawn the scourges of our God and man,
And now the top of th' altar did ascend
To crown the heav'nly piece with a bright end;
Whilst he, who in[1] seven languages gave law,
And always, like the Sun, his subjects saw,
Did, in his robes imperial and gold,
The basis of the doubtful ladder hold.
O Charls![2] a nobler monument than that,
Which thou thine own executor wert at!
When to our huffling Henry[3] there complain'd
A grieved earl, that thought his honor stain'd:
Away (frown'd he), for your own safeties, hast!

---

[1] Original reads *to.*   [2] Charles V.   [3] Henry VIII.

Q

In one cheap hour ten coronets I'l cast ;
But Holbeen's noble and prodigious worth
Onely the pangs of an whole age brings forth.[1]
Henry ! a word so princely saving said,
It might new raise the ruines thou hast made.

O sacred Peincture ! that dost fairly draw,
What but in mists deep inward Poets saw ;
'Twixt thee and an Intelligence no odds,[2]
That art of privy council to the gods !
By thee unto our eyes they do prefer
A stamp of their abstracted character ;
Thou, that in frames eternity dost bind,
And art a written and a body'd mind ;
To thee is ope the Juncto o' th' abysse,
And its conspiracy detected is ;
Whilest their cabal thou to our sense dost show,
And in thy square paint'st what they threat below.

Now, my best Lilly, let's walk hand in hand,
And smile at this un-understanding land ;
Let them their own dull counterfeits adore,
Their rainbow-cloaths admire, and no more.
Within one shade of thine more substance is,
Than all their varnish'd idol-mistresses :
Whilst great Vasari and Vermander shall
Interpret the deep mystery of all,
And I unto our modern Picts shall show,
What due renown to thy fair art they owe

---

[1] A story too well known to require repetition. The Earl is
not mentioned.—See WALPOLE's *Anecdotes of Painting*, ed. 1862,
p. 71.

[2] *i. e.* no difference. A compliment to Lely's spirituality.

In the delineated lives of those,
By whom this everlasting lawrel grows.
Then, if they will not gently apprehend,
Let one great blot give to their fame an end ;
Whilst no poetick flower their herse doth dresse,
But perish they and their effigies.

AN ANNIVERSARY ON THE

HYMENEALS OF MY NOBLE KINSMAN,[1]

THO. STANLEY, ESQUIRE.[2]

I.

THE day is curl'd about agen
    To view the splendor she was in ;
        When first with hallow'd hands
        The holy man knit the mysterious bands
When you two your contracted souls did move

---

[1] Lovelace was connected with the Stanleys through the Auchers. The Kentish families, about this time, intermarried with each other to a very large extent, partly to indemnify themselves from the consequences of gavelkind tenure (though many had procured parliamentary relief); and the Lovelaces, the Stanleys, the Hammonds, the Sandyses, were all more or less bound together by the ties of kindred. See the tree prefixed by Sir Egerton Brydges to his edition of *Hammond's Poems*, 1816, and the Introduction to *Stanley's Poems*, 1814. Sir William Lovelace, the poet's grandfather, married Elizabeth, daughter of Edward Aucher, Esq., of Bishopsbourne, near Canterbury, while Sir William Hammond, of St. Alban's Court, married, as his second wife, Elizabeth, daughter of Anthony Aucher, Esq., of Bishopsbourne, by whom he had, among other children, Mary, who became the wife of Sir Thomas Stanley, of Cumberlow, father of Thomas Stanley, the poet, historian, and translator of Bion, &c.

[2] See *The Poems of William Hammond*, 1655, edited by Sir E.

Like cherubims above,
        And did make love,
As your un-understanding issue now,
In a glad sigh, a smile, a tear, a vow.

II.

Tell me, O self-reviving Sun,
    In thy perigrination
        Hast thou beheld a pair
Twist their soft beams like these in their chast air?
As from bright numberlesse imbracing rayes
        Are sprung th' industrious dayes,
            So when they gaze,
And change their fertile eyes with the new morn,
A beauteous offspring is shot forth, not born.

III.

Be witness then, all-seeing Sun,
    Old spy, thou that thy race hast run
        In full five thousand rings;[1]
To thee were ever purer offerings
Sent on the wings of Faith? and thou, O Night,[2]
        Curtain of their delight,
            By these made bright,
Have you not mark'd their cœlestial play,
And no more peek'd the gayeties of day?

Brydges, 1816, p. 54, where there is a similar poem on Stanley and his bride from the pen of Hammond, who also claimed relationship with the then newly-married poet. The best account of Stanley is in the reprint of his Poems and Translations, 1814, 8vo.

[1] Meaning that the earth had made 5000 revolutions round the sun; or, in other words, that the sun was 5000 years old.

[2] Original reads *and thou of night.*

IV.

Come then, pale virgins, roses strow,
Mingled with Ios as you go.
The snowy ox is kill'd,
The fane with pros'lyte lads and lasses fill'd,
You too may hope the same seraphic joy,
Old time cannot destroy,
Nor fulnesse cloy;
When, like these, you shall stamp by sympathies
Thousands of new-born-loves with your chaste eyes.

ON SANAZAR'S BEING HONOURED

WITH SIX HUNDRED DUCKETS BY THE

CLARISSIMI OF VENICE,

FOR COMPOSING AN ELIGIACK HEXASTICK OF THE CITY.

A SATYRE.

WAS a blith prince[1] exchang'd five hundred crowns
For a fair turnip. Dig, dig on, O clowns!
But how this comes about, Fates, can you tell,
This more then Maid of Meurs, this miracle?

---

[1] Louis XI. of France was the prince here intended. See *Mery Tales and Quicke Answers*, No. 23 (ed. Hazlitt). I fear that if Lovelace had derived his knowledge of this incident from the little work mentioned, he would have been still more sarcastic; for Louis, in the *Tales and Quicke Answers*, is made to give, not 500 crowns for a turnip, but 1000 crowns for a radish.

Let me not live, if I think not St. Mark
Has all the oar, as well as beasts, in's ark!
No wonder 'tis he marries the rich sea,
But to betroth him to nak'd Poesie,
And with a bankrupt muse to merchandise ;
His treasures beams, sure, have put out his eyes.[1]
His conquest at Lepanto[2] I'l let pass,
When the sick sea with turbants night-cap'd was ;
And now at Candie his full courage shown,
That wan'd to a wan line the half-half moon.[3]
This is a wreath, this is a victorie,
Cæsar himself would have look'd pale to see,
And in the height of all his triumphs feel
Himself but chain'd to such a mighty wheel.

And now me thinks we ape Augustus state,
So ugly we his high worth imitate,
Monkey his godlike glories ; so that we
Keep light and form with such deformitie,

---

[1] Perhaps Lovelace is rather too severe on Sannazaro. That writer is said to have occupied twenty years in the composition of his poem on the Birth of the Saviour, for which he probably did not receive a sixth part of the sum paid to him for his hexastic on Venice ; and so he deserved this little windfal, which came out of the pocket of a Government rich enough to pay it ten times over. See Corniano's *Vita di Jacopo Sannazaro*, prefixed to the edition of his *Arcadia*, published at Milan in 1806. Amongst the translations printed at the end of *Lucasta*, and which it seems very likely were among the earliest poetical essays of Lovelace, is this very epigram of Sannazaro. As in the case of *The Ant*, I have little doubt that the satire was suggested by the translation.

[2] The battle of Lepanto, in which Don John of Austria and the Venetians defeated the Turks, 1571.

[3] The Turkish crescent.

As I have seen an arrogant baboon
With a small piece of glasse zany the sun.

   Rome to her bard, who did her battails sing,
Indifferent gave to poet and to king ;
With the same lawrells were his temples fraught,
Who best had written, and who best had fought ;
The self same fame they equally did feel,
One's style ador'd as much as t' other's steel.
A chain or fasces she could then afford
The sons of Phœbus, we, an axe or cord ;
Sometimes a coronet was her renown,
And ours, the dear prerogative of a crown.
In marble statu'd walks great Lucan lay,
And now we walk, our own pale statua.
They the whole year with roses crownd would dine,
And we in all December know no wine ;
Disciplin'd, dieted, sure there hath bin
Ods 'twixt a poet and a Capuchin.

   Of princes, women, wine, to sing I see
Is no apocrypha : for to rise high
Commend this olio of this lord 'tis fit :
Nay, ten to one, but you have part of it ;
There is that justice left, since you maintain
His table, he should counter-feed your brain.
Then write how well he in his sack hath droll'd,
Straight there's a bottle to your chamber roll'd,
Or with embroider'd words praise his French suit,
Month hence 'tis yours with his mans, to boot ;
Or but applaud his boss'd legs : two to none,
But he most nobly doth give you one.
Or spin an elegic on his false hair :

'Tis well, he cries, but living hair is dear.
Yet say that out of order ther's one curl,
And all the hopes of your reward you furl.[1]

Write a deep epick poem, and you may
As soon delight them as the opera,
Where they Diogenes thought in his tub,
Never so sowre did look so sweet a club.

You that do suck for thirst your black quil's blood,[2]
And chaw your labour'd papers for your food,
I will inform you how and what to praise,
Then skin y' in satin as young Lovelace plaies.
Beware, as you would your fierce guests, your lice,
To strip the cloath of gold from cherish'd vice ;
Rather stand off with awe and reverend fear,
Hang a poetick pendant in her ear,
Court her as her adorers do their glasse,
Though that as much of a true substance has,
Whilst all the gall from your wild[3] ink you drain,
The beauteous sweets of vertues cheeks to stain ;
And in your livery let her be known,
As poor and tatter'd as in her own.
Nor write, nor speak you more of sacred writ,
But what shall force up your arrested wit.
Be chast ; religion and her priests your scorn,
Whilst the vain fanes of idiots you adorn.
It is a mortal errour, you must know,
Of any to speak good, if he be so.

---

[1] Close, or shut up.
[2] *i.e.* write as a means of subsistence.
[3] Unrefined.

Rayl, till your edged breath flea[1] your raw throat,

And burn remarks[2] on all of gen'rous note;

Each verse be an indictment, be not free

Sanctity 't self from thy scurrility.

Libel your father, and your dam buffoon,

The noblest matrons of the isle lampoon,

Whilst Aretine and's bodies you dispute,

And in your sheets your sister prostitute.

   Yet there belongs a sweetnesse, softnesse too,

Which you must pay, but first, pray, know to who.

There is a creature, (if I may so call

That unto which they do all prostrate fall)

Term'd mistress, when they'r angry; but, pleas'd high,

It is a princesse, saint, divinity.

To this they sacrifice the whole days light,

Then lye with their devotion all night;

For this you are to dive to the abysse,

And rob for pearl the closet of some fish.

Arabia and Sabæa you must strip

Of all their sweets, for to supply her lip;

And steal new fire from heav'n, for to repair

Her unfledg'd scalp with Berenice's hair;

Then seat her in Cassiopeia's chair.

As now you're in your coach: save you, bright sir,

(O, spare your thanks) is not this finer far

Then walk un-hided, when that every stone

Has knock'd acquaintance with your ankle-bone?

When your wing'd papers, like the last dove, nere

Return'd to quit you of your hope or fear,

---

[1] Flay, excoriate.   [2] Original reads *all marks.*

But left you to the mercy of your host
And your days fare, a fortified toast.[1]

    How many battels, sung in epick strain,
Would have procur'd your head thatch from the rain?
Not all the arms of Thebes and Troy would get
One knife but to anatomize your meat,
A funeral elegie, with a sad boon,[2]
Might make you (hei!) sip wine like maccaroon;[3]
But if perchance there did a riband[4] come,
Not the train-band so fierce with all its drum:
Yet with your torch you homeward would retire,
And heart'ly wish your bed your fun'ral pyre.

    With what a fury have I known you feed
Upon a contract and the hopes 't might speed!
Not the fair bride, impatient of delay,
Doth wish like you the beauties of that day;
Hotter than all the roasted cooks you sat
To dresse the fricace of your alphabet,
Which sometimes would be drawn dough anagrame,[5]

---

  [1] A hard toasted crust.

  [2] A fee or gratuity given to a poet on a mournful occasion, and made more liberal by the circumstances of affliction in which the donors are placed.

  [3] Generally, a mere coxcomb or dandy; but here the poet implies a man about town who is rich enough to indulge in fashionable luxuries.

  [4] The ribbon by which the star of an order of knighthood was attached to the breast of the fortunate recipient. It sometimes also stood for the armlet worn by gentlemen in our poet's day, as a mark of some lady's esteem. See Shirley's *Poems* (Works, vi. 440).

  [5] A crude anagram.

Sometimes acrostick parched in the flame;[1]
Then posies stew'd with sippets, mottos by:
Of minced verse a miserable pye.
How many knots slip'd, ere you twist their name
With th' old device, as both their heart's the same!
Whilst like to drills the feast in your false jaw
You would transmit at leisure to your maw;
Then after all your fooling, fat, and wine,
Glutton'd at last, return at home to pine.

Tell me, O Sun, since first your beams did play
To night, and did awake the sleeping day;
Since first your steeds of light their race did start,
Did you ere blush as now? Oh thou, that art
The common father to the base pissmire,
As well as great Alcides, did the fire
From thine owne altar which the gods adore,
Kindle the souls of gnats and wasps before?

Who would delight in his chast eyes to see
Dormise to strike at lights of poesie?
Faction and envy now are[2] downright rage.
Once a five-knotted whip there was, the stage:
The beadle and the executioner,
To whip small errors, and the great ones tear;

---

[1] An imperfect acrostic. Few readers require to be told that anagrams and acrostics were formerly one of the most fashionable species of composition. Lovelace here pictures a poetaster "stewing" his brains with a poem of this description, which of course demanded a certain amount of tedious and minute attention to the arrangement of the name of the individual to whom the anagram or acrostic was to be addressed, and this was especially the case, where the writer contemplated a *double* acrostic.

[2] Original reads *is*.

Now, as er'e Nimrod the first king, he writes:
That's strongest, th' ablest deepest bites.
The muses weeping fly their hill, to see
Their noblest sons of peace in mutinie.
Could there nought else this civil war compleat,
But poets raging with poetick heat,
Tearing themselves and th' endlesse wreath, as though
Immortal they, their wrath should be so, too?
And doubly fir'd Apollo burns to see
In silent Helicon a naumachie.
Parnassus hears these at his first alarms;
Never till now Minerva was in arms.

O more then conqu'ror of the world, great Rome!
Thy heros did with gentleness or'e come
Thy foes themselves, but one another first,
Whilst envy stript alone was left, and burst.
The learn'd Decemviri, 'tis true, did strive,
But to add flames to keep their fame alive;
Whilst the eternal lawrel hung ith' air:
Nor of these ten sons was there found one heir.
Like to the golden tripod, it did pass
From this to this, till 't came to him, whose 'twas.
Cæsar to Gallus trundled it, and he
To Maro: Maro, Naso, unto thee;
Naso to his Tibullus flung the wreath,
He to Catullus thus did each bequeath.
This glorious circle, to another round,
At last the temples of their god it bound.

I might believe at least, that each might have
A quiet fame contented in his grave,
Envy the living, not the dead, doth bite:

For after death all men receave their right.[1]
If it be sacriledge for to profane
Their holy ashes, what is't then their flame?
He does that wrong unweeting[2] or in ire,
As if one should put out the vestal fire.

Let earths four quarters speak, and thou, Sun, bear
Now witnesse for thy fellow-traveller.
I was ally'd, dear Uncle,[3] unto thee
In blood, but thou, alas, not unto me;
Your vertues, pow'rs, and mine differ'd at best,
As they whose springs you saw, the east and west.[4]
Let me awhile be twisted in thy shine,
And pay my due devotions at thy shrine.

---

[1] Ovid, *El.* 15.

[2] Unwitting.

[3] The Lovelaces were connected, not only with the Hammonds Auchers, &c., but on the mother's side with the family of Sandys. See Berry's *Kent Genealogies*, which, however, are not by any means invariably reliable. The subjoined is partly from Berry:—

Edwin Sandys,=Cecilia, da. of Thomas
Archbishop of | Wilford, of Cranbrook,
York, ob. 1588. | Co. Kent, Esq. ob. 1610.

[Sir]=(4thly) Cath-	GEORGE, trans-	Anne=Sir William
Edwin	erine, da. of	lator of the	Barnes, of
Sandys	Sir R. Bulke-	Psalms, &c., ob.	Woolwich,
	ley, of Angle-	1643-4, Love-	the poet's
	sey.	lace's *great-*	maternal
		uncle.	grandfather.

Richard Sandys Esq.==Hester, da. of Edwin Aucher, second son of
Anthony Aucher, Esq., of Bishopsbourne.

[4] [George] Sandys published, in 1615, his " Relation of a Journey Begun A. D. 1610," &c., which became very popular, and was frequently reprinted.

Might learned Waynman[1] rise, who went with thee
Iu thy heav'ns work beside divinity,
I should sit still; or mighty Falkland[2] stand
To justifie with breath his pow'rful hand;
The glory, that doth circle your pale urn,
Might hallow'd still and undefiled burn: ·
But I forbear. Flames, that are wildly thrown
At sacred heads, curle back upon their own;
Sleep, heavenly Sands, whilst what they do or write,
Is to give God himself and you your right.

There is not in my mind one sullen[3] fate
Of old, but is concentred in our state:
Vandall ore-runners, Goths in literature:
Ploughmen that would Parnassus new-manure;
Ringers of verse that all-in-chime,
And toll the changes upon every rime.

---

[1] " There was Selden, and he sat close by the chair;
Wainman not far off, which was very fair."
SUCKLING's *Session of the Poets.*

[2] " Hales set by himself, most gravely did smile
To see them about nothing keep such a wil;
Apollo had spied him, but knowing his mind
Past by, and call'd *Falkland*, that sat just behind.
He was of late so gone with divinity,
That he had almost forgot his poetry,
Though to say the truth (and *Apollo* did know it)
He might have been both his priest and poet."
SUCKLING's *Session of the Poets.*

Lord Falkland was a contributor to *Jonsonus Virbius*, 1638, and
was well known in his day as an occasional writer.

[3] *Sullen* is here used in the sense of *mischievous*. In Worcester's
Dictionary an example is given of its employment by Dryden in
a similar signification.

A mercer now by th' yard does measure ore
An ode, which was but by the foot before ;
Deals you an ell of epigram, and swears
It is the strongest and the finest wears.
No wonder, if a drawer verses rack,
If 'tis not his, 't may be the spir't of sack ;
Whilst the fair bar-maid stroaks the muses teat,
For milk to make the posset up compleat.

  Arise, thou rev'rend shade, great Johnson, rise !
Break through thy marble natural disguise !
Behold a mist of insects, whose meer breath
Will melt thy hallow'd leaden house of death.
What was Crispinus,[1] that you should defie
The age for him ?[2] He durst not look so high
As your immortal rod, he still did stand
Honour'd, and held his forehead to thy brand.
These scorpions, with which we have to do,
Are fiends, not only small but deadly too.
Well mightst thou rive thy quill up to the back,

---

[1] Thomas Decker. the dramatist and poet, whom Jonson attacked in his *Poetaster*, 1602, under the name of *Crispinus*. Decker retorted in *Satiromastix*, printed in the same year, in which Jonson appears as *Young Horace*.

  [2] An allusion to the lines :
      " Come, leave the loathed stage,
        And the more loathsome age,"
prefixed to the *New Inne*, 1631, 8vo. Jonson's adopted son Randolph expostulated with him on this occasion in the ode beginning :—
      " Ben, doe not leave the stage,
        'Cause 'tis a loathsome age."
                    RANDOLPH's *Poems*, 1640, p. 64.
Carew and others did the same.

And scrue thy lyre's grave chords, untill they crack.
For though once hell resented musick, these
Divels will not, but are in worse disease.
How would thy masc'line spirit, father Ben,
Sweat to behold basely deposed men,
Justled from the prerog'tive of their bed,
Whilst wives are per'wig'd with their husbands head?
Each snatches the male quill from his faint hand,
And must both nobler write and understand,
He to her fury the soft plume doth bow:
O pen, nere truely justly slit till now!
Now as her self a poem she doth dresse.
And curls a line, as she would do a tresse;
Powders a sonnet as she does her hair,
Then prostitutes them both to publick aire.
Nor is 't enough, that they their faces blind
With a false dye; but they must paint their mind,
In meeter scold, and in scann'd order brawl,
Yet there's one Sapho[1] left may save them all.

But now let me recal my passion.
Oh! (from a noble father, nobler son)
You, that alone are the Clarissimi,
And the whole gen'rous state of Venice be,
It shall not be recorded Sanazar
Shall boast inthron'd alone this new made star;
You, whose correcting sweetnesse hath forbad
Shame to the good, and glory to the bad;
Whose honour hath ev'n into vertue tam'd

---

[1] Katherine Philips, the *matchless Orinda*, b. 1631, d. 1664.
Jeremy Taylor addressed to her his " Measures and Offices of
Friendship," 1657, and Cowley wrote an ode upon her death.

These swarms, that now so angerly I nam'd.
Forgive what thus distemper'd I indite:
For it is hard a *satyre* not to write.
Yet, as a virgin that heats all her blood
At the first motion of bad[1] understood,
Then, at meer thought of fair chastity,
Straight cools again the tempests of her sea:
  So when to you I my devotions raise,
  All wrath and storms do end in calm and praise.

COMMENDATORY VERSES,

PREFIXED TO VARIOUS PUBLICATIONS
BETWEEN 1652 AND 1657.

TO MY

DEAR FRIEND MR. E[LDRED] R[EVETT].[2]

ON HIS POEMS MORAL AND DIVINE.

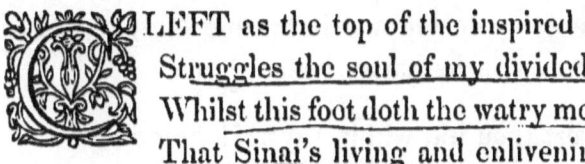

LEFT as the top of the inspired hill,
Struggles the soul of my divided quill,
Whilst this foot doth the watry mount aspire,
That Sinai's living and enlivening fire,

---

[1] By *motion of bad* I presume the poet means *wicked impulse*.

[2] Revett has some verses to the memory of Lovelace, which will be found among the Elegies at the end of the volume. The present lines were apparently written for a projected edition of Revett's poems, which, for some unknown reason, was never published. Revett has also verses prefixed to *The Royal Game of*

Behold my powers storm'd by a twisted light
O' th' Sun and his, first kindled his sight,
And my lost thoughts invoke the prince of day,
My right to th' spring of it and him do pray.

Say, happy youth, crown'd with a heav'nly ray
Of the first flame, and interwreathed bay,
Inform my soul in labour to begin,
Ios or Anthems, Pœans or a Hymne.
Shall I a hecatombe on thy tripod slay,
Or my devotions at thy altar pay?
While which t' adore th' amaz'd world cannot tell,
The sublime Urim or deep oracle.

Hark! how the moving chords temper our brain,
As when Apollo serenades the main,
Old Ocean smooths his sullen furrow'd front,
And Nereids do glide soft measures on't;
Whilst th' air puts on its sleekest, smoothest face,
And each doth turn the others looking-glasse;
So by the sinewy lyre now strook we see
Into soft calms all storm of poesie,
And former thundering and lightning lines,
And verse now in its native lustre shines.

How wert thou hid within thyself! how shut!
Thy pretious Iliads lock'd up in a nut!
Not hearing of thee thou dost break out strong,
Invading forty thousand men in song;

Chesse Play, 1656; to *Ayres and Dialogues,* by John Gamble,
1656; and to Hall's translation of the *Comment of Hierocles upon
the Golden Verses of Pythagoras,* 1657.

And we, secure in our thin empty heat,
Now find ourselves at once surprised and beat,
Whilst the most valiant of our wits now sue,
Fling down their arms, ask quarter too of you.

So cabin'd up in its disguis'd coarse[1] rust,
And scurf'd all ore with its unseemly crust,
The diamond, from 'midst the humbler stones,
Sparkling shoots forth the price of nations.
Ye safe unriddlers of the stars, pray tell,
By what name shall I stamp my miracle?
Thou strange inverted Æson, that leap'st ore
From thy first infancy into fourscore,
That to thine own self hast the midwife play'd,
And from thy brain spring'st forth[2] the heav'nly maid!
Thou staffe of him bore[3] him, that bore our sins,
Which, but set down, to bloom and bear begins!
Thou rod of Aaron, with one motion hurl'd,
Bud'st[4] a perfume of flowers through the world!
You[5] strange calcined[6] seeds within a glass,
Each species Idæa spring'st as 'twas!

---

[1] Original has *course*.

[2] This is only one instance among many which might be cited from *Lucasta* of the employment of an intransitive verb in a transitive signification.

[3] *i. e. that bore him.*   [4] *i. e. that bud'st.*   [5] Orig. has *thou.*

[6] This word, now employed only in a special sense, was formerly a very common and favourite metaphor. Thus Lord Westmoreland, in his *Otia Sacra*, 1648, p. 19, says:—

> "When all the vertue we can here put on
> Is but refined imperfection,
> Corruption calcined—"

See also p. 137 of the same volume.

Bright vestal flame that, kindled but ev'n now,
For ever dost thy sacred fires throw !

Thus the repeated acts of Nestor's age,
That now had three times ore out-liv'd the stage,
And all those beams contracted into one,
Alcides in his cradle hath outdone.

But all these flour'shing hiews, with which I die,
Thy virgin paper, now are vain as I :
For 'bove the poets Heav'n th' art taught to shine
And move, as in thy proper crystalline ;
Whence that mole-hill Parnassus thou dost view,
And us small ants there dabbling in its dew ;
Whence thy seraphic soul such hymns doth play,
As those to which first danced the first day,
Where with a thorn from the world-ransoming wreath
Thou stung, dost antiphons and anthems breathe ;
Where with an Angels quil dip'd i' th' Lambs blood,
Thou sing'st our Pelicans all-saving flood,
And bath'st thy thoughts in ever-living streams,
Rench'd[1] from earth's tainted, fat and heavy steams.
There move translated youth inroll'd i' th' quire,
That only doth with wholy lays inspire ;
To whom his burning coach Eliah sent,
And th' royal prophet-priest his harp hath lent ;
Which thou dost tune in consort unto those
Clap wings for ever at each hallow'd close :
Whilst we, now weak and fainting in our praise,
Sick echo ore thy Halleluiahs.

---

[1] Rinsed.

ON

THE BEST, LAST, AND ONLY REMAINING COMEDY OF MR. FLETCHER.

THE WILD GOOSE CHASE.[1]

'M un-ore-clowded, too ! free from the mist!
The blind and late Heaven's-eyes great
    Occulist,
  Obscured with the false fires of his sceme,
Not half those souls are lightned by this theme.

Unhappy murmurers, that still repine
(After th' Eclipse our Sun doth brighter shine),
Recant your false grief, and your true joys know ;
Your blisse is endlesse, as you fear'd your woe !
What fort'nate flood is this ! what storm of wit !
Oh, who would live, and not ore-whelm'd in it ?
No more a fatal Deluge shall be hurl'd :
This inundation hath sav'd the world.
Once more the mighty Fletcher doth arise,
Roab'd in a vest studded with stars and eyes
Of all his former glories ; his last worth
Imbroiderd with what yet light ere brought forth.
See ! in this glad farewel he doth appear
Stuck with the Constellations of his Sphere,

---

[1] " *The Wild-Goose Chase.* A Comedie: As it hath been acted with singular applause at the *Blackfriers.* Being the Noble, Last, and Onely *Remaines* of those Incomparable *Dramatists,* Francis Beaumont and John Fletcher, Gent. London: Printed for Humphrey Moseley, 1652," folio.

Fearing we numb'd fear'd no flagration,
Hath curl'd all his fires in this one *one ;*
Which (as they guard his hallowed chast urn)
The dull aproaching hereticks do burn.

Fletcher at his adieu carouses thus
To the luxurious ingenious, ·
As Cleopatra did of old out-vie,
Th' un-numb'red dishes of her Anthony,
When (he at th' empty board a wonderer)
Smiling she[1] calls for pearl and vinegar,
First pledges him in's *Breath,* then at one draught
Swallows *Three Kingdoms* of To *his best thought.*

Hear, oh ye valiant writers, and subscribe ;
(His force set by) y'are conquer'd by this bribe.
Though you hold out your selves, he doth commit
In this a sacred treason in your wit ;
Although in poems desperately stout,
Give up : this overture must buy you out.

Thus with some prodigal us'rer 't doth fare,
That keeps his gold still vayl'd, his steel-breast bare ;
That doth exceed his coffers all but's eye,
And his eyes' idol the wing'd Deity :
That cannot lock his mines with half the art
As some rich beauty doth his wretched heart ;
Wild at his real poverty, and so wise
To win her, turns himself into a prise.

---

[1] Singer reads *he,* but original *she,* as above. Of course Cleopatra is meant.

First startles her with th' emerald Mad-Lover[1]
The ruby Arcas,[2] least she should recover
Her dazled thought, a Diamond he throws,
Splendid in all the bright Aspatia's woes ;[3]
Then to sum up the abstract of his store,
He flings a rope of Pearl of forty[4] more.
Ah, see! the stagg'ring virtue faints! which he
Beholding, darts his Wealths Epitome ;[5]
And now, to consummate her wished fall,
Shows this one Carbuncle, that darkens all.

TO

MY NOBLE KINSMAN THOMAS STANLEY,[6] ESQ.;
ON HIS LYRICK POEMS COMPOSED
BY MR. JOHN GAMBLE.[7]

I.

HAT means this stately tablature,
　　The ballance of thy streins,
　Which seems, in stead of sifting pure,
　　T" extend and rack thy veins?

---

[1] Fletcher's *Mad Lover*.　　　[2] Fletcher's *Faithful Shepherdess*.

[3] *The Maid's Tragedy*, by Beaumont and Fletcher, 1619.

[4] Should we not read *fifty*, and understand the collected edition of Beaumont and Fletcher's Works in 1647?

[5] The *Wild-Goose Chase*, which is also apparently the *Carbuncle* mentioned two lines lower down.

[6] Thomas Stanley, Esq., author of the *History of Philosophy*, and an elegant poet and translator, v. *suprà*.

Lovelace wrote these lines for *Ayres and Dialogues*. To be sung to the *Theorbo, Lute, or Base-Violl*: By John Gamble. London, Printed by William Godbid for the Author, 1656, folio. [The words are by Stanley.]

[7] " Wood, in his account of this person, vol. i. col. 285, con-

Thy Odes first their own harmony did break :
For singing, troth, is but in tune to speak.

II.

Nor trus[1] thy golden feet and wings.
　　It may[2] be thought false melody[3]
T' ascend to heav'n by silver strings ;
　　This is Urania's heraldry.
Thy royal poem now we may extol,
As[4] truly Luna blazon'd upon Sol.

III.

As when Amphion first did call
　　Each listning stone from's den ;
And with his[5] lute did form the[6] wall,
　　But with his words the men ;
So in your twisted numbers now you thus
Not only stocks perswade, but ravish us.

IV.

Thus do your ayrs eccho ore
　　The notes and anthems of the sphæres,

---

jectures that many of the songs in the above collection (Gamble's
Ayres, &c. 1659), were written by the learned Thomas Stanley,
Esq., author of the *History of Philosophy,* and seemingly with
good reason, for they resemble, in the conciseness and elegant turn
of them, those poems of his printed in 1651, containing translations from Anacreon, Bion, Moschus and others."—HAWKINS.

[1] *Lucasta* and *Ayres and Dialogues* read *thus,* which leaves no
meaning in this passage.

[2] Old editions have *may it.*

[3] Harmonie—*Ayres and Dialogues,* &c.

[4] Original reads *and,* and so also the *Ayres and Dialogues.*

[5] Old editions have *the.*

[6] So the *Ayres and Dialogues. Lucasta* has *his.*

And their whole consort back restore,
   As if earth too would blesse Heav'ns ears :
But yet the spoaks, by which they scal'd so high,
Gamble hath wisely laid of *ut re mi.*

TO DR. F. B[EALE]; ON HIS BOOK
OF CHESSE.[1]

IR, now unravell'd is the golden fleece :
   Men, that could only fool at *fox and geese,*
   Are new-made polititians[2] by thy book,
   And both can judge and conquer with a look.
The hidden fate[3] of princes you unfold ;
Court, clergy, commons, by your law control'd.
Strange, serious wantoning all that they
Bluster'd and clutter'd for, you *play.*

---

[1] These lines, among the last which Lovelace ever wrote, were originally prefixed to "The Royal Game of Chesse-Play. Sometimes the Recreation of the late King, with many of the Nobility. Illustrated with almost an hundred gambetts. Being the Study of Biochino, the famous Italian [Published by Francis Beale.]" Lond. 1656, 12mo.

[2] The text of 1656 has, erroneously no doubt, *politians.*

[3] Text of 1656 has *fates.*

TO THE GENIUS OF MR. JOHN HALL.

ON HIS EXACT TRANSLATION OF HIEROCLES HIS
COMMENT UPON THE GOLDEN VERSES
OF PYTHAGORAS.[1]

 IS not from cheap thanks thinly to repay
  Th' immortal grove of thy fair-order'd bay
  Thou planted'st round my humble fane,[2]
    that I
Stick on thy hearse this sprig of Elegie:
Nor that your soul so fast was link'd in me,
That now I've both, since't has forsaken thee:
That thus I stand a Swisse before thy gate,
And dare, for such another, time and fate.
Alas! our faiths made different essays,
Our Minds and Merits brake two several ways;
Justice commands I wake thy learned dust,
And truth, in whom all causes center must.

 Behold! when but a youth, thou fierce didst whip
Upright the crooked age, and gilt vice strip;

---

[1] These lines were originally prefixed to " Hierocles upon the
Golden Verses of Pythagoras. Teaching a Virtuous and Worthy
Life. Translated by John Hall, of Durham, Esquire. *Opus
Posthumum.*" Lond. 1657, 12mo. (The copy among the King's
pamphlets in the British Museum appears to have been purchased
on the 8th Sept. 1656.) The variations between the texts of
1656 and 1659 are chiefly literal, but a careful collation has
enabled me to rectify one or two errors of the press in *Lucasta.*

[2] Lovelace refers to the lines which Hall wrote in commenda-
tion of *Lucasta,* 1649.

A senator prætext,[1] that knew'st to sway[2]
The fasces, yet under the ferula ;
Rank'd with the sage, ere blossome did thy chin,
Sleeked without, and hair all ore within,
Who in the school could'st argue as in schools :
Thy lessons were ev'n academic rules.
So that fair Cam saw thee matriculate,
At once a tyro and a graduate.

At nineteen, what *Essayes*[3] have we beheld !
That well might have the book of Dogmas swell'd :
Tough Paradoxes, such as Tully's, thou
Didst heat thee with, when snowy was thy brow,
When thy undown'd face mov'd the Nine to shake,
And of the Muses did a decad make.
What shall I say ? by what allusion bold ?
None but the Sun was ere so young and old.

Young reverend shade, ascend awhile ! whilst we
Now celebrate this posthume victorie,
This victory, that doth contract in death
Ev'n all the pow'rs and labours of thy breath.
Like the Judean Hero,[4] in thy fall
Thou pull'st the house of learning on us all.
And as that soldier conquest doubted not,
Who but one splinter had of Castriot,[5]

---

[1] The *Horæ Vacivæ* of Hall, 1646, 16mo., are here meant.

[2] See Beloe's translation of *Aulus Gellius*, ii. 86.

[3] *Horæ Vacivæ*, or Essays and some Occasional Considerations. Lond. 1646, 16mo., with a portrait of Hall by William Marshall, *an. æt.* 19. [4] Sampson.

[5] Scanderbeg, whose real name was George CASTRIOT. *Castriot* is also one of the *dramatis personæ* in Fletcher's *Knight of Malta.*

But would assault ev'n death so strongly charmd,
And naked oppose rocks, with his[1] bone[2] arm'd;
So we, secure in this fair relique, stand[3]
The slings and darts shot by each profane hand.
These soveraign leaves thou left'st us are become
Scar clothes against all Times infection.

Sacred Hierocles, whose heav'nly thought
First acted ore this comment, ere it wrote,[4]
Thou hast so spirited, elixir'd, we
Conceive there is a noble alchymie,
That's turning of this gold to something more
Pretious than gold, we never knew before.
Who now shall doubt the metempsychosis
Of the great Author, that shall peruse this?
Let others dream thy shadow wandering strays
In th' Elizian mazes hid with bays;
Or that, snatcht up in th' upper region,
'Tis kindled there a constellation;
I have inform'd me, and declare with ease:
Thy Soul is fled into Hierocles.

---

[1] So the text of 1656, *i. e.* of the lines as originally written by the poet. *Lucasta*, 1659, erroneously has *this.*

[2] "And he found a new jawbone of an ass, and put forth his hand and took it, and slew a thousand men therewith."—*Judges*, xv. 15.

[3] *i. e.* withstand.

[4] So the text of 1656. *Lucasta* has *wrought.*

TRANSLATIONS.

TRANSLATIONES.

SANAZARI HEXASTICON.

VIDERAT Adriacis quondam Neptunus in
    undis
    Stare urbem et toto ponere Jura mari:
Nunc mihi Tarpeias[a] quantumvis, Jupiter,
    Arces
Objice et illa mihi mœnia Martis, ait,
Seu pelago Tibrim præfers, urbem aspice utramque,
Illam homines dices, hanc posuisse deos.

IN VIRGILIUM. PENTADII.

PASTOR, arator, eques; pavi, colui, superavi;
    Capras, rus, hostes; fronde, ligone, manu.

DE SCÆVOLA.

LICTOREM pro rege necans nunc mutius ultro
    Sacrifico propriam concremat igne manum:
Miratur Porsenna virum, pænamque relaxans
    Maxima cum obsessis fædera a victor init,
Plus flammis patriæ confert quam fortibus armis,
    Una domans bellum funere dextra suâ.

---

[a] Rome.

TRANSLATIONS.

SANAZAR'S HEXASTICK.

IN Adriatick waves when Neptune saw,
The city stand, and give the seas a law:
Now i' th' Tarpeian tow'rs Jove rival me,
And Mars his walls impregnable, said he;
Let seas to Tyber yield; view both their ods!¹
You'l grant that built by men, but this by gods.

IN ENGLISH.

A SWAIN, hind, knight: I fed, till'd, did command:
Goats, fields, my foes: with leaves, a spade, my hand.

ENGLISHED.

THE hand, by which no king but serjeant² dies,
Mutius in fire doth freely sacrifice;
The prince admires the Hero, quits his pains,
And Victor from the seige peace entertains;
Rome's more oblig'd to flames than arms or pow'r,
When one burnt hand shall the whole war devour.³

---

¹ Points of difference or contrast. For *let seas*, &c., we ought
to read *shall seas*, &c.

² A somewhat imperfect rendering of *Lictor*.

³ The reader will easily judge for himself of the valueless
character of these translations; but it is only just to Lovelace to
suggest that they were probably academic exercises only, and at

DE CATONE.

Invictus victis in partibus omnia Cæsar
　　Vincere qui potuit, te, Cato, non potuit.

ITEM.

Ictu non potuit primo Cato solvere vitam ;
　　Defecit tanto vulnere victa manus :
Altius inseruit digitos, qua spiritus ingens
　　Exiret, magnum dextera fecit iter.
Opposuit fortuna moram, involvitque, Catonis
　　Scires ut ferro plus valuisse manum.

ITEM.

Jussa manus sacri pectus violare Catonis
　　Hæsit, et inceptum victa reliquit opus.
Ille ait, infesto contra sua vulnera vultu :
　　Estné aliquid, magnus quod Cato non potuit ?

ITEM.

Dextera, quid dubitas ? durum est jugulare Catonem ;
　　Sed modo liber erit : jam puto non dubitas !
Fas non est vivo quenquam servire Catone,
　　Nedum ipsum vincit nunc Cato si moritur.

PENTADII.

Non est, fulleris, hæc beata non est
Quod vos creditis esse, vita non est :
Fulgentes manibus videre gemmas
Et testudineo jacere lecto,

---

the same time to submit that they are not much worse than
Marlowe's translation of Ovid, and many other versions of the
Classics then current.

OF CATO.

THE world orecome, victorious Cæsar, he
That conquer'd all, great Cato, could not thee.

ANOTHER.

ONE stabbe could not fierce Cato's[1] life unty;
Onely his hand of all that wound did dy.
Deeper his fingers tear to make a way
Open, through which his mighty soul might stray.
Fortune made this delay to let us know,
That Cato's hand more then his sword could do.

ANOTHER.

THE hand of sacred Cato, bad to tear
His breast, did start, and the made wound forbear;
Then to the gash he said with angry brow:
And is there ought great Cato cannot do?

ANOTHER.

WHAT doubt'st thou, hand? sad Cato 'tis to kill;
But he'l be free: sure, hand, thou doubt'st not still!
Cato alive, 'tis just all men be free:
Nor conquers he himself, now if he die.

ENGLISHED.

IT is not, y' are deceav'd, it is not blisse
What you conceave a happy living is:
To have your hands with rubies bright to glow,
Then on your tortoise-bed your body throw,

---

[1] Cato of Utica.

S

Aut plumâ latus abdidisse molli,
Aut auro bibere, aut cubare cocco ;
Regales dapibus gravare mensas,
Et quicquid Lybico secatur arvo ;
Non unâ positum tenere cella :
Sed nullos trepidum timere casus,
Nec vano populi favore tangi,
Et stricto nihil æstuare ferro :
Hoc quisquis poterit, licebit illi
Fortunam moveat loco superbus.

AD M. T. CICERONEM.
Catul Ep. 50.

DISERTISSIME Romuli nepotum,
Quot sunt, quotque fuere, Marce Tulli,
Quotque post alios erunt in annos,
Gratias tibi maximas Catullus
Agit, pessimus omnium poeta :
Tanto pessimus omnium poeta,
Quanto tu optimus omnium patronus.

AD JUVENCIUM. CAT. EP. 49.

MELLITOS oculos tuos, Juvenci,
Si quis me sinat usque basiare,
Usque ad millia basiem trecenta ;
Nec unquam videat satur futurus :
Non si densior aridis aristis,
Sit nostræ seges osculationis.

DE PUERO ET PRÆCONE. CATUL.

CUM puero bello præconem qui videt esse,
Quid credat, nisi se vendere discupere ?

And siuk your self in down, to drink in gold,
And have your looser self in purple roll'd ;
With royal fare to make the tables groan,
Or else with what from Lybick fields is mown,
Nor in one vault hoard all your magazine,
But at no cowards fate t' have frighted bin ;
Nor with the peoples breath to be swol'n great,
Nor at a drawn stiletto basely swear.
He that dares this, nothing to him's unfit,
But proud o' th' top of fortunes wheel may sit.

TO MARCUS T. CICERO.
In an English Pentastick.

TULLY to thee, Rome's eloquent sole heir,
The best of all that are, shall be, and were,
I the worst poet send my best thanks and pray'r :
Ev'n by how much the worst of poets I,
By so much you the best of patrones be.

TO JUVENCIUS.

JUVENCIUS, thy fair sweet eyes
  If to my fill that I may kisse,
Three hundred thousand times I'de kisse,
  Nor future age should cloy this blisse ;
No, not if thicker than ripe ears
The harvest of our kisses bears.

CATUL.

WITH a fair boy a cryer we behold,
What should we think, but he would not be sold ?[1]

---

[1] Lovelace has made nonsense of this passage. We ought to
read rather, " but that he would be sold !"

PORTII LICINII.

Sɪ Phœbi soror es, mando tibi, Delia, causam,
    Scilicet, ut fratri quæ peto verba feras :
Marmore Sicanio struxi tibi, Delphice, templum,
    Et levibus calamis candida verba dedi.
Nunc, si nos audis, atque es divinus Apollo,
    Dic mihi, qui nummos non habet unde petat.

SENECÆ EX CLEANTHE.

Dᴜᴄ me, Parens celsique Dominator poli,
Quocunque placuit, nulla parendi mora est ;
Adsum impiger ; fac nolle, comitabor gemens,
Malusque patiar facere, quod licuit bono.
Ducunt volentem Fata, nolentem trahunt.

QUINTI CATULI.

Cᴏɴsᴛɪᴛᴇʀᴀᴍ exorientem Auroram forte salutans,
    Cum subitò á lævâ Roscius exoritur.
Pace mihi liceat, cœlestes, dicere vestrâ,
    Mortalis visu pulchrior esse deo.
Blanditur puero satyrus vultuque manuque ;
    Nolenti similis retrahit ora puer :
Quem non commoveat, quamvis de marmore? fundit
    Penè preces satyrus, penè puer lachrymas.

FLORIDI. DE EBRIOSO.

Pʜœʙᴜs me in somnis vetuit potare Lyæum,
    Pareo præceptis : tunc bibo cum vigilo.

ENGLISHED.

If you are Phœbus sister, Delia, pray,
This my request unto the Sun convay:
O Delphick god, I built thy marble fane,
And sung thy praises with a gentle cane,[1]
Now, if thou art divine Apollo, tell,
Where he, whose purse is empty, may go fill.

ENGLISHED.

Parent and Prince of Heav'n, O lead, I pray,
Where ere you please, I follow and obey.
Active I go, sighing, if you gainsay,
And suffer bad what to the good was law.
Fates lead the willing, but unwilling draw.

ENGLISHED.

As once I bad good morning to the day,
O' th' sudden Roscius breaks in a bright ray:
Gods with your favour, I've presum'd to see
A mortal fairer then a deitie.
With looks and hands a satyre courts the boy,
Who draws back his unwilling cheek as coy.
Although of marble hewn, whom move not they?
The boy ev'n seems to weep, the satyre, pray.

OF A DRUNKARD.

Phœbus asleep forbad me wine to take:
I yield; and now am only drunk awake.

---

[1] Reed or pipe.

DE ASINO QUI DENTIBUS ÆNEIDEM CONSUMPSIT.

CARMINIS iliaci libros consumpsit asellus;
   Hoc fatum Troiæ est: aut equus, aut asinus.

AUSONIUS LIB. EPIG.

TRINARII quodam currentem in littoris orâ
   Ante canes leporem cœruleus rapuit;
At[a] lepus: in me omnis terræ pelagique rapina est,
   Forsitan et cœli, si canis astra tenet.

AUSONIUS LIB. EPIG.

POLLA, potenta, tribon, baculus, scyphus: arcta supellex
   Hæc fuerant Cinici, sed putat hanc nimiam:
Namque cavis manibus cernens potare bubulcum,
   Cur, scyphe, te, dixit, gusto supervacuum?

AUSONIUS LIB. I. EPIG.

THESAURO invento qui limina mortis inibat,
   Liquit ovans laqueum, quo periturus erat;
At qui, quod terræ abdiderat, non repperit aurum,
   Quem laqueum invenit nexuit, et periit.

A LA CHABOT.

OBJECT adorable et charmant!
Mes souspirs et mes pleurs tesmoignent mon torment;
Mais mon respect[b] m'empeche de parler.
Ah! que peine dissimuler!
Et que je souffre de martyre,
D'aimer et de n'oser le dire!

---

[a] Qu. a contraction of *ait.*   [b] Original has *mes respects.*

THE ASSE EATING THE ÆNEIDS.

A WRETCHED asse the Æneids did destroy :
A horse or asse is still the fate of Troy.

ENGLISHED.

On the Sicilian strand a hare well wrought
Before the hounds was by a dog-fish caught ;
Quoth she : all rape of sea and earth's on me,
Perhaps of heav'n, if there a dog-star be.

ENGLISHED.

The Cynicks narrow houshould stuffe of crutch,
A stool and dish, was lumber thought too much :
For whilst a hind drinks out on's palms o' th' strand
He flings his dish : cries : I've one in my hand !

ENGLISHED.

A TREASURE found one, entring at death's gate,
Triumphing leaves that cord, was meant his fate ;
But he the gold missing, which he did hide,
The halter which he found he knit : so dy'd.

TO THE SAME AYRE IN ENGLISH, THUS,

Object adorable of charms !
My sighs and tears may testifie my harms ;
But my respect forbids me to reveal.
Ah, what a pain 'tis to conceal !
And how I suffer worse then hell,
To love, and not to dare to tell !

THEOPHILE BEING DENY'D HIS ADDRESSES TO KING JAMES, TURNED THE AFFRONT TO HIS OWN GLORY IN THIS EPIGRAM.

Si Jaques, le Roy du scavior,
Ne trouue bon de me voir,
    Voila la cause infallible !
Car, ravy de mon escrit,
Il creut, que j'estois tout esprit
    Et par consequent invisible.

AUSONIUS.

Vane, quid affectas faciem mihi ponere, pictor,
    Ignotamque oculis solicitare manu ?
Aeris et venti sum filia, mater inanis
    Indicii, vocemque sine mente gero.
Auribus in vestris habito penetrabilis echo ;
    Si mihi vis similem pingere, pinge sonos.

AUSON[IUS].

Toxica zelotypo dedit uxor maecha marito,
    Nec satis ad mortem credidit esse datum ;
Miscuit argenti lethalia pondera vivi,
    Ut celeret certam vis geminata necem.
Ergo, inter sese dum noxia pocula certant,
    Cessit lethalis noxa saltuiferi.
Protinus in vacuos alvi petiere recessus,
    Lubrica dejectis quae via nota cibis.
Quam pia cura Deûm ! prodest crudelior uxor.
    Sic, cùm fata volunt, bina venena juvant.

LINEALLY TRANSLATED OUT OF THE FRENCH.

If James, the king of wit,
To see me thought not fit,
    Sure this the cause hath been,
That, ravish'd with my merit,
He thought I was all spirit,
    And so not to be seen.

IN ENGLISH.

Vain painter, why dost strive my face to draw
With busy hands? a goddesse eyes nere saw.
Daughter of air and wind, I do rejoyce
In empty shouts; (without a mind) a voice.
Within your cars shrill echo I rebound,
And, if you'l paint me like, then paint a sound.

IN ENGLISH.

Her jealous husband an adultresse gave
Cold poysons, which to[o] weak she thought for's grave;
A fatal dose of quicksilver then she
Mingles to hast his double destinie;
Now whilst within themselves they are at strife,
The deadly potion yields to that of life,
And straight from th' hollow stomack both retreat
To th' slippery pipes known to digested meat.
Strange care o' th' gods the murth'resse doth avail!
So, when fates please, ev'n double poysons heal.

AUSONIUS EPIG.

Emptis quod libris tibi bibliotheca referta est,
 Doctum et grammaticum te, philomuse, putas.
Quinetiam cytharas, chordas et barbita conde :
 Mercator hodie, cras citharœdus, eris.

AVIENI[a] V. C. AD AMICOS.

Rure morans, quid agam, respondi, pauca rogatus :
Maue, deum exoro famulos, post arvaque viso,
Partitusque meis justos indico labores ;
Inde lego, Phœbumque cio, Musamque lacesso ;
Tunc oleo corpus fingo, mollique palœstrâ
Stringo libens animo, gaudensque ac fœnore liber
Prandeo, poto, cano, ludo, lavo, cœno, quiesco.

AD FABULLUM. CATUL. LIB. I. EP. 13.

Cœnabis bene, mi Fabulle, apud me
Paucis, si dii tibi favent, diebus ;
Si tecum attuleris bonam atque magnam
Cœnam, non sine candidâ puellâ,
Et vino, et sale, et omnibus cachinnis.
Hæc si, inquam, attuleris, Fabulle noster,
Cœnabis bene : nam tui Catulli
Plenus sacculus est aranearum.
Sed, contrâ, accipies meros amores,
Seu quod suavius elegantiusve est :
Nam unguentum dabo, quod meæ puellæ
Donârunt Veneres Cupidinesque ;
Quod tu cum olfacies, deos rogabis,
Totum te faciant, Fabulle, nasum.

---

[a] Rufus Festus Avienus, the Latin poet.

IN ENGLISH.

BECAUSE with bought books, sir, your study's fraught,
A learned grammarian you would fain be thought;
Nay then, buy lutes and strings; so you may play
The merchant now, the fidler, the next day.

ENGLISHED.

Ask'd in the country what I did, I said:
I view my men and meads, first having pray'd;
Then each of mine hath his just task outlay'd;
I read, Apollo court, I rouse my Muse;
Then I anoynt me, and stript willing loose
My self on a soft plat, from us'ry blest;
I dine, drink, sing, play, bath, I sup, I rest.

ENGLISHED.

Fabullus, I will treat you handsomely
Shortly, if the kind gods will favour thee.
If thou dost bring with thee a del'cate messe,
An olio or so, a pretty lass,
Brisk wine, sharp tales, all sorts of drollery,
These if thou bringst (I say) along with thee,
You shall feed highly, friend: for, know, the ebbs
Of my lank purse are full of spiders webs;
But then again you shall receive clear love,
Or what more grateful or more sweet may prove:
For with an ointment I will favour thee
My Venus's and Cupids gave to me,
Of which once smelt, the gods thou wilt implore,
Fabullus, that they'd make thee nose all ore.

MART. LIB. I. EPI. 14.

CASTA suo gladium cum traderet Arria Pæto,
 Quem de visceribus traxerat ipsa suis;
Si qua fides, vulnus quod feci non dolet, inquit:
 Sed quod tu facies, hoc mihi, Pæte, dolet.

MART. EPI. XLIII. LIB. 1.

CONJUGIS audîsset fatum cum Portia Bruti,
 Et substracta sibi quæreret arma dolor,
Nondum scitis, ait, mortem non posse negari,
 Credideram satis hoc vos docuisse patrem.
Dixit, et ardentes avido bibit ore favillas.
 I nunc, et ferrum turba molesta nega.

MART. EP. XV. LIB. 6.

DUM Phaetonteâ formica vagatur in umbrâ,
 Implicuit tenuem succina gutta feram,
Dignum tantorum pretium tulit illa laborum:
 Credibile est ipsam sic voluisse mori.

MAR. LIB. IV. EP. 33.

ET latet et lucet, Phaetontide condita guttâ
 Ut videatur apis nectare clausa suo.
Sic modo, quæ fuerat vitâ contempta manente,
 Funeribus facta est jam preciosa suis.

ENGLISHED.

WHEN brave chast Arria to her Pœtus gave
The sword from her own breast did bleeding wave :
If there be faith, this wound smarts not, said she ;
But what you'l make, ah, that will murder me.

IN ENGLISH.

WHEN Portia her dear lord's sad fate did hear,
And noble grief sought arms were hid from her :
Know you not yet no hinderance of death is,
Cato, I thought, enough had taught you this,
So said, her thirsty lips drink flaming coales :
Go now, deny me steel, officious fools !

ENGLISHED.

WHILST in an amber-shade the ant doth feast,
A gummy drop ensnares the small wild-beast,
A full reward of all her toyls hath she ;
'Tis to be thought she would her self so die.

IN ENGLISH.

BOTH lurks and shines, hid in an amber tear,
The bee, in her own nectar prisoner ;
So she, who in her life time was contemn'd,
Ev'n in her very funerals is gemm'd.

MART. LIB. VIII. EP. 19.

Pauper videri Cinna vult, et est pauper.

OUT OF THE ANTHOLOGIE.[a]

Ἔσβεσε τὸν λύχνον μῶρος ψύλλων ἀπὸ πόλλων
Δακνόμενος, λεξας· οὐκ ἔτί με βλέπετε.

IN RUFUM. CATUL. EP. 64.

Noli admirari, quare tibi fœmina nulla,
    Rufe, velit tenerum supposuisse femur ;
Non ullam raræ labefactes munere vestis,
    Aut pellucidulis deliciis lapidis.
Lædit te quædam mala fabula, quâ tibi fertur
    Valle sub alarum trux habitare caper.
Hunc metuunt omnes, neque mirum : nam mala valde est
    Bestia, nec quicum[b] bella puella cubet.
Quare aut crudelem nasorum interfice pestem,
    Aut admirari desine, cur fugiant.

CATUL. EP. 71.

De Inconstantiâ fœminei amoris.

Nulli se dicit mulier mea nubere velle,
    Quam mihi : non, si Jupiter ipse petat ;
Dicit ; sed mulier cupido quod dicit amanti,
    In vento et rapidâ scribere oportet aquâ.

---

[a] This is from Lucian.   [b] An archaic form of *quocum*.

IN ENGLISH,

Cinna seems[1] poor in show,
And he is so.

IN AN ENGLISH DISTICK.

A FOOL, much bit by fleas, put out the light;
You shall not see me now (quoth he); good night.

TO RUFUS.

THAT no fair woman will, wonder not why,
Clap (Rufus) under thine her tender thigh;
Not a silk gown shall once melt one of them,
Nor the delights of a transparent gemme.
A scurvy story kills thee, which doth tell,
That in thine armpits a fierce goat doth dwell.
Him they all fear full of an ugly stench:[2]
Nor 's 't fit he should lye with a handsome wench;
Wherefore this noses cursed plague first crush,
Or cease to wonder, why they fly you thus.

FEMALE INCONSTANCY.

My mistresse sayes she'll marry none but me;
No, not if Jove himself a suitor be.
She sayes so; but what women say to kind
Lovers, we write in rapid streams and wind.

---

[1] A very inadequate translation of *videri vult.*
[2] Original has *stinch.*

AD LESBIAM, CAT. EP. 73.

DICEBAS quondam, solum te nosse Catullum,
    Lesbia, nec præ me velle tenere Jovem;
Dilexi tum te, non tantum ut vulgus amicam,
    Sed pater ut gnatos diligit et generos.
Nunc te cognovi, quare et impensius uror,
    Multo mi tamen es vilior et levior.
Qui potis est inquis, quod amantem injuria talis
    Cogat amare magis, sed bene velle minus?
Odi et amo; quare id faciam, fortasse requiris;
    Nescio; sed fieri sentio, et excrucior.

IN LESBIAM CAT. EP. 76.

HUC est mens deducta tuâ, mea Lesbia, culpâ,
    Atque ita se officio perdidit ipsa suo.
Ut jam nec bene velle queam tibi, si optima sias:
    Nec desistere amare, omnia si facias.

AD QUINTIUM. CAT. EP. 83.

QUINTI, si tibi vis oculos debere Catullum,
    Aut aliud si quid carius est oculis,
Eripere ei noli, multo quod carius illi
    Est oculis, seu quid carius est oculis.

DE QUINTIA ET LESBIA. EP. 87.

QUINTIA formosa est multis, mihi candida, longa,
    Recta est; hæc ego sic singula confiteor:

ENGLISHED.

THAT me alone you lov'd, you once did say,
Nor should I to the king of gods give way.
Then I lov'd thee not as a common dear,
But as a father doth his children chear.
Now thee I know, more bitterly I smart;
Yet thou to me more light and cheaper art.
What pow'r is this? that such a wrong should press
Me to love more, yet wish thee well much lesse.
I hate and love; would'st thou the reason know?
I know not; but I burn, and feel it so.

ENGLISHED.

By thy fault is my mind brought to that pass,
That it its office quite forgotten has:
For be'est thou best, I cannot wish thee well,
And be'est thou worst, then I must love thee still.

TO QUINTIUS.

Quintius, if you'l endear Catullus eyes,
Or what he dearer then his eyes doth prize,
Ravish not what is dearer then his eyes,
Or what he dearer then his eyes doth prize.

ENGLISHED.

Quintia is handsome, fair, tall, straight: all these
Very particulars I grant with ease:

Tota illud formosa nego : nam multa venustas ;
  Nulla in tam magno est corpore mica salis.
Lesbia formosa est quæ, cum pulcherrima tota est,
  Tum omnibus una omneis surripuit veneres.

DE SUO IN LESBIAM AMORE. EP. 88.

NULLA potest mulier tantum se dicere amatam
  Verè, quantum a me Lesbia amata mea est ;
Nulla fides ullo fuit unquam fœdere tantâ,
  Quanta in amore suo ex parte reperta meâ est.

AD SYLONEM. EP. 104.

AUT sodes mihi redde decem sestertia, Sylo,
  Deindo esto quam vis sævus et indomitus ;
Aut si te nummi delectant, desine, quæso,
  Leno esse, atque idem sævus et indomitus.

But she all ore 's not handsome ; here's her fault :
In all that bulk there's not one corne of salt,
Whilst Lesbia, fair and handsome too all ore,
All graces and all wit from all hath bore.

ENGLISHED.

No one can boast her self so much belov'd,
Truely as Lesbia my affections prov'd ;
No faith was ere with such a firm knot bound,
As in my love on my part I have found.

ENGLISHED.

Sylo, pray pay me my ten sesterces,
Then rant and roar as much as you shall please ;
Or if that mony takes [you,]¹ pray, give ore
To be a pimp, or else to rant and roar.

---

¹ Original has *takes*, but a word is wanting to complete the metre, and perhaps the poet wrote *takes you, i. e.* captivates you.

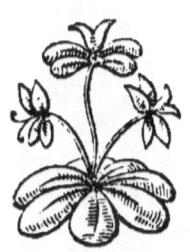

ELEGIES
sacred
to y^e memory
of
R. Lovelace
Esq:

P. Lilly Inu.   W. Faithorne sculp.

ELEGIES

SACRED

To the Memory of the

AUTHOR:

By feveral of his Friends.

Collected and Publifhed

BY

D. P. L.

Nunquam ego te vitâ frater ambilior
Adfpiciam pofthac; at certè femper amabo.
Catullus.

London, Printed 1660.

ELEGIES.

TO THE MEMORY OF MY WORTHY FRIEND,

COLL. RICHARD LOVELACE.[1]

TO pay my love to thee, and pay it so,
 As honest men should what they justly owe,
 Were to write better of thy life, then can
 The assured'st pen of the most worthy man.
Such was thy composition, such thy mind,
Improv'd from vertue, and from vice refin'd ;
Thy youth an abstract of the world's best parts,
Invr'd to arms and exercis'd to arts,
Which, with the vigour of a man, became
Thine and thy countries piramids of fame.
Two glorious lights to guide our hopeful youth
Into the paths of honour and of truth.

 These parts (so rarely met) made up in thee,
What man should in his full perfection be :
So sweet a temper into every sence

---

[1] These lines may be found, with some verbal variations, in
the poems of Charles Cotton, 1689, p. 481-2-3.

And each affection breath'd an influence,
As smooth'd them to a calme, which still withstood
The ruffling passions of untamed blood,
Without a wrinckle in thy face, to show
Thy stable breast could a [1] disturbance know.
In fortune humble, constant in mischance ;
Expert in both, and both serv'd to advance
Thy name by various trialls of thy spirit,
And give the testimony of thy merit.
Valiant to envy of the bravest men,
And learned to an undisputed pen ;
Good as the best in both and great, but yet
No dangerous courage nor offensive wit.
These ever serv'd the one for to defend,
The other, nobly to advance thy friend,
Under which title I have found my name
Fix'd in the living chronicle of fame
To times succeeding : yet I hence must go,
Displeas'd I cannot celebrate thee so.
But what respect, acknowledgement and love,
What these together, when improv'd, improve :
Call it by any name (so it express
Ought like a tribute to thy worthyness,
And may my bounden gratitude become)
Lovelace, I offer at thy honour'd tomb.

And though thy vertues many friends have bred
To love thee liveing, and lament thee dead,

---

[1] This reading is adopted from Cotton's Poems, 1689, p. 482.
In *Lucasta* we read *no disturbance.*

In characters far better couch'd then these,
Mine will not blott thy fame, nor theirs encrease.
'Twas by thine own great merits rais'd so high,
That, maugre time and fate, it shall not dye.

Sic flevit.

CHARLES COTTON.

UPON THE POSTHUME AND PRECIOUS POEMS
OF THE NOBLY EXTRACTED GEN-
TLEMAN MR. R. L.[1]

 HE rose and[2] other fragrant flowers smell
best,
    When they are pluck'd and worn in hand
        or brest,
So this fair flow'r of vertue, this rare bud
Of wit, smells now as fresh as when he stood ;
And in these Posthume-Poems lets us know,
He on[3] the banks of Helicon did grow.
The beauty of his soul did correspond
With his sweet out-side : nay, it went[4] beyond.

---

[1] These lines, originally printed as above, were included by
Payne Fisher in his collection of Howell's Poems, 1663, 8vo.,
where they may be found at p. 126. Fisher altered the super-
scription in his ill-edited book to " Upon the Posthume-*Poems*
of Mr. Lovelace."

[2] *With*—Howell's Poems.

[3] *That he upon*—ibid.

[4] *If not go beyond*—ibid.

Lovelace, the minion[1] of the Thespian dames,
Apollo's darling, born with Enthean flames,
Which in his numbers wave and shine so clear,
As sparks refracted from[2] rich gemmes appear;
Such flames that may inspire, and atoms cast,
To make new poets not like him in hast.[3]

JAM. HOWELL.

AN ELEGIE,

SACRED TO THE MEMORY OF MY LATE HONOURED FRIEND, COLLONELL RICHARD LOVELACE.

PARDON (blest shade), that I thus crowd to be
'Mong those that sin unto thy memory,
And that I think unvalu'd reliques spread,
And am the first that pillages the dead;
Since who would be thy mourner as befits,
But an officious sacriledge commits.
How my tears strive to do thee fairer right,
And from the characters divide my sight.
Untill it (dimmer) a new torrent swells,
And what obscur'd it, falls my spectacles

---

[1] Fr. *Mignon*, darling.
[2] So in Howell's Poems. *Lucasta* has *in*.
[3] " Such sparks that with their atoms may inspire
    The reader with a pure *poetick* fire."

HOWELL'S Poems.

Let the luxurious floods impulsive rise,
As they would not be wept, but weep the eyes,
The while earth melts, and we above it lye
But the weak bubbles of mortalitie ;
Until our griefs are drawn up by the Sun,
And that (too) drop the exhalation.
How in thy dust we humble now our pride,
And bring thee a whole people mortifi'd !
For who expects not death, now thou art gone,
Shows his low folly, not religion.

Can the poetick heaven still hold on
The golden dance, when the first mover's gon ?
And the snatch'd fires (while circularly hurl'd)
In their strong rapture glimmer to the world,
And not stupendiously rather rise
The tapers unto these solemnities ?

Can the chords move in tune, when thou dost dye,
At once their universal harmony ?
But where Apollo's harp (with murmur) laid,
Had to the stones a melody convey'd,
They by some pebble summon'd would reply
In loud results to every battery ;
Thus do we come unto thy marble room,
To eccho from the musick of thy tombe.

May we dare speak thee dead, that wouldest be
In thy remove only not such as we ?
No wonder, the advance is from us hid ;
Earth could not lift thee higher then it did !
And thou, that didst grow up so ever nigh,
Art but now gone to immortality !
So near to where thou art, thou here didst dwell,

The change to thee is less perceptible.
  Thy but unably-comprehending clay,
To what could not be circumscrib'd, gave way,
And the more spacious tennant to return,
Crack'd (in the two restrain'd estate) its urn.
That is but left to a successive trust ;
The soul's first buried in his bodies dust.

  Thou more thy self, now thou art less confin'd,
Art not concern'd in what is left behind ;
While we sustain the losse that thou art gone,
Un-essenc'd in the separation ;
And he that weeps thy funerall, in one
Is pious to the widdow'd nation.

  And under what (now) covert must I sing,
Secure as if beneath a cherub's wing ;
When thou hast tane thy flight hence, and art nigh
In place to some related hierarchie,
Where a bright wreath of glories doth but set
Upon thy head an equal coronet ;
And thou, above our humble converse gon,
Canst but be reach'd by contemplation.

  Our lutes (as thine was touch'd) were vocall by,
And thence receiv'd the soul by sympathy,
That did above the threds inspiring creep,
And with soft whispers broke the am'rous sleep ;
Which now no more (mov'd with the sweet surprise)
Awake into delicious rapsodies ;
But with their silent mistress do comply,
And fast in undisturbed slumbers lye.

  How from thy first ascent thou didst disperse
A blushing warmth throughout the universe,

While near the morns Lucasta's fires did glow,
And to the earth a purer dawn did throw.
We ever saw thee in the roll of fame
Advancing thy already deathless name;
And though it could but be above its fate,
Thou would'st, however, super-errogate.

Now as in Venice, when the wanton State
Before a Spaniard spread their crowded plate,
He made it the sage business of his eye
To find the root of the wild treasury;
So learn't from that exchequer but the more
To rate his masters vegetable ore.
Thus when the Greek and Latin muse we read,
As but the[1] cold inscriptions of the dead,
We to advantage then admired thee,
Who did'st live on still with thy poesie;
And in our proud enjoyments never knew
The end of the unruly wealth that grew.
But now we have the last dear ingots gain'd,
And the free vein (however rich) is drein'd;
Though what thou hast bequeathed us, no space
Of this worlds span of time shall ere embrace.
But as who sometimes knew not to conclude
Upon the waters strange vicissitude,
Did to the ocean himself commit,
That it might comprehend what could not it,
So we in our endeavours must out-done
Be swallowed up within thy Helicon.

Thou, who[2] art layd up in thy precious cave,

---

[1] Original has *the but.* [2] Original has *ow.*

And from the hollow spaces of thy grave,
We still may mourn in tune, but must alone
Hereafter hope to quaver out a grone ;
No more the chirping sonnets with shrill notes
Must henceforth volley from our treble throtes ;
But each sad accent must be humour'd well
To the deep solemn organ of thy cell.

 Why should some rude hand carve thy sacred stone,
And there incise a cheap inscription ?
When we can shed the tribute of our tears
So long, till the relenting marble wears ;
Which shall such order in their cadence keep,
That they a native epitaph shall weep ;
Untill each letter spelt distinctly lyes,
Cut by the mystick droppings of our eyes.

EL. REVETT.[1]

AN ELEGIE.

ME thinks, when kings, prophets, and poets dye,
  We should not bid men weep, nor ask them
   why,
  But the great loss should by instinct impair
The nations, like a pestilential ayr,
And in a moment men should feel the cramp
Of grief, like persons poyson'd with a damp.

---

[1] I have already pointed out, that the author of these truly
wretched lines was probably the same person, on whose *Moral
and Divine Poems* Lovelace has some verses in the *Lucasta.* The
poems of E. R. appear to be lost, which, unless they were far
superior to the present specimen, cannot be regarded as a great
calamity.

All things in nature should their death deplore,
And the sun look less lovely than before ;
The fixed stars should change their constant spaces,
And comets cast abroad their flagrant[1] faces.
Yet still we see princes and poets fall
Without their proper pomp of funerall ;
Men look about, as if they nere had known
The poets lawrell or the princes crown ;
Lovelace hath long been dead, and he[2] can be
Oblig'd to no man for an elegie.
Are you all turn'd to silence, or did he
Retain the only sap of poesie,
That kept all branches living ? must his fall
Set an eternal period upon all ?
So when a spring-tide doth begin to fly[3]
From the green shoar, each neighbouring creek grows
     dry.
But why do I so pettishly detract
An age that is so perfect, so exact ?
In all things excellent, it is a fame
Or glory to deceased Lovelace name :
For he is weak in wit, who doth deprave
Anothers worth to make his own seem brave ;
And this was not his aim : nor is it mine.
I now conceive the scope of their designe,
Which is with one consent to bring and burn
Contributary incence on his urn,
Where each mans love and fancy shall be try'd,
As when great Johnson or brave Shakespear dyed.

---

[1] Burning.   [2] Original has *we*.   [3] A fine image !

Wits must unite: for ignorance, we see,
Hath got a great train of artillerie:
Yet neither shall nor can it blast the fame
And honour of deceased Lovelace name,
Whose own *Lucasta* can support his credit
Amongst all such who knowingly have read it;
But who that praise can by desert discusse
Due to those poems that are posthumous?
And if the last conceptions are the best,
Those by degrees do much transcend the rest;
So full, so fluent, that they richly sute
With Orpheus lire, or with Anacreons lute,
And he shall melt his wing, that shall aspire
To reach a fancy or one accent higher.
Holland and France have known his nobler parts,
And found him excellent in arms and arts.
To sum up all, few men of fame but know,
He was *tam Marti, quam Mercurio.*[1]

TO HIS

NOBLE FRIEND CAPT. DUDLEY LOVELACE

UPON HIS EDITION OF HIS BROTHERS
POEMS.

HY pious hand, planting fraternal bayes,
Deserving is of most egregious praise;
Since 'tis the organ doth to us convey
From a descended sun so bright a ray.

---

[1] The motto originally employed by George Gascoigne, who,
like Lovelace, wielded both the sword and the pen.

Clear spirit! how much we are bound to thee
For this so great a liberalitie,
The truer worth of which by much exceeds
The western wealth, which such contention breeds!
Like the Infusing-God, from the well-head
Of poesie you have besprinkled
Our brows with holy drops, the very last,
Which from your Brother's happy pen were cast:
Yet as the last, the best; such matchlesse skill
From his divine alembick did distill.
Your honour'd Brother in the Elyzian shade
Will joy to know himself a laureat made
By your religious care, and that his urn
Doth him on earth immortal life return.
Your self you have a good physician shown
To his much grieved friends and to your own,
In giving this elixir'd medecine,
For greatest grief a soveraign anodine.

    Sir, from your Brother y' have convey'd us bliss;
Now, since your genius so concurs with his,
Let your own quill our next enjoyments frame;
All must be rich, that's grac'd with Lovelace name.

SYMON OGNELL M.D.[1] Coningbrens.

---

[1] This person is not mentioned in Munk's Roll of the Royal College of Physicians, 1861.

ON THE

TRULY HONOURABLE COLL. RICHARD LOVELACE,
OCCASIONED BY THE PUBLICATION
OF HIS POSTHUME-POEMS.

ELEGIE.

GREAT son of Mars, and of Minerva too!
With what oblations must we come to woo
Thy sacred soul to look down from above,
And see how much thy memory we love,
Whose happy pen so pleased amorous ears,
And, lifting bright *Lucasta* to the sphears,
Her in the star-bespangled orb did set
Above fair Ariadnes coronet,
Leaving a pattern to succeeding wits,
By which to sing forth their Pythonick fits.
Shall we bring tears and sighs? no, no! then we
Should but bemone our selves for loosing thee,
Or else thy happiness seem to deny,
Or to repine at thy felicity.
Then, whilst we chant out thine immortal praise,
Our offerings shall be onely sprigs of bays;
And if our tears will needs their brinks out-fly,
We'l weep them forth into an elegy,
To tell the world, how deep fates wounded wit,
When Atropos the lovely Lovelace hit!
How th' active fire, which cloath'd thy gen'rous mind,
Consum'd the water, and the earth calcin'd

Untill a stronger heat by death was given,
Which sublimated thy poor soul to heaven.
Thou knew'st right well to guide the warlike steed,
And yet could'st court the Muses with full speed
And such success, that the inspiring Nine
Have fill'd their Thespian fountain so with brine.
Henceforth we can expect no lyrick lay,
But biting satyres through the world must stray.
Bellona joyns with fair Erato too,
And with the Destinies do keep adoe,
Whom thus she queries: could not you awhile
Reprieve his life, until another file
Of poems such as these had been drawn up?
The fates reply'd that thou wert taken up,
A sacrifice unto the deities;
Since things most perfect please their holy eyes,
And that no other victim could be found
With so much learning and true virtue crown'd.
Since it is so, in peace for ever rest;
'Tis very just that God should have the best.

Sym. Ognell M.D. Coningbreus.

ON MY BROTHER.

LOVELACE is dead! then let the world return
    To its first chaos, mufled in its urn;
    The stars and elements together lye,
Drench'd in perpetual obscurity,
And the whole machine in confusion be,

As immethodick as an anarchie.
May the great eye of day weep out his light,
Pale Cynthia leave the regiment of night,
The galaxia, all in sables dight,
Send forth no corruscations to our sight,
The Sister-Graces and the sacred Nine,
Statu'd with grief, attend upon his shrine,
Whose worth, whose loss, should we but truly rate,
'Twould puzzle our arithmetic to state
Th' accompt of vertu's so transcendent high,
Number and value reach infinity.
Did I pronounce him dead! no, no! he lives,
And from his aromatique cell he gives
Spice-breathed fumes, whose oderiferous scent
(In zephre-gales which never can be spent)
Doth spread it self abroad, and much out-vies
The eastern bird in her self-sacrifice ;
Or Father Phœbus, who to th' world derives
Such various and such multiformed lives,
Took notice that brave LOVELACE did inspire
The universe with his Promethean fire,
And snatcht him hence, before his thread was spun,
En'ving that here should be another Sun.   T. L.[1]

---

[1] Thomas Lovelace, one of the poet's brothers.

ON THE DEATH OF MY DEAR BROTHER.

EPITAPH.

READ (reader) gently, gently ore
The happy dust beneath this floor:
For in this narrow vault is set
An alablaster cabinet,
Wherein both arts and arms were put,
Like Homers Iliads in a nut,
Till Death with slow and easie pace
Snatcht the bright jewell from the case;
And now, transform'd, he doth arise
A constellation in the skies,
Teaching the blinded world the way,
Through night, to startle into day:
And shipwrackt shades, with steady hand,
He steers unto th' Elizian land.

DUDLEY POSTHUMUS-LOVELACE.

THE END.

CHISWICK PRESS:—PRINTED BY WHITTINGHAM AND WILKINS,
TOOKS COURT, CHANCERY LANE.